DRAWN TO THE BEAST

Brides of Northumbria #2

CATE MELVILLE

"No man ever steps in the same river twice, for it's not the same river, and he's not the same man."
Heraclitus

Chapter One

BEAUFORDE CASTLE

Early January, 1156

Vacant eyes stared back at her. Gone was the father she had known all her life. In his place was a shell with little resemblance to the robust man of three days earlier. The inhabitants of Beauforde Castle had been celebrating the twelve days of Christmas and the marriage of Ranulf d'Argentan to Cicele's younger half sister, Isabeau, when their father fell from his horse while hunting.

There was little recognition reflected in the once lively green eyes that stared vacantly at her. Suddenly his body twitched and he refocused. His eyes never left hers as he grasped her hand and began to speak.

Despite his flesh being consumed by the fever that had ravaged his body for the past few days, his grip was surprisingly strong. The same couldn't be said for his voice. Cicele leaned in close to hear him, then recoiled as a cough shook his feeble body. The castle's physician pushed her aside and dribbled a watery substance into her father's mouth, but even the tiny trickle that passed between his lips was too much. His body convulsed with a hacking, choking cough. Agonizing minutes passed before he regained the power of speech.

"Enough!" he wheezed. His hand snaked out and again took hers in a fierce grip. "You will marry, and you will do it today."

Cicele looked at the faces of those standing vigil beside her dying father's bed. Her half sister, Isabeau, wore an expression of genuine sympathy, but Isabeau's husband, Ranulf, refused to meet Cicele's eye.

Shaking herself from the waking nightmare unfolding before her, Cicele gathered her courage. She refused to be bullied by her father, even if it was to be his dying wish that she marry. Grasping hold of the only thing that might offer her a reprieve, she bargained for more time. "I cannot marry while you linger close to death, Father, it is improper." There was a slim hope he would listen to propriety, but then again, he had never been one to care over much for appearances.

What hope did she have? He had ignored her most of her life, and even now when he lay dying he refused to consider her, and her feelings.

Her father still held her hand in his, but turned his head to look at Ranulf. She saw her brother by marriage give her father a slight nod before he spoke. "Your groom is unable to make the journey in time," he said as he gave her father another glance. Then he turned back to face her. "The king has ordered that you marry with your father as witness. Therefore, I will stand in your husband's stead."

"You are proxy?" Cicele asked, incredulous that she had once again been maneuvered into an unwanted marriage by her father. No one, not even her sister, had informed her she was to marry, again. Cicele hadn't been fool enough to think she would not be forced into marriage, but she hadn't expected it to be so soon. Nicholas, God grant him peace, had only died in July, giving her only five months to mourn. Not that she mourned her late husband.

But she had thought to be free from another marriage for at least a year. Fate, it seemed, had intervened. Again.

Resentment, deep and acidic, stung her throat, making it difficult for her to reply. What could she say? There was no one in this room who dared go against a dying man's wishes. Or the king's. Her father and Ranulf both owed him fealty and for that alone they would do the king's bidding.

God in heaven how had her life come to this? Like a silly chit, she had assumed that if her father did die from his injuries, then she could delay any marriage proposal till after a mourning period. A pox on her father, and a pox on her new husband, whoever he was. And a pox on her brother by marriage for agreeing to such a thing. She dared not curse the king. That was a step too far.

Ranulf caught her attention and for a moment something passed behind his eyes, but it disappeared too quickly for Cicele to be sure, but she suspected pity. God, she hated that he pitied her. They were not friends but because of her sister Cicele always made an effort to be civil to her brother by marriage. Once again, his expression became shuttered as he bowed his head in her direction.

It took her several deep breaths before she gained enough control to speak. A surge of pleasure flowed through her when her father shrank from her glare. "You arranged this without my knowledge, and now you expect me to obey you like a meek lamb led to slaughter? Well I shall not be led into another marriage against my will." She was so angry her hands shook. But still her father's grasp prevented her from pulling away.

A long dormant rage began to bubble in her chest, threatening to break free of her carefully erected walls. To her surprise, she had neither the will nor inclination to contain it. Her father, her duplicitous, pox-ridden father, had once again trapped her, and she couldn't do a damned thing about it. She didn't often curse, but forbidden words formed in her mind. Oh, if only she were brave enough to give them air. But she knew herself too well. Never would she give her father the satisfaction of seeing how much his decision angered her.

Memories of her previous marriage, and the rage that burned in her belly towards her father for forcing her into it, almost had her screaming and yelling like the poor addle-brained crone that used to live on the edge of the woods near Lesbury Castle, her childhood home. The memory sent shivers up her spine. No. She would never become as desperate, or deranged, as that.

Her father tugged her hand to make her face him. "You must marry the king's choice. And I am out of time." Her father began to cough again, but he refused the physician's ministrations. When he had control of his voice he continued, "I will not have my lands and title discharged back to the crown because you defy me."

"Your land and titles? They are my mother's, and you cared so little for her that you married another when she was not buried a month." Now that she had spoken she couldn't hold the torrent back. "You value wealth and reputation more than your daughter," she spat, her temper almost at breaking point. She had to find the resolve to remain in control of her emotions, but God help her, she could not. "You care so little for me that you would force me to do your will, although you know how I feel?"

Her father was shocked at your unexpected outburst, but he wasn't cowed. "You will do your duty."

Cicele looked again to her brother by marriage. "Is there no other way?" She heard the pleading in her own voice, but was beyond caring.

Ranulf looked back at her father with barely concealed loathing before he focused on her. "The king has ordered it, and it must be done while your father still lives." He cast a look at her father lying on the bed. "The archbishop is waiting."

So, her father had once again won. He had decided her fate while leaving her ignorant.

Only ten days ago Cicele had watched the archbishop celebrate a nuptial mass for her sister's wedding in the chapel here at Beauforde Castle. The king had ordered a public celebration to bear witness to the marriage between Isabeau and Ranulf. Foolishly they had married in secret and without the king's permission, but King Henry had been willing to overlook the insult to his authority if Ranulf would agree to a public marriage. Ranulf had also been lucky not to have his lands confiscated. It was very clear this new king would not tolerate defiance.

Now it seemed she too was subject to his wishes. God help her.

A mere ten days and now her father lay dying after falling from his horse while hunting. Something had ruptured, so the physician had said, and he was unlikely to survive the night.

She might be able to fight her father, but could she fight Fate? It seemed Fortuna was spinning her wheel, and Cicele had the desperate feeling that her future would be one she would never have chosen for herself.

Pragmatism and the ability to hide her emotions were skills Cicele had honed over years of being manipulated by her father. A chess piece moved about a board between players who cared little for her, or her desires.

Well, she would become her own player, making sure her new husband understood that she was not willing to be any man's pawn. Cicele had learned to play chess and had become a fierce opponent. She would develop a strategy to deal with her new husband. That was what chess had taught her. Strategy. And patience.

"Very well, it seems I have no choice. Proceed." She didn't look at her sister standing on the other side of the huge bed. One look at Isabeau and Cicele's resolve would falter. Cicele pulled her hand free of her father's grip and stood by the hearth, waiting for others to once again lead her where she didn't wish to go.

Within the hour, she stood before the archbishop in the bedchamber where her father's wheezing breath punctuated every word the archbishop spoke as he intoned the sacred prayers that would bind her to a man she had never met. Cicele was only partially listening when a name caught her attention.

"Who did you say?"

The archbishop looked up and seemed to be confused by her question. "I beg your pardon, my lady, but I address Sir Ranulf on behalf of your husband."

"Yes, Your Grace, I understand, but forgive me I must have misheard. Who is it exactly I am marrying?"

The archbishop cast a glance at Ranulf, who stood solemnly beside her in her soon-to-be-husband's stead, before returning his attention back to her. "Sir Ranulf stands in proxy for Sir Guyon le Loup, the newly appointed Baron Bolham, my lady." Then he continued to the blessing, pronouncing her married.

A buzzing began in her ears, growing in intensity until the chamber started to spin. Cold, cruel fingers of panic closed around her throat making it impossible to breathe. Powerless to stop her body's reaction to the devastating news her stomach heaved.

"Quick, she is about to vomit," someone said, but Cicele didn't know who.

She retched into the proffered bowl, vaguely aware of gentle hands rubbing her back and murmuring soothing words as her stomach emptied itself.

Oh God. Of all the cruel twists of fate she was now married to the one man she loathed above all others.

Slowly the strength in her legs gave way and she sank to the floor.

Fate was cruel, and she was doomed.

THE NEXT AFTERNOON Cicele stood beside her sister as they watched the wagon bearing their father's body leave the upper bailey. The archbishop had conducted the last rights sometime during the night, but instead of being buried in the vault at Beauforde Castle, it had been her father's wish to be buried back at his castle in Redesdale. There he would have his funeral and be buried in the vault in the castle's chapel.

"I should have gone with him." Listless and numb, Cicele couldn't gather any strength of conviction as she uttered what was expected of her.

"He is dead, and you are required here." Isabeau placed her arm around Cicele. "And you and I both know he didn't want us in life, so he surely won't want us in death."

Cicele had to agree. Her father had never really shown her any attention. And he had abandoned her sister, Isabeau, to an abbey as an infant to save the honor of his wife and himself.

"He was a poor excuse for a man, but he was our father."

"Being the one to impregnate our mothers hardly seems to imply he is a father." Isabeau had forgiven her father, but she hadn't liked him.

Trying to change the subject, Cicele turned and looked at her sister. "Yes, you are right." Cicele gestured to her sister's growing belly. "Now in your case the one who has planted that child will make an extraordinary father." She gave her sister a provocative smile.

Isabeau's cheeks turned a dark shade of red. Cicele loved to tease her. That's what sisters did, and Cicele would enjoy the teasing and the closeness for as long as she could.

"I wonder when I will hear from my new husband?" Cicele changed the subject. No one except her maid, Maude, knew of her past with Guyon le Loup, and it would stay that way. Try as she might she couldn't bring herself to name him out loud. That wasn't a great start to a marriage, but defiance was all she had, and she would not relinquish it.

Isabeau absentmindedly stroked the ear of the great black hound that stood at her side. "Ranulf had expected a missive advising of his arrival, but he has had no word since before the wedding." Isabeau watched as her husband rode behind the wagon bearing their father.

Turning back to Cicele, Isabeau clasped her hand. "Sister, you must believe me, I had no idea Father, or the king, was going to make you marry." Her sister's expression was pleading for Cicele to believe her.

Cicele placed her hand on her sister's arm to reassure her. "I do believe you, and besides what could I have done had I known their plans?" She was as powerless over her future as was the night to hold back the day. She kissed Isabeau's cheek. "Come, you must be tired, and Godiva will have my heart on a platter if I keep you standing out here talking of my woes."

Isabeau smiled and took Cicele's hand as they walked back up the steps and into the hall.

"I shall miss you when you are gone," Isabeau confessed quietly as they made their way through the hall and towards the tower stairs.

A lump formed in Cicele's throat, which she couldn't dislodge, so instead squeezed her sister's hand in response. She couldn't imagine what the next few months would be like. To be married to the man who had broken her heart was too cruel a fate to contemplate. She had barely slept the previous night thinking about the man who was now her husband. Once she had longed for them to be married, but now…

Perhaps she could seek to live a separate life. Without the ability to bear children he would have no use for her. Would she tell him the whole truth? Probably not. He did not deserve any consideration. Six years ago he had promised her the world, only to break her heart and leave her ruined. What a young, naive fool she had been. A fool in love, who had willingly believed him to be a better man than he actually was. Ignoring her maid's repeated warnings to stay away from a man who had a reputation for womanizing, Cicele had all but thrown herself at Guyon, believing his honeyed words of love and marriage. But true to her maid's warning he had betrayed her, leaving her heartbroken and ruined.

Trust and respect were the foundations on which a good marriage was built. Cicele would never trust him again. And respect? He was a man without honor, and totally underserving of her respect.

It was too much to think about, and fret upon, and it was making her ill. Cicele was talented at many things that people underestimated: putting on a mask of indifference was one of her most exceptional talents, so she simply pushed all her fears to one small corner of her mind and presented the face of a woman surrendered to her fate. It seemed to be working.

After delivering Isabeau to her chamber Cicele decided to go to the stables and see the mare she would have to leave behind. Vite ran at her feet, the little dog sniffing and peeing on every surface his small height allowed, as she walked through the upper bailey and down into the lower bailey to where the stables were situated.

Beauforde Castle had been her home now for several months, and she had been happy here. Having her sister's love had assuaged much of Cicele's pain and grief, but now that pain threatened to consume her. God's bones, she was weary of it all.

Back when she had first met Guyon—the name almost made her choke—she had confessed her dream to breed horses. He had listened, and together they talked about the palfreys she would breed and sell all over the kingdom. *Naive fool. There's another reason to be mocked and ridiculed for your stupidity.* Humiliation scorched her cheeks.

Her first husband had presented her with a beautiful palfrey as a marriage gift, but it was never hers. Her dream of breeding fine horses, like her dream of wanting to marry the man she had once loved, were as ash on a cold hearth. The irony of her situation was not lost on her. Never would she love her new husband.

Everything she had when married to Nicholas was taken from her on her husband's death. Yes, she had her dower lands, but her father had reclaimed them after Nicholas died. Most of her personal possessions, and much of her clothing, were owned by her husband and had been taken from her and given to the new Lord of Ellingham. Six years of marriage, and she was left with nothing save a gown and some trinkets.

The only possession she could truly call her own was the psalter her mother had left her.

When she had learned that she had a sister, and that she could stay with her and her husband, she had been overjoyed. The thought of going back to her father's castle to be ignored at best, and reviled as useless, would have been too much to endure.

Now she was in the same position. Everything she was to inherit became her husband's. Once again, she was a mere chattel. A rich and titled chattel, but a possession to dispense with as her husband saw fit.

Ever since she was a child she wanted to do something for herself, and breeding fine horseflesh seemed like a good idea. Jabbe, the long dead huntsman at Lesbury, her childhood home, had taught her all he knew about horses. He had called her his "lady apprentice." They had been some of the happiest days of her lonely childhood. If she could persuade her new husband to let her live a quiet life at Lesbury where she could breed horses, and hunt and fish, then she would be happy. A small spark of hope sprang to life in the barren places of her heart. Yes. That was a plan she could work with. *Please, God, make him willing.* It was a prayer she would pray diligently until it was granted.

Arriving at the stables Cicele walked down the stalls patting heads as she passed. She came to Isabeau's mare Cloud.

"She's a bonny wee thing."

The mare nodded her agreement. She was a gentle creature, and soothed Cicele's anxious thoughts with a soft nuzzle and a playful nudge.

Cicele would miss so much about Beauforde, especially the horses. She had no idea what to expect when her husband arrived and took her away. It didn't do to dwell on things she had no power to change, so she called Vite and left.

Standing in the lower bailey, she paused. Too restless and irritable to return to the lady's solar to stitch and listen to Elizabet and Beatrice cooing over their babies, Cicele decided to walk to the pele yard and on to the orchard. It was a lovely morning, and surprisingly warm for early January. Vite ran ahead as she walked. Men-at-arms nodded to her, but most of the inhabitants of the castle were too busy about their morning tasks to take much notice of her.

"Do you want to come and watch me practice?" an excited voice asked from somewhere behind her. Cicele turned to see Tillie dressed in boy's clothing, and a generous smile plastered on her plain little face.

Isabeau had told Cicele about Tillie, and yet Cicele still had trouble connecting the scared little girl of Isabeau's story to the child that stood smiling at her now.

"Yes, Tillie, I think I would like that very much. But do you mind if I practice with you?"

The little girl looked shocked. "You throw knives?"

Cicele tried not to laugh at the little girl's stunned expression. "I learned to throw when I was about your age from my huntsman. It is an important skill for a woman, and one I have always maintained."

Tillie nodded. "That is what Sir Ranulf says."

Cicele spent the rest of the morning practicing with Tillie as they threw knives at the poor unsuspecting pell, while Vite wandered about peeing on every post he could find. It was perfect.

Chapter Two

WALLINGFORD CASTLE, ENGLAND

The day after Epiphany

It was official. By God's splintered cross, it was a disaster. Guyon schooled his face into a neutral expression. The last thing he wanted was to reveal his concerns to the man sitting in front of him. Henry would exploit any weakness to his advantage and Guyon wasn't willing to give even more of himself to his king.

Shrewd unblinking eyes assessed Guyon. "I see you are somewhat a reluctant groom?" The king took a deliberate sip of wine from his silver goblet, but his eyes never left Guyon. "Marriage to Lady Cicele is a coup, even for you. In one sweep, you have titles and land even your vast ambition could not have dreamed of." Henry leaned forward and fingered the parchment lying on the table. "You wish it wasn't so?" he said trying to bait him.

Guyon kept his expression neutral. He'd signed the contract, placed his seal on the accursed thing, and as of four days ago was married. There wasn't a bloody thing he could do about it.

"I am your servant, Sire." Guyon was careful to keep his tone impartial, but he walked a fine line with the young king who sat watching him.

Henry didn't respond immediately. He ran his finger around the rim of the cup of wine he had been sipping from, seemingly deep in thought. It was unusual to have a private audience with the king. The only other inhabitants of the small audience chamber were the king's newly appointed Lord Chancellor, Thomas Becket, and a clerk who was busy scribbling the details of the interview. Henry recorded everything.

Becket stood to the right of Henry's shoulder, watching, but he never spoke. Guyon would have to watch himself with Thomas Becket. The man had a hungry, ambitious look to his eyes that warned Guyon to be careful.

He swiveled his eyes away from the chancellor and back to Henry who looked up at Guyon. His eyes held none of their previous warmth.

"As I predicted." He gave him a cold stare. "Cessford is dead, and you are now *jure uxoris* the Earl of Cessford, courtesy of the Lady Cicele."

Guyon refused to be cowed by Henry's uncompromising gaze, and although sweat slid down his spine he remained still, fighting the instinct to move back. God only knew how Cicele was feeling being married to him. If he could go back and change what had happened that summer in Rouen he would, but it was beyond him to change the past.

Finally, Henry held out the charter. "Here is the charter to your new title, and lands, Sir Guyon," he purred, but didn't relinquish the sealed parchment as Guyon's fingers sought to claim it. "You have served your king well."

Guyon didn't take his eyes off the king, or release his grip from the proffered parchment. But he did wait. He had spent the better part of twenty years serving this man's family. First his father, Geoffrey of Anjou, then his mother, the Empress Matilda, and now their son, King Henry. The king of England might be young, but he was no fool. And neither was Guyon. He would do everything in his power to make the marriage work, although he had the distinct feeling it would be almost impossible. Past decisions, foolish male arrogance, and an accursed body, were all responsible for what had transpired, but he saw no easy way to explain them to his new wife. He wasn't even sure he could explain it to himself. God's bones, his life was complicated.

Of course, Henry knew nothing of the past that would sour Guyon's marriage to Lady Cicele. Politics propelled the king's decision to award Guyon with an earldom. Unfortunately, it also propelled Guyon into a marriage he never wanted.

It would seem Fate, aided by the king, had brought Cicele and himself back around to face the past head on. A pox on the man, king or not, for embroiling him in his quest for power and control of the north.

"My lord." A curt nod was all Guyon offered.

Henry relinquished the parchment, but he didn't take his eyes off Guyon. There was something calculating in his gaze that warned Guyon that what he was about to communicate was ominous. His stomach clenched as he waited for his king to continue. God's teeth, he was a good as trapped, and there wasn't a thing he could do to save himself.

Henry took a sip of wine, swirled it in his mouth then swallowed. "Understand me well, Sir Guyon, I cannot allow another to take control of the north." Henry cast Guyon a sly look.

Guyon knew that look, and it didn't bode well for any man for whom it was directed. He could feel Henry's schemes closing about his neck as surely as a hangman's noose sitting against his skin. Fighting the shiver that slid up his spine, he waited.

Henry tapped the map that lay across the table. "It is imperative you swive your good wife and ensure William's schemes to usurp my God-given right to the throne are not realized. I hold the north because of good men, but not all are as loyal to me as you, and your new brother in marriage, Ranulf d'Argentan."

What Henry omitted to mention was that Guyon, as Lady Cicele's husband, now controlled vast swaths of land in the north. Henry had obviously decided he could control Guyon, but not William. It was no secret that King Stephen's son, William, wanted his father's throne. Henry had the rightful claim, but when did that matter if powerful men were hungry for power?

Guyon decided to test his theory. "You doubt his loyalty, Sire?" William had sworn his oaths to Henry when old King Stephen had died, and named Henry the heir to the crown, but William wanted his father's throne and he was desperate to reclaim what he considered his birthright.

Henry sneered, "I have just signed the death warrants for traitors who plotted with the Scots king to take possession of the north. I will not tolerate another." Henry rapped his fingers on the table. "Now that you have married, and control estates in the north, you will do your duty and make sure the Scots keep out of my lands. I leave for London, then Rouen on the tide. In my absence you must ensure the north is secure." Henry gave Guyon a sly smile. "There are rumors your old adversary, the Earl of Lincoln, threatens the peace from his castle in Warkworth." Henry held Guyon's gaze.

"Lincoln sides with King Malcolm?" Probably William was also involved, but Guyon kept that thought to himself.

"I suspect he does," Henry snarled.

"I shall ride north immediately, Sire." Guyon was Henry's loyal tenant-in-chief, and would give his life for his liege lord. God knows he didn't want to contemplate what the rest of his life would look like shackled to Lady Cicele, but a perverse side of him relished the idea of inflicting some pain on the worthless blackguard Lincoln. The man's ambitions knew no bounds.

Henry cast Guyon a menacing glare. "My spies tell me Lincoln is securing his castles. He is up to something, and I want him stopped." Henry smiled as he toyed with his goblet. "Perhaps your wife will again prove a temptation." Henry stopped playing with his goblet to meet Guyon's eyes. "You will rid me of this threat."

Guyon didn't think he had heard Henry correctly, so he just looked at him for several moments. Six years ago, in Rouen, Lincoln had tried to abduct Cicele and force her to marry him. Guyon had thwarted his plan. When Lincoln had been renounced at court, and sent back to England in disgrace, Lincoln had vowed he would not rest until he destroyed Guyon. Until then Lincoln and Guyon had been fast friends, but since Rouen they had become sworn enemies.

Henry smiled. "Ah, I see you are thinking, 'did your king suggest you kill a nobleman?' It can be done, surely, if you are the High Sheriff of Northumbria?"

It was a significant honor to be given the role of high sheriff, but Guyon didn't want to begin his tenure with innocent blood on his hands. True, Lincoln was no innocent, but Guyon would not murder, even for the king.

Henry barked a laugh. "You disapprove of my tactics? Come now, it is not in your nature to be so scrupulous."

I've become his puppet. You fucking idiot, you've been bought by a title, and wealth, and now you are trapped. Impotent rage gnawed in Guyon's gut. Justice was a scarce commodity, so it seemed.

"You will consummate your marriage immediately, and then take her to Alnwick where you will administer my justice. And you will rid me of any threat to my authority." Henry's tone was unequivocal, but he smiled as he toyed with his goblet.

"Your mother's family have been lords of Alnwick since my grandsire's time. It would please me, and ease your transition, if you were to take her name. I will have my clerics write the charter." A sly smile creased the young king's face. "But for now, I think your own reputation will ensure the north is controlled." Henry's face changed in an instant. His features became serious, and his eyes took on a furious intensity. "Do I make myself clear, my lord?"

Guyon had been outmaneuvered, and by a lad of just two and twenty. Yet the "lad" was the son of two of the most powerful people in Christendom. His respect for the king increased as he watched him recline on his grand chair.

"Yes, my liege, I understand," he replied, with clipped precision, "I will not fail." Guyon didn't want to take his mother's name, but admitted that the idea had merit. The de Vesci name was synonymous with Alnwick, and power. The irony was not lost on Guyon; his mother had lost her dower lands when she married a man who had neither title or wealth. His parents had married for love, and neither mourned the loss of her family's favor. Guyon's father was the grandson of a wolf catcher who happened to save old King Henry from an injured wolf while out hunting. The le Loup family had land, but were not of noble blood, and that was what had infuriated his mother's sire. But Guyon was the last survivor of the de Vesci blood.

Would it grieve him to lose his father's name? The name le Loup would not be of great advantage in Alnwick, but being a de Vesci would go a long way to gathering much needed support.

So, Fate had spun her wheel—he was not only married to a woman who probably wanted to cut his balls off, but he was also forced to change his name. He had to remind himself he had chosen this, and he was not about to cry foul. He would accept Fate's hand, and obey his king. God help him.

Henry barked a laugh. "I know you will not fail. You are not called 'la Bête' for nothing. I suspect Lincoln is already shitting himself knowing you now possess the woman who could have made him rich as Croesus."

Guyon smiled at the epithet; it was a play on his name, "le Loup," which meant "the wolf." He had earned it in the many battles between King Stephen and Henry. His tactic of stalking his enemies, then pouncing on unsuspecting soldiers, leaving none alive but one to relay the message of la Bête's terror. Fear of "the Beast" had spread throughout Stephen's ranks. Henry had once joked that that was one of the reasons why the barons had put pressure on King Stephen to agree to a peace between the two factions.

Now Stephen was dead, and Henry was king. And for Guyon's vicious tactics he had been awarded the office of high sheriff, his maternal uncle's estates, and an earldom. God's blood, he also had a wife who was apt to be as cold and hard as winter.

Henry rose from his chair and cast Guyon a dangerous look. "Remember, Lincoln must not succeed, is that clear?"

"As always, you may rely on me, and my men." A chill slithered down Guyon's spine. Would Lincoln risk abducting Cicele before Guyon reached Beauforde?

Henry cut across Guyon's thoughts. "It will not go well for you if you fail me in this." The king's voice was quiet, but the threat was undeniable.

How had his life become so complicated? A marriage to an unwilling bride, and the destruction of an enemy he had once called friend. God's bones, he was tired.

He bowed to Henry, then turned on his heel and strode from the small, private chamber.

"A bloody pox on the man," he spat under his breath. He was as good as trapped, and the infuriating thing of it was he'd been the one to walk into it.

Marriage to Lady Cicele promised to be his most pressing challenge. An image of a younger Cicele as he bade her farewell, promising to come back and marry her, filled his mind. He'd failed her, and she was not likely to forgive or forget. "Hell's teeth, what a godawful mess."

However, things were never easy, and his ability to retain all that Henry had awarded him meant he couldn't let anyone, not even his wife, see just how vulnerable he really was. No matter how many masses were said, the guilt and shame would never be assuaged.

GUYON STRODE out into the daylight, making for the stables where his men waited. He took a shuddering breath to calm the frustration Henry's scheming roused in him. Without looking at his men he shouted, "We're leaving!" He took the reins of his horse from his squire and stalked to the mounting block. None of the men spoke; they merely did as their lord demanded. In silence three knights, their squires, and twenty mounted men-at-arms, with their grooms, five packhorses, Guyon's destrier, and two wagons, all formed a column behind Guyon.

Silence descended as they made their way from the castle, through the town, and towards the king's road which would take them north. Guyon wasn't inclined to conversation. He would tell them his plan in good time.

He needed to think about his next move. If he wasn't careful King Henry, Lincoln, or the Lady Cicele might prove his undoing.

When they reached the road Guyon reined in his horse and waited for his sergeant to join him. The two men had served together as squires; now twenty years later Thomas de Mares was like a brother to him.

"It looks like you've done battle with the devil himself." Thomas's laughter bubbled under the surface. "Will we be expecting the fiend to give chase any time soon?"

Ignoring the smirk on his friend's face, Guyon turned to his squire. "Warin, take two men and scout for trouble. We make for Beauforde, and we'll be moving fast."

His plan was simple, but he needed to gain ground, which meant he had to drive his men hard for the six days it would take them to reach Beauforde Castle. None would complain; each one, man and beast alike, was war-hardened. They'd been pushed beyond their endurance many times, and survived. The previous summer had been spent waging a war on King Stephen and his followers. That had been bloody and vicious. This was akin to a leisurely saunter about his estates. Albeit a miserable one.

THE RAIN STARTED SOON after they left Wallingford and didn't stop for three days. It lashed man and beast, soaking through to drench everything, including their baggage. Impossible to escape the incessant wet, clothing chafed against damp skin, and the mail began to show signs of rust. Each man sat grim-faced and resolute, praying the weather would turn. Winter rains could last for days, making travel miserable, as well as dangerous. There was always the danger a horse could come up lame, or worse, break a leg, if it lost its footing.

There is a God in heaven, after all. Guyon heaved a sigh of relief as he woke on the morning of the fourth day to an unseasonably warm dawn. The decision had been made to leave half the men-at-arms to guard the wagons and spare horses on the second day, their pace too slow in the rain-drenched ground. Guyon and his remaining retinue continued north at a faster pace.

Now, as the sun shone on their backs, Guyon allowed himself to relax. Fertile land covered with every shade of green imaginable spread out to the east. On the western side of the road lay thick forest, its bare tree branches looking like skeletal limbs against a pale blue sky.

The road was in truth little more than a track. Merchants plied their trade along its length, although prudent travelers were sure to spend coin on security to ensure their goods, and lives, were not plundered. Only a fool would travel without protection.

The further north they traveled the more likely they were to be attacked. Bands of mercenaries or disenfranchised peasants roamed the forest and lanes, in hopes of stealing something of value to barter for food to relieve their incessant hunger. The years of war between King Stephen and the Empress Matilda had been brutal to many. Starvation made desperate men reckless. As he surveyed the forest he was confident his retinue was safe from attack. Their numbers were assurance, but nevertheless he had his men form a tight column.

By mid-afternoon on the fifth day he reined in and waited for Thomas to come alongside him. "Hexham is just over that next hill." He motioned with his head in the direction of the town where they would spend the night.

Both men squinted against the watery sun to see if they could catch sight of the town's cathedral, with its ornate tower.

They had passed the previous night at the village of Ovingham, in the hall of the bailiff, Sir Rupert Fitzwilliam. The man was only too pleased to offer hospitality to Guyon and his men. That was part of Guyon's plan, to announce that the new high sheriff had arrived. He would repeat it at Hexham.

"Are you clear about what you must do?" Guyon scanned the surrounding countryside with a critical eye.

"I'd prefer it if you took more than Warin; I don't like the idea of you out there by yourself."

"God's truth man, I don't need you to nursemaid me." Impatience made his voice sharp, while irritation clawed at his resolve. "I'll be fine, and besides, if I encounter any trouble I'll set Warin on them." He gave his squire a wink.

"I'm not sure if it's wise to make yourself so vulnerable. The pox-ridden cur wishes you dead." Thomas's annoyance made his tone petulant.

Thomas was referring to Lincoln who would not hesitate to skewer Guyon, then take Cicele to wife, if he had the chance.

Guyon turned his head and observed his sergeant. "'Tis but a day's hard ride to Beauforde. All will be well. Besides, they will be expecting *you*," he reminded his friend. "I'm not anticipating any trouble." It was his meeting with an angry and reluctant Lady Cicele, rather than an encounter with Lincoln, that clawed at his insides.

"You might not be expecting it, but in all the years I've known you, it finds you." Thomas's brows were drawn together in a scowl to match Guyon's.

Guyon laughed. "Aye, it does."

In truth, Guyon wasn't expecting any trouble, but an uneasy feeling had been gnawing at his guts for days. There was one thing he had learned early in life—trust his intuition for danger. It had never proved him wrong. He'd be careful.

HEXHAM WAS A BUSTLING TOWN, its markets and abbey the reason the town prospered. Hundreds of pilgrims flocked to pray, and seek succor from the saint buried in the abbey's vault. It was said that when King Ælfwald was murdered a great light shone on the place where he lay. Heaven, it seemed, had stamped its authority on the man, and now the abbey prospered from divine favor. The indulgences collected from such veneration were one of the reasons the abbey was undergoing renovations. The new bishop seemed to have a head for increasing revenue, but Guyon couldn't fault him for it. His ambition was evident. His Grace, the Bishop of Hexham, lived in a palace to rival Henry's court. The previous bishop had been tried for treason and was in the tower of London awaiting his death, the poor sot. He hoped the new bishop had better sense than to plot against the king.

Guyon looked at the impressive buildings, but wasn't inclined to believe God paid much attention to the frenzied ambitions of mere mortals. Still he had no objection to the bishop's enterprise. Perhaps Guyon could encourage the abbot of St. Andrew's Priory to unearth the relics of an ancient saint. It was close enough to Alnwick to benefit both the town and the priory. The revenue would help pay for his expenditure as sheriff.

Turning his thoughts back to the present, Guyon paid for lodging at the sizable inn on the town square. The Sheep's Head boasted a large upper room where he and his men could sleep the night. It suited his purpose to be seen by as many people as possible. Guyon, as the new Lord High Sheriff of Northumbria, would dine with the town's aldermen and merchant guild, hear their grievances, and ply them with wine. Then, come morning, Thomas would swap places with him, taking on his identity, and ride in state towards Beauforde. Hopefully, if Lincoln was planning an ambush, Thomas and his men would be the decoy, while Guyon became a nameless bachelor knight heading north.

Before dawn they left the inn and rode north towards Beauforde, where his wife would be waiting. An hour out of Hexham, Guyon, along with his squire, took to the byways, while the rest of his retinue, under the command of Thomas, headed on the main road north towards Otterburn where they would wait for the wagons. Then he would ride to Beauforde.

Guyon didn't expected Lincoln to come to Alnwick and acknowledge him as Alnwick's new lord. But he would be watching and waiting for Guyon to make a mistake. He had to get to the safety of Alnwick as soon as possible. By Guyon's reckoning that was at least three days away. Enough time to retrieve his wife, consummate his marriage, and travel to Alnwick and establish himself in the castle.

It was a simple plan. Nothing, he assured himself, could go wrong.

Chapter Three

As he had anticipated, Guyon arrived at Beauforde Castle without incident. But before he entered the castle he wanted to ensure Lincoln didn't have men hiding in the woods. Beauforde was a secure castle, but Guyon didn't take anything for granted. Within the past two weeks Beauforde had been playing host to every titled noble within a fifty-mile radius. It was the perfect opportunity for a whoreson like Lincoln to exploit.

It wouldn't take long to scout the land and woods close to the castle, then a bath and a fresh change of clothes before confronting his wife. At the thought of being clean he scratched himself, imagining vermin already taking up residence in his filthy clothing. He didn't want to think about what crawled in the long whiskers covering his chin. Only a few short years ago six days in the saddle would have mattered not the least to him.

He sighed. A bath and a shave would have to wait. *I'm getting old and soft*. Murmuring to himself he tied his horse to a tree under the cover of the woods and walked towards the river that flowed around the northern side of the castle. He had told Warin to search the village and meet him by the postern gate. There was perhaps another two hours of full daylight left. Guyon would take advantage of that daylight to ensure there were no nasty surprises waiting for him.

As he slowly walked through the woods he surveyed the area for signs of trouble. Moving through the bracken that covered the forest floor, memories of a much younger Cicele de Saussay flooded his mind. She had arrived at Geoffrey and Matilda's court in Rouen, with her father, to secure a marriage. Although Cicele was one and six, and a bit old to not be betrothed, Guyon had never seen a more beautiful woman. He huffed a small laugh remembering her haughty demeanor as she was introduced to him. Her expression suggested she knew that her face and figure were her greatest assets, and wouldn't be given away cheaply.

He had watched her as she moved through the hall—chin held high—her eyes never focusing on anyone as she walked through a sea of men, each one coveting her titles. Like the addle-brained fool he was, he hadn't been able to take his eyes off her. Hair the color of chestnuts, and eyes that seemed to pierce through flesh to bone, she was a vision that left him gasping for breath.

He wasn't the only man to succumb to Lady Cicele's charms. Lincoln had made a spectacle of himself, fawning over her and spouting chivalric poetry to the amusement of the whole court. And it was Lincoln who Guyon had found trying to abduct her one morning when she was out riding. Matilda had ordered Guyon to act as a guard for the beautiful young heiress, and thankfully he was there to protect her from Lincoln's scheme to abduct and rape her, then force her to marry him. If he had been successful he would have been one of the most powerful men in England. But Guyon had destroyed Lincoln's plans.

Lincoln fled Rouen and scurried back to England rather than face Matilda and Geoffrey. When he returned to England, he betrayed Matilda by joining forces with Stephen, marrying one of Stephen's nieces.

Guyon shuddered as he remembered Lincoln's words as Guyon forced him away from Cicele. "I will destroy you, and everything you hold dear. That is a vow, Guyon le Loup."

Chances were that Lincoln wanted to settle that score and destroy Guyon before he had a chance to establish himself at Alnwick and assert his authority. "Not if I can help it."

Six years had passed and Guyon was a different man. It was probably too much to hope that Lincoln was also different. Only a fool would believe that Lincoln would be content with his lands and title, and the forgiveness of his new king. Henry's orders echoed in Guyon's head. It was inevitable that Guyon and Lincoln would cross swords again. And probably soon.

King Henry's veiled warning about Lincoln stirred something in the back of Guyon's mind. Was it Fate, or something more sinister, that both Lincoln's wife and Cicele's husband had died in the space of three months?

A cold chill settled in Guyon's bones. The thought, once it had taken root, wouldn't budge. *Satan's cods! Surely Lincoln wouldn't kill his own wife, would he?* No, it was too heinous, even for a cur like Lincoln.

Guyon's quickly conceived plan to ride hard to Beauforde to claim his wife seemed a godsend. If Lincoln was capable of murder, then Cicele was in grave peril.

Scanning the riverbank by the castle's postern gate he spied movement close to the river where it wound its way behind the cliff on which the castle sat. Something about the movement below piqued his curiosity, so he picked his way through the trees, always keeping low to the ground, and investigated.

He had seen many things in his travels—strange beasts, and even stranger men. He was also accustomed to women, but nothing had prepared him for the spectacle he was confronted with as he came to a halt several feet from the ledge that overlooked the wide, slow-moving river.

Shock, amusement, and a stab of lust all rolled together as his eyes beheld a woman with bare legs and a head of flowing chestnut hair. A small black dog yipped at her from the riverbank. Her chemise was gathered between her long slender legs as she waded out of the small weir. She bent over to retrieve her hose, offering Guyon a tantalizing view of her arse. His pulse coursed through his body, while his jaw clenched, making his ears ache.

He wasn't sure what he was feeling—lust, incredulity, or anger? Anger won out. What in God's name was she doing prancing about in the river almost naked? And with no protection. His tongue seemed stuck to the roof of his mouth, making speech impossible. *Move, you bloody great hulk.* Thankfully his legs obeyed as he began to walk, but it would take him some time to reach her. And when he did he would march her back inside the keep, where she would be safe.

Guyon was unlike most men who believed a beautiful woman had new washed wool between her ears—all white and fluffy, with absolutely no substance. Lady Cicele had a formidable mind, and a sharp tongue that could cut a man to pieces. He had told her once that she could use it to better advantage as a cheese knife. Her reaction had been instant, and very enjoyable.

Turning his attention back to the weir he was inclined to think her wits had deserted her. Her actions made a mockery of his belief that she was a woman in possession of superior wit. God help him.

He continued to watch for trouble as he made his way towards the steep path that led to the weir.

Oblivious to his presence, or the danger of being out of the castle unprotected, she hummed a melancholy tune, and chattered to her little dog.

Put some bloody clothes on!

He reached the path that led directly to the riverbank below and paused to watch as Cicele pulled her chemise down over her wet legs. His mouth went dry and his hands shook as she gathered up her kirtle to pull on her hose. Her fingers slid over the silk-soft skin of her legs as she pulled the woolen hose up and over her knee. Like one of the trout gasping for breath that she had thrown on the bank he watched all boggle-eyed as she tied a ribbon over her knee, securing the hose. He remembered what that skin felt like. Every muscle in his stomach and groin tensed. His need for her hadn't diminished over the years. *Shit!*

By the time she had fastened her shoes on her feet, and stood, his body was trembling with suppressed tension.

Although he was consumed with the sight of the woman before him, Guyon was a trained killer, and it was that instinct that saved him. The sound of mail jingling alerted him to approaching men. Guyon spun to see where the threat lay, but from his position he didn't have a clear view of the riverbank. He surged forward, desperate to get to his wife, every sense on alert and tingling with anticipation. Keeping low to the ground he ran down the track, but as he rounded a small bend he stopped. A group of men had surrounded Cicele.

The compulsion to leap forward and confront the intruders was strong, but it was too late. There were too many for him to fight.

Guyon remained hidden and calmed his breathing. He would have to wait for his chance to savage those who dared touch *his* wife.

Chapter Four

The past week had been a trial. She wanted to be free of her sister's constant sympathy, so she stole out of the castle and went to the weir she had made with Tillie's help two weeks before.

Vite had darted off into the woods eager to catch an unsuspecting coney. The dog's unbridled vigor for life was a constant source of amusement. No matter where he was, he embraced the situation with exuberance. In her more wistful moments she wondered what it might be like to show the kind of excitement her dog displayed. Too often she held her emotions close. A lifetime of being scrutinized had made her self-conscious. Of course, that didn't stop her from doing things when she knew she could get away with it.

"I don't know why you insist on doing this, my lady, when there are others who should be." Agatha's tone held a note of reproach which Cicele chose to ignore.

"I like doing something useful." Cicele sat down on the bank to remove her shoes. "And besides, I'm good at it."

"But you are a lady," her maid said with an impatient tone.

"And it is unseemly to be half naked outside your chamber. What if someone was to come upon you?"

Cicele looked up at her maid. "And who would come by and see me?" She had taken the precaution of constructing the weir at a bend in the river and under a large overhang. No one from the castle would be able to see what she was doing.

Cicele loved this time of the day, the precious hours at the end of the day before supper, when the castle was quiet. She could slip out undetected and gather fish, or hunt with her bow and arrows.

Taking advantage of her new husband's absence, she would enjoy her freedom while it lasted. *God knows he will be here soon enough.*

Careful to keep her kirtle and hose dry, Cicele flung them on the riverbank next to where her maid stood scowling. Standing up, Cicele caught her chemise up between her legs, and secured it into her belt. Then she stepped into the large weir to gather the trapped fish and eels, gasping as the cold water made her breath catch.

Reaching down, she took hold of a large brown trout and tossed it onto the riverbank.

It landed next to an unsuspecting Agatha, who jumped back in horror. "I wish you wouldn't do that!" she snapped.

Cicele laughed at her maid's censure. Agatha hated the outdoors. Oh, she liked hunting, and riding, well enough, but she was happiest inside reading or stitching all day. The thought of being cooped up inside, even for a few hours, drove Cicele to desperation.

This was Cicele's secret time, and she would share it with no one. If Isabeau found out, she could probably talk her sister into keeping her secret safe. But Ranulf. Well, he was another matter entirely. If he found out he would undoubtedly forbid her. No, she would savor her time here with no one to criticize her.

"You are welcome to go back and sew, I am happy to be by

myself," Cicele called over her shoulder. She didn't want Agatha to spoil it.

Her maid stood on the bank with her arms folded over her chest. Her stance defiant. "You shouldn't be here, my lady, it isn't safe," Agatha implored while looking about.

Cicele shook her head. She didn't need anyone to watch out for her. In fact, she resented the constant attention. She just wanted to have time to herself with no one berating her, or telling her what she could or couldn't do. And no responsibility. Surely, that was not too much to ask?

Agatha's mood had been sullen of late. Skimming her hands through the cool water searching for fish it occurred to Cicele that her maid had become more and more anxious since Cicele had been forced to marry. Did Agatha think she would turn her out? The young woman was a widow, with no family. Cicele would never discard her.

Something was wrong, but whenever Cicele asked her maid what vexed her she would deny that she was unhappy. Cicele chose to ignore her maid's ill favor and resumed fishing. She savored the time she was spending here with her sister, Isabeau. It was the first time in her life that Cicele had other women with whom to talk and gossip. Elizabet, and especially Beatrice, were constant companions, and if she were honest she would miss them almost as much as she would miss her sister. When Guyon arrived, and he would arrive soon—of that she was in no doubt, she would have to leave. But for now, she would enjoy their company.

Her year had started in ignorance of her sister, but now she couldn't imagine life without her. Perhaps it was God's way of blessing her. First her husband had died just before Easter. Her father had informed her of her younger half brother's death in August. Although not close to Roland, she had mourned her sibling. Then several weeks later a missive arrived from a woman claiming to be her sister, Roland's twin. All her life she had been told Roland was her only sibling. What a jolt it had been to learn she had a sister, and that her father had lied about her existence for years. It was difficult to forgive her father for keeping such a secret. And although he was dead, the familiar twinge of anger she harbored towards her father abandoning Isabeau reminded her that she was a long way from truly forgiving him. Dead or not.

Upon receiving the missive from her sister, Cicele had left her dead husband's home to travel to Beauforde and meet her sister. That was in September. Now the new year had begun, and Cicele's life was to take a major turn once more. But whereas she had begun the previous year with a dying husband and an estranged father and brother, Cicele was thankful for having a sister she had truly come to love. Now she looked forward to being part of Isabeau's life. And she would be an aunt as Isabeau would deliver a child sometime before winter's end. Isabeau's good fortune of having a husband she loved and a babe on the way warmed Cicele's heart. She might not have those things herself, but she would never begrudge her sister.

God alone knew how Isabeau had fared all those years believing she was an abandoned orphan. Cicele's childhood may not have been ideal but at least she knew who she was, and who her parents were.

She may have been unloved, ignored, and barely tolerated by her father, but Cicele had her identity. That had been denied her sister.

Although her father had not really loved her, and both her mother and stepmother had died while she was too young to remember them, Cicele had known what it was to be loved. Her nurse, Maude, who was now her maid had lavished her with affection, and even the old huntsman, Jabbe, had been kind to her, in his own gruff way. But if she was honest, panic over her recent marriage plagued her.

Resentment still lingered at the heavy-handedness of her father and the king. The thought of living the rest of her life with the man who had rejected and abandoned her was almost too much to be borne. The Fates had outdone themselves this time. Six years had passed and a lifetime of indignities had been forced upon her. All thanks to a beast who knew nothing of honor.

Forcing her mind back to the present, she decided to enjoy her time out here, without her maid's constant worry, or her own memories, to ruin it.

"Agatha, please go back and ask Maude to have a bath prepared for me before supper," Cicele called, "and ask Alys to come and collect the basket of fish."

Agatha's body stiffened at Cicele's request. Was she going to refuse? "My lady, you can't stay out here alone. Please come back with me," Agatha pleaded, wringing her hands as she cast furtive glances about the riverbank.

Astounded at her maid's behavior, Cicele held her tongue and waited for Agatha to obey. Silence in the face of anger was a ploy she had learned early. Her father would fly into a fury, but presented with her silence he would usually capitulate and walk away.

Finally, her maid's eyes lowered, and she gave Cicele a curt nod. "Yes, my lady."

Agatha stalked back towards the postern gate. Perhaps it was time for Agatha to remarry. Isabeau might know of a good match for the young maid who had served Cicele for several years.

I won't think on that now. Instead she breathed in the cool afternoon air, letting the confrontation with Agatha recede to the back of her mind.

The sleek body of an eel slid by her ankles. As a girl she had hated the feeling of the eels and fish squirming around her legs. Jabbe had teased her when she had squealed in disgust, and it was that teasing that made her swallow her terror and show no sign of fear. Now she savored the freedom to wade up to her knees in the weir as fish writhed in the small enclosure. No doubt her new husband would never allow her such freedom.

Shaking off her fears for the future, Cicele concentrated on fishing. All thought of her husband, a pox on the man, were pushed far from her mind.

Careful to release the smaller fish and eels back into the river, Cicele made short work of collecting a bountiful harvest. She wouldn't take the fish to Master Dugas herself. The castle's cook was bound to have apoplexy if she arrived at the kitchen with a basket of fish and dressed in filthy servants' clothing. Her well-guarded secret must remain just that. A secret.

Vite's barking, the high-pitched bark the dog reserved for the arrival of friends, interrupted her humming. Alys, the little kitchen maid, appeared with Vite at her heels. "Ye have done well, milady." Alys's eyes boggled as she watched Cicele throw the last of the fish into the basket. It landed on the bank instead of the basket.

The little girl quickly picked up it up and threw it in with the others.

"It will be heavy, you might want to get one of the kitchen lads to come and get it." Cicele kept her tone impassive.

Alys's face transformed from light and bright into a scowl. Her small chest puffed out much like a rooster about to crow. "I don't need no boy to help me." Her tone conveyed what she thought of Cicele's suggestion.

The little girl pulled out a padded square of cloth from her pocket, and placed it on her head, then she heaved the basket onto her head and walked back towards the castle.

"She's as stubborn as a burr."

Vite yipped in agreement.

"Yes, you should know." Every evening Cicele picked the prickly little seed heads from the dog's fur.

Reaching down, she flicked the dog's ears in a playful gesture, deciding to enjoy a moment's peace before she donned her clothing and headed back towards the confines of the castle.

Things were changing, and she was to expect her husband soon.

His missive had arrived three days ago saying he was on his way. Although ashamed, Cicele didn't grieve her father's death. It still rankled that he had forced her to marry.

She had managed to push the missive she had received from her new husband three days ago to the back of her mind. He would be taking her to Alnwick. It was only a few days ride between Alnwick and Beauforde. Cicele and Isabeau could see each other often. *I'll make sure of it.*

Now, as she stilled from her labor at the weir, the contents of the missive clambered for her attention. That she was wed again, and to a man she once had loved, but now despised with every fiber of her being, was almost too much for her to bear. She remembered the summer she traveled to Rouen with her father to secure a betrothal.

She had allowed herself to be seduced. A few words, a lavish amount of charm, and she was lost. She had warmed his bed without a second thought. Saints in heaven, she had been a fool. Even now, the memory still made her skin prickle with humiliation. However, she was resolute. She would never be compliant. He had forfeited that right when he destroyed her life.

Instead of lingering where she knew her thoughts would lead, she closed her eyes and listened to the birds as they went about their day. Their songs filled her with pleasure. She hummed a song her nurse had taught her as a child. It was a sad song of lost love. Taking a deep breath, she relaxed into the serenity of the woods. During her first marriage, her only real joy had been to roam about the woods at Acomb almost every day. Her husband, although not a bad man, had been too distracted with running his vast estates to wonder where she was, which left her free to hunt and fish in the castle's vast forest. She suspected that that luxury would be lost to her when her lord husband finally showed up and took her to Alnwick.

At least she had had a few months to live with her sister here at Beauforde, ostensibly to mourn her first husband, and now her father. What she hadn't wanted was to be sent back to court. Her time in Rouen had taught her to loathe the king's court. She hated the gossip, the intrigue, and the endless men who proposed secret assignations. As a widow they would have been at her like dogs to a bitch in heat. She shuddered at the thought.

As she thought back to her marriage with Sir Nicholas she realized that marriage to Guyon couldn't be any worse. She had been filled with dread on her wedding night, and rightly so. It had been an unmitigated disaster. But it had won her time, and for that she had been grateful.

After five years of marriage, and no child, there was no point in pretending that what the castle's physician had said was not true. She was unable to get with child.

Armed with that sad fact she would refuse Guyon her bed, and eventually she would live a separate life at Lesbury. Hopefully she would only have to see him once or twice a year.

Once again, she was reminded that she was a mere pawn in a man's game—her father, the king, and even Guyon controlled her future. Henry had contracted her to a marriage that he had said would bring peace. "Peace, wouldn't that be a change," she sighed. She doubted peace would be won by her marrying Guyon. Now that her father had died, and she inherited her mother's title and lands, it would be Guyon who controlled a huge swath of northern England. The king, like most men, was only concerned with the politics of the marriage. And Guyon le Loup, now Earl of Cessford, Baron Bolham, and High Sheriff of Northumbria, would be a very powerful ally.

She was pulled back to her surroundings when Vite came scampering back, his nose nudging her calf, his little tongue poking from the tip of his foaming muzzle.

She paused as she pulled on her shoes. "You are a fool," she said, smiling as she bent to stroke his ears and inquire after his adventures. "Did you happen to catch something useful to bring to the table?" The dog's crestfallen demeanor was evidence enough. "Hmm, methinks you need to learn some stealth if you hope to be a mighty hunter." No sooner had she spoken when the little dog tensed, emitting a low growl as his ruff stiffened along the ridge of his spine. Cicele immediately shrank down and began to scan the trees for danger.

The dog emitted another menacing growl. Cicele took hold of the fur around his neck and pulled him to her. "Quiet!" she commanded, barely above a whisper. The dog obeyed instantly.

As she strained to listen she heard something that sent fingers of fear crawling up her spine. The metallic jingle of mail. It was faint, but as she concentrated she knew without doubt that armed men were advancing towards her. And that she was trapped.

Staying low to the ground, she crawled towards the tree where she had placed her bow and arrows, pulling Vite beside her. She had to defend herself if she had any hope of returning to the castle.

Heart thumping, she thrust four arrows in the dirt and notched one to her bow string. She hid herself behind the tree and waited just like Jabbe had taught her. It didn't take long for her to see through the dense woods. A small group of armed men were making their way towards her.

Without warning, Vite darted forward and began barking and snarling at the approaching men. That's when Cicele realized all was lost.

Chapter Five

BEFORE SHE COULD RUN SHE WAS SURROUNDED BY SIX MEN WHO looked as though they had come from Hades itself. Dressed in black from head to toe, they were a terrifying sight.

"Well, what do we have here?" A man with eyes the color of the darkest pit of hell stood over her and ripped her bow from her hands. A violent shiver shook her spine, but before she could react he grabbed her arm in a fierce grip that would leave bruises. "Shut that dog up before the guards come down on us like avenging angels," he yelled over his shoulder to his men.

"No!" Cicele screamed. She wrestled her arm free and rushed towards a gap, desperately trying to get to the dog before he was killed.

A rough hand grabbed her around her neck and dragged her back. "If you try that again I'll cut the tongue from your mouth," he snarled, baring his teeth. Increasing his grip on her neck, he marched her along a track that led into the woods. They moved fast and Cicele tripped several times before they stopped where their horses had been hobbled. Without ceremony, he released her and pushed her to the ground. "Stay there, and don't move.

"Get that bloody dog, and don't come back until it's dealt with," he shouted at the back of a man who was already darting into the woods giving chase to Vite. Another man joined him.

Terrified, Cicele decided it best to keep quiet, and hope—no pray—for her little dog. "Please God, keep him safe," she whispered.

Four men remained. They were a rude, filthy lot with manners suited to the pigpen. Except for the one who had caught her. He was obviously the leader, as his clothing suggested he was of some consequence. His face was clean shaven, but he had the look of a man who would rip her heart out if she didn't do as bid. Too terrified to speak she remained quiet. She had learned early in life that it was best to remain calm, and wait for the opportunity to act. There was always a chance, and she was sure it would come sooner if she complied. Her heart raced and sweat trickled down her stomach. *Don't panic. Oh God, help me please.* She dared not think about her little dog alone with those men.

"On your feet!" A small, wiry man with greasy, matted hair, and rotten teeth clutched her arm and dragged her to a horse. Without warning he flung her up on the saddle, then climbed up behind her. Try as she might, Cicele couldn't prevent the shudder that convulsed her body as the man's chest touched her back.

"Aye, I likes to make a bitch shudder, 'tis part of my charm," he sniggered, leaning close to her ear.

Cicele could feel his breath on her neck, making her stomach hitch. Saliva gathered in her mouth and her stomach gave a heave. Making sure not to vomit on her clothing, she leaned to the side of the horse and emptied her stomach, retching several times until it was completely empty.

"Ah, Pate, you have a way with the ladies." A man guffawed, but Cicele couldn't see who he was.

"Quiet, you idiots," the leader hissed.

Without another word they mounted their horses, and moved deeper into the woods, and away from the castle.

"We don't go without the others," the one they called Pate said behind her, his tone defiant.

"We move, and we move fast."

"But…"

The leader rode up beside them and glared at the man behind Cicele. "You will do as I say, or here is where you die."

Pate must have agreed because within a heartbeat they were moving, and fast. Further and further away from the castle.

Fear coursed through her body. No one would wonder where she was until it was dark. Agatha would wait before letting anyone know she hadn't returned. Unfortunately, Agatha wouldn't suspect anything was wrong until it was too late. Cicele often didn't return to the castle until it was almost dark.

When Agatha told Isabeau that Cicele was gone, it would be too late for Ranulf to track her. *God in heaven, what have I done?* Cicele berated herself for not listening to her maid. But it was too late for recriminations. She had to keep her wits about her and hope for a miracle.

The group led Cicele further and further away from her sister's home. They traveled fast for hours, finally stopping by a stream as the gloaming turned the day into night.

"I go no further until my brothers come," came the voice of the man sitting behind her. His breath stirred her hair and she trembled in revulsion.

The mood between the men had changed. Anger bristled among the small group. She could feel the tension in the man sitting behind her.

"We keep going," the leader shouted.

The two men who sat on horses beside her folded their arms over their chests and refused to move. "Not until me brothers come."

"You," the leader barked at the smallest of the three, "go back; see if you can find them."

The man looked at Pate before he reined his horse around, and retreated back the way they had just come.

The leader looked around the small clearing. "Make a fire."

Her body was stiff and sore. And her head ached, but Cicele refused to slump in the saddle. If she sat straight, she barely felt the odious presence behind her.

When she dismounted, he led her to a tree and told her to stay. She had an idea they were heading southeast, but she couldn't be sure. By her reckoning she was at least ten miles from Beauforde castle. Perhaps she could escape in the night and make her way back. She was familiar with the woods, and had a good chance of remaining undetected. Who were they? What did they want? Her thoughts tumbled about in her mind. With a sinking feeling she realized she was in real danger. Once before she had been abducted and almost raped, but Guyon had saved her. Unshed tears stung the back of her eyes. *Oh, Guyon, where are you when I really need you?*

"Go, do what ye must do, then get back here," Pate said. "I'll be watching, so don't do anything foolish." He smiled in a way that suggested he would like nothing better than to chase her down.

Her body was so stiff she had to move onto her hands and knees before she could stand. Cicele made her way towards a cluster of bracken, and although private, her captors could still see her head above the vegetation.

When she returned, she was told to sit, and then a rope was tied around her waist, but the end lay on the ground next to her. It didn't take long to discover what that meant.

The leader sauntered over and crouched in front of her. "Here." He offered her a small flagon of ale and bread. "I don't want you going hungry, milady," he sneered. His mocking voice filled her ears, making her head dizzy.

"Who are you, and what do you want?" She didn't manage to keep the quiver of fear from her voice.

"You'll find out soon enough," he replied, his smile akin to a cat about to devour its prey.

She couldn't help it; her whole body shuddered. Gathering her strength, she tilted her chin up a fraction to give the impression she was looking down her nose at him and asked, "What do you want with me?"

He regarded her with a calculating gaze. "My master wants you before la Bête gets to you first," he replied, then walked back to his men as they settled for the night.

La Bête? What did Henry's beast of war want with her? She had heard rumors about the murderous knight who created fear wherever he went. She would rather submit herself to Guyon's care than yield to the one they called "the beast."

For the first time in six long, harrowing years Cicele wanted Guyon. She didn't trust him, and wanted to kill him. But he would keep her safe. Of that, she was absolutely sure. Never had he done anything to suggest that he was a threat to her. Well, not to her physically, anyway. Her heart was an entirely different matter.

Terrified, she watched as the men made their camp. Who was their master? They were a dangerous lot, uncouth and ill-bred. She gave an involuntary shudder as she remembered her ride with Pate breathing down her neck.

Tired and frightened, she turned her attention to the bread and ale she had been given. Doubting she could eat anything, she decided to drink the ale. Her mouth was so dry she found it difficult to swallow, but the cool liquid soothed her throat and slaked her thirst. She decided to stash the bread in her pocket for later.

With nothing else to do she sat down on the leaf litter at the base of the tree and tried not to panic. The leader came and crouched before her. "We stay here the night, and in the morrow you will be taken to my master." He tied the end of the rope around the tree where she was sitting, then flung a blanket and a sheep skin at her. Grateful that she would at least be warm she lay the skin, wool side up, on the ground then sat on it, then wrapped the blanket over herself. The night was already cold and a damp mist was settling over the trees. By morning she would be freezing, but at least dry.

The three men were standing around a small fire. "I don't like this," Pate moaned.

Cicele was pleased to hear anxiety in his voice. Could she hope that someone had discovered she had been abducted and given chase? God in heaven, she prayed it might be so. She didn't want to think about what tomorrow would bring. Memories of when Remeys de Roumare had tried to abduct her flew through her mind. He was the Earl of Lincoln now, but he had whispered to her when Guyon had caught him trying to rape her that he would find her and she would be his. She shivered at the memory. Was Lincoln responsible for this? Her blood ran cold. She had to escape. She would never let that animal anywhere near her. Never again.

"I'll take first watch. If any of you touch her I will skin you alive. Do you understand me?" He glowered at the two men, who looked to their feet, each nodding their understanding. Dear God, who was this man that he could invoke such terror? Pate had been beyond brave, or stupid, to insist they wait for his men.

When he'd gone, she moved to get settled but the rope tugged. She would have to sleep sitting up. A sense of despair settled over her. Try as she might she couldn't stop her heart from breaking over the loss of her little dog. Vite. Such a fast and joyful little creature.

When she had lost her baby, and told Nicholas that the castle physician said she would, all likelihood, never be able to have another, the grief threatened to overwhelm her. It was then that Nicholas had given her the little black pup. It was perhaps the only thing her late husband had done that could be construed as thoughtful. She choked back a sob as she leaned back against the tree and closed her eyes.

The two men who lay around the fire spoke in low whispers, but she wasn't close enough to hear what they were saying. Something about their demeanor suggested they were anxious.

She opened her eyes and looked at them. "When my brother by marriage comes to rescue me, you will wish you had never been born." She would never had said that if the "leader" had been there, but Pate and the other man didn't frighten her as much.

In the firelight she could see their expressions as they looked at each other. Good; she was pleased they were worried.

Terrified and uncomfortable, and although her body ached for oblivion, she couldn't sleep. A pox on her captors who seemed to have no trouble. If she could get free of the rope, she just might be able to disappear into the forest. Slowly she moved her hands to the knife she had hidden in her boot. If she could cut through the rope tied around her waist she just might have a chance.

"I wouldn't do anything stupid if I were you." A voice growled in the darkness. Pate stood up and walked to where she lay. "Give it to me." He stretched his hand out, waiting.

She had little choice but to give him the knife. A sob caught in her throat as he took it from her trembling hand.

Taking the knife, he returned to where he had been lying by the fire. "We have a hard ride on the morrow, so you best sleep."

She heard him shift his weight, and inhaled the pungent stench of his unwashed body as he moved a little closer to where she sat.

"I can't lie down, and it is too uncomfortable to sleep." She swallowed her fear and pride and pleaded. "Please."

Grunting, his dark shadow rose over her and released the rope around the tree at her back enough for her to lie down before she heard him retie it.

She settled on her side. "Thank you."

He muttered something under his breath as he lay back down.

It seemed like an eternity while she waited for his breathing to become slow, and even. Terror made her aware of every sound.

She tried not to fret, but couldn't stop her mind churning in panic. No one knew where she was, but by now they would know she had been abducted. Ranulf, although fearless, was no fool. The security of the castle was his responsibility and he would have to wait until dawn. He wouldn't risk going out at night. She had to escape.

Several hours later the leader came back and sent another to keep watch. Without a word, he settled down and within minutes she heard his snores.

Time crawled by, her fear growing as the forest settled into darkness. She had never been so terrified. *You must escape*, she counseled herself, but terror drained what little strength she had.

Hours later, perhaps well after midnight, a faint sound somewhere behind her had her rigid with alarm. She kept still, listening for the sound to repeat, but only the normal noise of the forest night dwellers could be heard. Owls hooted from their perches overhead, and the scurrying of tiny creatures made the leaf litter rustle as they foraged on the forest floor. She gulped down her rising panic when she heard a spine-chilling scream. Cicele chided herself for being so silly when she realized it was only a fox and nothing more sinister.

She strained to listen for the unfamiliar noise that had alerted her to a presence lurking in the darkness. She had spent so many nights out in the forest as a young girl, she knew what was common, and what was not.

She had begun to think the noise was in her imagination when a hand snaked out from behind her and clasped her mouth. Her body became instantly rigid, fear making her heart pound.

Slowly the hand slid from her mouth, and a voice so low and close, sent shivers down her neck. "Don't move or make a sound. I'm here to rescue you."

She gave the tiniest of nods to show she understood. Relief flooded her body making her eyes water.

It took all her resolve not to fight when she felt his hands slide under the blanket and move down her body until they found the rope tied around her waist. A small tug, and then she felt the rope skim her waist. She was free.

Chapter Six

GUYON HAD BEEN FORCED TO WATCH, KNOWING IT WOULD BE
pointless to try and overcome six men. He didn't want to jeopardize
Cicele's safety, so he clenched his teeth and kept hidden.

It was unbearable to be rendered so useless. Their rough
handling of Cicele made his hands tremble, as his anger burned red-
hot. He forced himself to keep still as she cried out for her dog. That
small, desperate cry, struck him with such force he had to shake his
head to dislodge a momentary lapse in concentration.

Why was nothing ever straightforward? Guyon didn't want to
go after the dog, but he knew he must.

It didn't take long. The fools sent to dispatch the animal were so
inept they were no match for the little imp.

Guyon watched with some amusement as the little black creature ran in circles evading the clumsy sots. One of them had stopped
by a tree to take a piss. With swift, practiced ease Guyon punched
him in the side of the head. As the body fell he grabbed the head
and pulled upwards in one vicious heave, then twisted the head until
he heard the gratifying snap of the man's neck.

One down. Guyon kept to the cover of the trees as he pursued the last man. It was obvious the dog possessed the superior intelligence. He watched as the creature darted hither and thither, using very little energy, whereas the man was worn to exhaustion.

Guyon decided, after several minutes of watching the farce, to end it and take the dog with him. He needed to track the larger party if he had any hope of getting to Cicele while there was still daylight.

The first part of the plan was easy. As the fellow rested against a tree, trying to catch his breath, Guyon crept up behind him and slit his throat in one swift action. He didn't even bother to watch the body crumble to the ground before he squared off with the little black devil.

"I'm not averse to letting you scamper about the woods all night looking for her." Bloody hell, he was talking to a dog.

Without warning the dog sauntered up to him and looked at Guyon with bright intelligent eyes that made Guyon think he was somewhat out of his depth. Then the animal walked over to the body lying at the base of the tree. The little dog gave it a cursory sniff, then lifted his leg and pissed on the man's prone body.

Guyon barked a laugh, "My sentiments exactly." Guyon shook his head; he had never encountered a dog quite like this one. What a remarkable little fellow. Guyon crouched down, resting on his heels, and invited the dog to sniff his hands, which it did without a moment's pause. "I think we should be going if we plan to save your mistress." Guyon raised his eyebrow at the dog, who nuzzled his hand as if to confirm the plan.

Guyon made his way back to where he had hobbled his horse, the little dog trotting at his heels. As they were going to have to travel some distance Guyon chose to carry him by making a sling from his cloak and crossing it across his chest, then placing the dog inside it. "I hope it's to your liking?"

The little dog settled into the sling with only its head visible. Guyon hadn't realized just how small the animal was until he picked him up. He was no bigger than a coney.

It didn't surprise Guyon to find that the men hadn't bothered to cover their tracks. The gobdaws were beyond stupid. He hoped that boded well for his attempt to snatch Cicele out from under their noses. There was no time to find Warin or alert Ranulf. Guyon would have to do this himself. If all went well he should have Cicele back at Beauforde by dawn. If they didn't encounter any trouble.

WAITING WAS THE HARDEST. He hated the inactivity of being still, but he had learned patience. It was a skill that could determine life or death. So, he waited as the group settled for the night.

Perhaps an hour before he'd heard a horse coming along the track, so Guyon hid. He recognized the man as one of Cicele's captors. Without pause Guyon nudged his horse forward, keeping to the shelter of the trees and drew the blade at his belt—with skill honed by years of practice Guyon flicked the knife as the man walked his horse past where Guyon hid.

The man lurched forward over the horse's neck. Dead. Feeling the weight on its neck the horse stopped and waited. Slowly Guyon rode over and reclaimed his knife sticking out of the man's neck. He pushed the dead man off the horse and dragged him into the trees. He didn't want any evidence. Then he slapped the horse's rump making it bolt along the track and out of sight. It would make its way back to Beauforde, he was sure of it. Horses were herd animals and the lure of the castle's horses would be too strong to ignore.

When he reached the camp it was fully dark, but there was enough light from a small fire to see the leader. Guyon recognized him immediately. Eustace de Sayre, Lincoln's captain, strode back towards the camp. He ordered another to stand watch. Then he lay next to the fire and slept.

The bastard. This time Lincoln had gone too far. Forcing

himself to forget about Lincoln and concentrate on rescuing Cicele, Guyon waited.

It was after the moon reached its height that Guyon decided it was time to make his move. The sentry had his back towards Guyon, which made it easy to catch him unawares. Once again taking the razor-sharp dagger from his belt, he slit the man's throat. He held the body upright and took the length of rope he carried over his shoulder and tied it under the man's arms to make it look like he sat against the tree. Guyon hoped he had hours before the other two men realized their guard was dead.

Like a night wraith he crept towards the place where Cicele lay against a tree. Hopefully she wouldn't do something stupid and scream. That was a possibility, but he had to take his chances.

She was smarter than he dared hope, and quick to discern what he was up to. Clever wench.

Just as he thought he had managed the impossible, all hell broke loose.

SHE WAS FREE. Cicele had just lifted the blanket from her shoulders when her ankle was caught in a vice-like grip.

"Where do you think you're going?" one of her captors asked in a low growl that made her skin crawl. It was too dark to see his face but she recognized his voice. The leader. Dear God.

Immediately the forest erupted. A dark figure sprang from behind the tree where she sat and lunged at the man holding her leg.

The two scuffled on the ground. Grunts and curses punctuated their deadly embrace. It took several heartbeats for her to regain her senses and dart behind the tree to watch the scene before her unfold.

Her rescuer, whoever he was, seemed to be having the upper hand. That was until the other of her captors sprang into action. She turned to see if the sentry would join in, but she suspected he was dead as he hadn't moved.

She had to do something. There was no telling what would happen if she didn't escape, and the one man that could help her seemed to be having some trouble fending off her two captors. Frantically she groped around for anything she could use. Her hand fell on a large stone—that would have to do.

Carefully, so as not to collide with them she stalked around the three men waiting for her opportunity.

They no longer brawled on the ground, but now stood fighting. She could see the flash of metal as knives caught the moonlight. One of her captors must have been hurt because he staggered from the fight. She had an instant to inflict damage and she took it. While he stood trying to regain his balance she flung herself at him and smashed the stone into his head. They both went down. Unfortunately, he had grabbed her as she fell forward from the momentum of her attack. Now he held her while he regained his senses.

There was a grunt, then one of them fell to the ground on his knees. God in heaven, she hoped it wasn't her would-be rescuer.

She let out an audible sigh when she recognized the one they called Pate lying on the ground. His eyes were open but lifeless.

"Don't move or I'll slit your fucking throat." A voice close to her ear snarled. With a sudden lurch he gained his feet, dragging her by the hair with him.

Off balance she leaned into him. A piercing pain in her scalp made her gasp as he twisted her hair in his fist, exposing her throat. The tip of his knife pressed against her flesh. She dared not even breathe.

"Put down your knife or she dies," he spat at her rescuer as he stood before them.

Silence.

Cicele could see that the man before her was too far away and wouldn't be able to disarm her captor without the risk of the knife being plunged into her throat. She swallowed, and felt the tip of the knife scratch her throat. She couldn't think. Her mind was numb with fear.

"Put down your knife," the man shouted as the knife at her throat nicked her skin. The smell of blood filled her nostrils. Fear—acidic and feral—surged through her as she fought to keep control of her emotions. It was a deadly combination, and one Cicele might not survive.

The other man stood motionless, but still didn't speak. He just waited.

Cicele needed to break the deadlock and give her rescuer a chance to overpower her captor. Her hands were free but she couldn't dislodge his grasp without risking her own neck.

She was desperate. Her breath came in short, shallow gasps. She was almost too frightened to breathe, but her instincts to survive overrode her desire to hold her breath. Panicking, she did the first thing that came into her head. She leaned all her weight on her outside leg and then stomped back with her other foot connecting with her captor's foot. All her weight was focused in that one small act and she prayed it would be enough.

The man grunted and for an instant slackened his hold. It was enough.

In a blur her rescuer lunged forward and pushed her sideways as he caught her captor under the chin. All three of them went spiraling to the ground.

It was over too fast for Cicele to determine what had happened but when she gained her feet her captor was lying on the ground tightly curled into a ball.

Without speaking, her rescuer bent down and dragged the man, who was now moaning piteously, over to the tree where she had been tied.

With quick, rough efficiency he was tied to the tree.

Her rescuer crouched before him. "De Sayre, I suggest you stop your godawful whining, or you'll have wolves upon you before your master arrives to rescue your worthless hide."

He knew him? Who, in God's name, was her rescuer?

The man took his advice, but not before lashing out with his feet and catching her rescuer unawares. He fell back on his backside and laughed.

What, in the name of God, was he doing laughing? Perhaps he had been hit in the head and it had addled his brain.

That wasn't good.

A sensation began crawling through her chest and up into her throat, restricting her ability to breathe. *Don't panic. Don't panic. All will be well.*

"I'm glad to see you have some spirit left, you may have need of it before the dawn brings relief." Her rescuer spoke quietly to the cur who had held a knife to her throat.

A violent shudder run through Cicele's body. Never in her life had she been so frightened, or sure of her own death. In the distance a wolf howled, making the hairs on the back of her neck prickle.

"I have a message for your master." He kicked his prisoner. "Are you listening?"

The prisoner spat on the ground in answer.

"Tell him 'la Bête' doesn't share."

He walked over to where she stood and tilted her chin up to examine her neck. It was too dark to get a look at his face.

"It is only a small scratch. You will be well until we reach Beauforde." Then he walked back towards the forest and out of the small clearing, but not before he retrieved his knife, and untied the horses and shooed them into the forest.

"Wait!" she called. She wanted some answers, and she wanted them now.

To her relief he stopped and glanced at her over his shoulder.

"Who are you, and where are you taking me?" He had mentioned Beauforde, but she wanted to make sure.

"To your husband."

She glanced towards the area where the horses had disappeared into the forest. "Why not take one; it would mean we travel faster."

"I have my own." He didn't bother waiting, but began to disappear into the trees. "We need to go," he snapped as the night swallowed him.

A hacking laugh caught her attention. It was coming from the man who was tied to the tree. "La Bête will rip your throat out, milady. He's done it before. If I were you I'd run, and run fast, and pray he doesn't catch you."

Her body convulsed in fear, but she managed to keep her chin high as she regarded him. "I will be safer with him than with you and your master."

Then she ran to catch up with the man who was rumored to kill without conscience. As she hurried away the sound of laughter filled the air.

She prayed to all the saints she could think of that she would be safe. Unfortunately, she didn't think it would be enough if la Bête truly was the beast everyone claimed him to be.

THANKFUL that she didn't stand and argue, Guyon led her away from the camp and into the forest. Time was running out; they had to make it to the horse and away before Lincoln found his man. Guyon was sure de Sayre would have reinforcements arriving. And soon.

"We have to move fast," Guyon grunted over his shoulder as he continued to stride through the forest. He had pulled the cowl of his short cloak over his head to hide his face. He didn't want her to recognize him until he was ready.

She grunted as she tried to catch up to him, but he ignored it. The moon gave enough light to reveal the track leading back towards where he had hobbled the horse. He anticipated they would reach it soon. Then they would make better time. He doubted he could rely on any divine help to aid their escape. God had proved to be blind, deaf, and mute to his pleas for help long ago. His own ability, and a good dollop of luck, was all he had.

So far so good.

A muffled yelp drew his attention. That sound told him that his luck had changed.

Muttering a curse, he turned and walked back to where Cicele lay crumpled on the forest floor.

"I've turned my ankle," she hissed through her teeth. She spat the words as though it was his fault.

"Can you walk?"

"No, I can't walk, you…"

Guyon didn't wait for her to finish; he picked her up and tossed her over his shoulder and began to run.

It had been a good while since he had hauled a woman over his shoulder. It would be uncomfortable and humiliating for her but it couldn't be helped. They didn't have time to limp back to the horse. They had to keep moving, and fast. Carrying her like this was his only solution, although he knew he'd be on the receiving end of her sharp tongue when she got the chance.

Surprisingly he relished the idea of crossing words with her. Fool that he was.

Chapter Seven

She felt like a sack of oats as he hoisted her over his shoulder. Of all the indignities, this was the limit.

"Put me down this instant," she hissed. It was hard to put the scowling note she intended into her voice when she was hanging upside down over his shoulder.

He didn't bother to answer, but kept trotting through the forest while her head bounced against his back, her free hand resting against his backside. If she was taller and had a larger mouth, with sharp teeth, she would have liked to take a bloody great chunk out of it. Well, she could dream. Relief to be away from her abductors and heading back to Beauforde made her a little reckless. She should have been grateful that he had rescued her, but fear had given way to outrage.

Did this brute work for her husband? La Bête was Henry's man, so surely she was safer with him than the men who had abducted her? She hadn't see his face clearly as he fought, or when he examined her neck. Not even when he turned and faced her before lifting her over his shoulder, but something about him seemed familiar.

God in heaven, her mind must be addled. She had, until now, never met the notorious la Bête.

A strange, blurry world began to dance in front of her eyes as she bobbed along. Finally, she decided to lever herself up to get some blood into her head. Placing her hand on his waist was all she could do, and immediately she felt his muscles tense. "What are you about?" It sounded like a snarl.

"I need to put my head up or I will faint," she ground out. It was getting harder to talk, let alone think.

Without warning he pulled her back and placed her on her feet. Thankfully she had the presence of mind not to put weight on her ankle. As she stood upright her head swam and she began to crumble. Her knees were too weak to hold her. Without warning she was supported with his hands around her waist.

"Unhand me." She was furious at his rough handling. And she wanted answers.

Now.

He didn't let go.

"Who are you?" She had to close her eyes as the world swam around her. When she opened them, she couldn't make out his features although she sensed his eyes staring at her. She blinked, trying desperately to maintain her sense of calm. "And what do you want?" She sounded breathless, and pathetic. She hated that.

"I should have thought it obvious what I was doing." He didn't take his eyes off hers. They reflected dark menace as the moon peeked through the trees.

"And it should be just as obvious we need to keep going," he drawled.

She was in no position to argue; he had saved her from those... those pox-ridden, flea-bitten dogs. Still, she wasn't about to acquiesce to a stranger's demands without some answers.

"Are you la Bête?" She swallowed her fear, instead trying for a tone that might be construed as imperious, but it came out a bit of a squeak instead. Ignoring her humiliation, she managed to tilt her chin up a fraction more, and glared back at the man.

She couldn't be sure, but she suspected she saw a flicker of white teeth. The villain was laughing at her, which annoyed her beyond belief. The moon's light partially illuminated his eyes, but not his face. She gave an involuntary shudder, and looked away.

She heard a muffled curse.

"We need to hurry if we are to get back to Beauforde before dawn." His head jerked back, indicating the direction where her sister's castle would be. Then without a "by your leave" he picked her up and hoisted her back over his shoulder.

Everything within her wanted to flail and yell until he put her down and talked to her. But she had the distinct impression that wouldn't help. The temptation to rail at him was strong, but she needed to rein in her temper, and wait. She was prepared to trust him. For now.

Cicele didn't understand what had happened, or why. Yes, she was now the countess, but she was also married to Guyon. She may not like him, or forgive him for what he did, but he was powerful, and only a fool would bait him by abducting his wife.

Unless? Yes, that made more sense. Many barons had reneged on their fealty to Henry and had turned to the youngest surviving son of King Stephen. And the Scots. The war between Stephen and Henry was settled now that Stephen had died. Still, Stephen's son, William, was probably a threat. She had heard rumors that William was secretly wooing barons to his side. Barons who had been loyal to his father, and were disinclined to return castles that had been awarded under Stephen's reign. Was she to be the leverage?

As the blood once again began to pool in her head it made her incapable of keeping her thoughts straight. Black dots began to form behind her eyes. Too weak and tired to struggle, she drifted into a semiconscious waking dream.

Just as she was about to surrender to the welcoming wave of

numbness she was unceremoniously pulled upright and lowered to the ground and leaned against a tree. She sat while the forest spun around her. The Beast had lowered her to the ground with a modicum of care for her pained ankle. So, he was considerate. Who would have thought?

It took a moment for her vision to clear. She was so exhausted she wanted to collapse into a ball and sleep. Pain and fear had robbed her of her last reserves. Giving in to the temptation, she closed her eyes. That's when she heard it. A faint whimper, and then a wet nose bumped her hand. Cicele's eyes sprang open.

"Vite!" She couldn't help it, tears ran down her cheeks as she gathered the wriggly little dog onto her lap. He was so excited his whole body was a writhing mass of muscle. His tongue licked her nose, and darted into her mouth as she laughed. She didn't want to think about where that tongue had been. She was too pleased to see him to care.

When they both calmed down, she looked at the man who now stood in front of her. "You found him." It wasn't a question, exactly. But she did know that Vite couldn't have made it by himself, so it was this great brute of a man standing in front of her who was responsible for her dog's sudden appearance.

"Thank you." She lowered her eyes, a sudden blush heating her cheeks. She wasn't used to being so openly scrutinized by anyone.

"You need to rest." He didn't bother to hide his impatience.

Cicele was exhausted, but she refused to be cowed by the man standing in front of her. Her brain was so addled it took her a few moments to think clearly. Beast, or not, he had rescued Vite, so perhaps he possessed some honor. They must keep going; Isabeau would be anxious, and Cicele didn't want anything to threaten Isabeau's unborn baby. The sooner they got to Beauforde the better.

The moon had almost disappeared, and the sun's faint rays were beginning to color the eastern sky. She could hardly keep her eyes open, but she forced herself to stand, wobbled, and almost fell.

. . .

"SIT BEFORE YOU FALL DOWN." He didn't mean to be so abrasive, but something about her indignant expression irritated him. "Foolish wench," he murmured under his breath as he walked back to the horse and retrieved a blanket.

"How did you know to rescue me from those… those?"

His back was to her, as he undid the saddle bag, but smiled at her gall. What an imperious tone she used. She must be tired, and scared, yet she refused to be cowed by her circumstances. God help him, he rather admired her for it.

He had purposely kept the cowl of his cloak pulled over his head to obscure his face, but now he must face her. To his dismay, her proximity had made his body react to her in ways he had hoped to avoid, so he gathered his defenses about him and removed his hood.

He turned around, after he had retrieved a skin of wine and a parcel of bread and cheese from his saddle bags, and faced her. "Hello, Cicele." He kept his voice neutral.

She stared at him. Her lips parted, but not a sound escaped her. Good. She was shocked into silence.

Guyon placed the skin of wine in front of her and unwrapped the waxed linen that contained the bread and cheese. The little dog didn't take his eyes off the viands, but he lay down next to his mistress. His eyes were alert and his tongue was busy licking his nose. Without thinking, Guyon cut a small piece of cheese and threw it to him. It landed by his paws, but he didn't take the morsel, instead he looked at his mistress, waiting for her to give the command to eat.

"Good boy," she cooed, then she gave him a nod. The dog devoured the cheese in one gulp. "You greedy brute," she scolded, but there was no heat in her tone. The smile she bestowed on the dog made Guyon's pulse skip. Her eyes softened, and her lips separated to show a small glimpse of her white teeth. He still dreamed about that mouth and those teeth. Guyon had to shake his head to clear the image.

Then she shifted her gaze to him. No warmth in their golden hue. What had he expected? She had brought her knees up to her chest, and her arms were clasped about them. It was a protective gesture. Her eyes slid from his face back to her clasped hands about her knees.

"*You* are la Bête?"

Of all the questions she could ask, it had to be this one. There was an edge to her comment that Guyon didn't like.

"Aye."

She chewed her bottom lip, and her eyes blinked with unshed tears. "You never came back." She turned her face from him and looked at the dog by her feet.

"I had no choice." Although it had been six years, he still lived with the sting of his actions. Then, as now, he regretted so much.

Instead of fighting back, she cuffed the tears that had begun to slide down her cheeks.

He shouldn't have cared that he'd made her cry, but he did. Bollocks! Seeing her and having her so close created a hunger in him that made him angry. He didn't want to rekindle the longing. The hope. It would make their marriage so much easier to bear if he could shut out his infernal longing for what would never be.

Frustrated, he ran his fingers through his hair. Why, in God's name, couldn't he keep his distance? He couldn't afford to let her back into his heart, but her face looked so crestfallen. His defenses began to crumble.

Guyon took a moment to get his emotions under control. "You should eat, then we have to go," he said, keeping his tone indifferent. "We have an hour or so ride ahead of us, and we need to go soon."

She shrugged, but didn't say anything else. They ate in silence.

She never raised her eyes from the food on the ground before her. When they had finished, he stood and retrieved the waxed linen and skin. "We will set out again soon, but for now rest." Then he turned and walked to the horse to stow the skin and linen in his bags.

"Why agree to marry me now?"

He turned to face her. Her expression had changed from woeful to cool and haughty. He much preferred this Cicele to the one who wept at his thoughtless words.

How much to tell? "I should imagine your response to the marriage was much the same as mine." He looked at her, a wretched expression on her face. "We both did our duty to our king." He took a breath to gather his thoughts. "Make no mistake, Cicele, whether you or I like the arrangement, I am your husband."

"Were those Lincoln's men?" Her tone was matter-of-fact, but her eyes betrayed her confusion, and God forbid, her pain. She seemed to think for a moment, then continued. "He can gain my lands and title if he forces marriage on me, but that's not his only motive, surely?"

Guyon forced his face into an impassive mask. "The king is worried that Lincoln might entertain plotting against him. You are the key to having the northern barons unite under his banner." If Lincoln was successful there would be all-out war. Guyon had the uneasy feeling that in agreeing to marry Cicele, he had put her at great risk. What a bloody mess.

Cicele's eyes bored into him, but she nibbled her lower lip as she considered what he had said.

He dragged his eyes away from her mouth. He couldn't afford to become distracted by those bewitching lips. "You need to get some rest. I'll keep watch," he grunted. "We ride hard to Beauforde."

"And then?"

He looked at her beautiful face, and felt his heart lurch. Her hair was a mess, and there was dirt on her face, but she had never looked more ravishing. It took a moment for him to recover. "To Alnwick. I have inherited my uncle's title and lands. You will be at my side." He had no time to be discussing this. She was his wife, and would have to accept his authority, and do as she was told.

She nodded, as she sat quietly, but her eyes reflected a sadness that caught him unawares.

He remembered the first time those eyes had been turned on him; they had taken his breath away. She possessed the most mesmerizing eyes of any woman he had ever seen. When he first met her, he thought they were brown, but as they spent more time together he discovered they sometimes looked a light brown rimmed with green and sprinkled with gold flecks. Now, as she searched his face waiting for answers he could not give, he basked in the golden hues of those extraordinary eyes.

He took a step towards her before he realized what he had done. He uttered a curse under his breath, and forced himself to stay where he was. He couldn't afford to become distracted. He had to remember what was at stake.

He wouldn't let his heart be destroyed all over again. Instead he focused on the dog lying at her side. Guyon gathered in a breath, then he released it slowly. "Now, you must rest." He turned on his heel and strode out into the forest to keep watch.

"Lincoln can't marry me." She sounded incredulous. "He's my brother by marriage. The church would never sanction such a union." She stared at Guyon wide-eyed.

Guyon had returned to the small clearing to make ready to leave. Instead of resting, it seemed Cicele had been thinking. As always, when Cicele thought, it was with an intelligence that Guyon admired. Her mind as sharp as her tongue.

Guyon swiveled his head around to look at her. Cicele's face paled as her eyes grew large. They had a hollow look about them that tore at Guyon's heart.

"Legally he can't marry you, but even so, if he manages to abduct you and force you to marry him the church may take months, if not years, to rule the marriage illegal. By then he could have an heir and…" One look at her face and he decided to stop. God knows the threat of abduction was real.

Only a few years ago Henry's brother Geoffrey, with the help of Theobald, had tried to abduct Eleanor to gain her lands before Henry could marry her. Henry outsmarted his brother, and Guyon would do the same to Lincoln.

Guyon took a deep breath. "It seems Lincoln has a spy in Henry's court; he probably wanted to get to you before we consummated our marriage." He couldn't look at her, so he focused on the forest to make sure they were safe. "I'm thinking Lincoln will try to force my hand. If he can kill me and marry you, he has won."

Cicele turned her gaze on him. "Guyon, how could you do those things? You were never that cruel or callous."

It took a moment for him to catch her meaning. He had forgotten she could shift from one topic to another without warning.

He watched as her face changed from an expression of horror into a mask of impassivity. He had seen her become detached before, and it tore at his heart that she would wear it for him. *Fool! She has no affection for you. And why would she after what you did?*

"I have only ever done what my liege lord has asked. It is all any knight would do," he said belligerently, allowing anger to seep into his tone. He would not apologize for doing his duty.

"But all those innocent people? How could you murder clerics?"

That brought his head up with a start. "What atrocities would you accuse me of?" He had to keep his temper harnessed, but it was difficult. Yes, he had killed, all in the name of war, but to be accused of unjustified atrocities. That he would not tolerate.

She studied his face. The tip of her tongue ran along her bottom lip and his stomach lurched in want.

"My maid said she had heard tell that in retaliation for the lack of support from the steward at Bury St. Edmunds you attacked the abbey. Several monks were herded into the chapel, and when the steward refused to surrender you ordered it burned to the ground." She was visibly shaking as she spoke.

Guyon ran his hand through his hair, but controlled his outrage at such a heinous lie. "I did put the monks into the chapel, for their protection, but I never set it afire," he choked, as he remembered one of the worst days of his life. "The abbey surrendered, and the captives were all released." He took a breath to calm himself. "When my men had gone, King Stephen's son, who was chasing us down, plundered the place. It was he who set fire to the chapel. God be praised, he died that same night—choked on a piece of eel. His pig of a brother, William, put it about that I was guilty of the crime, and that his 'sainted' brother died of a broken heart." Guyon took a steadying breath to calm himself. "We were ambushed as we came back to see why there was smoke. Of course, it was too late to save the poor sots trapped in the burning church." His palms were sweating in his gloves as he looked at her. By all that was holy he needed to have her believe him incapable of such evil.

After what seemed an eternity her cool gaze softened and she nodded. "I believe you incapable of such atrocities, but others will not. It seems you have attracted the derision of many. Lincoln is a very powerful enemy," she announced, in her cool detached way.

He sighed in relief, not wanting to think why her trust meant so much to him.

"Why does he hate you so?"

Surely, she had not forgotten that Guyon had saved her from Lincoln's attack in Rouen? Deciding to skirt the obvious he chose to be vague. "I have something Lincoln wants, and he can't seem to let it go." He wasn't about to tell her the whole story, although he would have to one day. Lincoln and Guyon were trapped in a never-ending circle of violence. One day they would face each other, and only one would survive.

It didn't help that Guyon was now married to Cicele, one of the wealthiest heiresses in England. Lincoln needed her titles if he hoped to have the barons rally to his side. God's blood, what a complicated life Fate had spun for him.

Guyon didn't give her a chance to question him further. They needed to move, and quickly.

Chapter Eight

It was early morning when she saw the distant towers of Beauforde castle through the thinning trees. Heaving a sigh of relief, she let her body relax.

Her calm was almost immediately destroyed when she heard the thundering of many hooves. Without warning the horse stopped suddenly, almost toppling her off its rump, where she had endured hours of discomfort.

Grunting, she tried to keep herself steady. And failed.

"We have company," he rasped as he caught her thigh to stop her slipping sideways off the horse.

She peered around him, almost falling again when she lost her balance. He flung his arm out to steady her.

He muttered something under his breath, but she chose to ignore it.

Through the trees several mounted men were approaching them. She recognized Ranulf, but the other man riding beside him was unknown.

Both men wore mail coifs, as did the group of men-at-arms riding with them.

"We came to rescue you, my lord, but I see there is no need." The young stranger smiled as he greeted Guyon. Then he turned to her and bowed his head. "My lady."

She acknowledged him with a slight nod, but didn't reply.

Ranulf walked his mount forward until he was parallel to her. "Are you well, Cicele?" he asked in a gruff tone.

She was about to reply but was cut off.

"We need to get inside the keep before we are set upon." Guyon's tone bristled with impatience. Ranulf looked at her but didn't say anything. A wry smile danced on his lips as he looked from her to her husband. "Good to see you, my friend."

Guyon grunted, but clasped Ranulf's outstretched arm.

Ranulf cast her a quick glance; a small smile danced at the corner of his mouth. He found something amusing, but must have decided to keep it to himself.

She, on the other hand, didn't find anything amusing. Giving a huff of displeasure, she glared back at him.

When they reached the inner bailey, she waited for Guyon to dismount before she could slip her leg over the saddle and slide from the horse. Vite had run back to her when he had been removed from the sling he had been carried in.

"Hello, little one," she purred as the dog yipped louder in response. As she hit the ground with both feet she almost lost her balance. Her legs were like wax, and her ankle objected to her weight. A searing pain stabbed up her leg, but she refused to ask for help. Instead she clenched her jaw tight, and hissed through her teeth as she put pressure on her injured ankle. Without warning strong arms encircled her waist and picked her up. She was grateful, but she was reluctant to give the brute the satisfaction of knowing it. However, she was too tired to demand he put her down, so she rested against the wall of his chest.

～

GUYON WANTED to lie down and close his eyes. Every muscle screamed *enough*! Fatigue hung like a saturated woolen blanket about his shoulders, making his body sluggish. Refusing to heed his body's need for rest he dismounted, released the dog from its sling, then turned back to his horse. Cicele remained seated behind his saddle, looking like he felt—exhausted and decidedly disheveled. For some reason, which Guyon wasn't ready to examine, an unwelcome urge to compliment her for her bravery rose unbidden to his lips, but he didn't speak.

She had done well. Better than he had expected. When he first met her, she had presented herself as an arrogant, spoiled young woman who didn't seem to care for the suitors her father paraded before her. But the more time he spent with her he began to see another woman altogether, passionate, determined, sharp-tongued, and possessed of a wry wit.

The woman before him now was a strong, stubborn harpy. He hadn't liked her fiery nature at first, but once he began to really know her he enjoyed their verbal sparring. In truth her stubborn insistence that she needed no one had intrigued him. But after a night without sleep he was bone weary and didn't need the aggravation. She had wanted to fight him at every turn, but it seemed Cicele de Saussay—no Cicele le Loup now—had a pragmatic side to her.

The dog had promptly dashed back to his mistress, and began yipping at the horse's hooves. With feigned indifference, Guyon watched as she dismounted and acknowledged the dog. When she tried to walk, she stumbled. Without thinking Guyon walked over and picked her up, cradling her in his arms.

He felt her body stiffen. *The stubborn wench is going to demand I put her down.* No sooner had the thought presented itself, when he felt her body relax into him. That was another thing Guyon realized, with slight alarm. He liked the warm, satisfied feeling of having this woman in his arms again.

Ignoring his inclination to hold her tighter into his chest he strode over to the wooden stairs that led into the hall. As he entered its darkened interior he was met by two women. Both beauties. One had fiery red hair and a ferocious scowl that creased her brow, her clothing identifying her as the Lady Beauforde. The other, a maid, with the face of an angel. Her eyes were almost identical to Cicele's as they stared in cold disapproval at him. She too wore a scowl of concern and censure.

"My lady, what happened to you? Are you well?" Both women fired questions that were making his head ache.

"Lady Cicele needs a bath and something to eat, then rest," he growled, giving them a scowl of his own. At his expression they both stood still and looked to Ranulf who was standing by his side.

"Do as he says." Ranulf's voice sounded resigned.

Lady Beauforde gave her husband a slight nod, then turned and led Guyon, still cradling Cicele in his arms, through the hall, along a short corridor, then up the tower stairs and into a large, light chamber. He deposited her on the chair by the fire.

When she sat down, she looked so small and vulnerable. He took her chin in his fingers. "I will leave you with your women. When we have both had a chance to rest and recover, we will speak." He didn't wait for a reply. Turning on his heel he walked from the chamber. Her eyes on him had almost been his undoing. He needed to take some time to compose himself before he was ready to face her again. He was tired, angry, and confused. Never a good combination. Guyon wanted strong wine, a bath, and sleep. Hopefully Ranulf would supply all three.

He walked back into the hall and over to where Ranulf stood before a large fire. The hall was preparing for the noon meal. Benches were being placed in front of the high table, while servants were laying white linen table cloths over the high table on the dais.

Ranulf placed his hand on Guyon's shoulder. "I've had your squire prepare you a bath. There is wine and viands in yonder chamber." His head indicated a curtained area behind the raised dais. "When you are refreshed, we will talk."

Cicele opened her eyes and glanced at the window where she could see the sun making its way to the western horizon. It wouldn't be long before it set. With a start, she realized she must have slept all afternoon. A clamor outside the chamber that had probably woken her from sleep warned that she had better dress. Stretching as she sat up in her bed, she reached for her chemise when she heard a knock on the chamber door. Vite was watching from the nest he had made of the furs that covered the large bed. Slipping the linen garment over her naked body she rose, steadied herself on the bedpost to protect her aching ankle, and waited.

Guyon entered and stopped abruptly when he saw she was only partially dressed.

Trying to cover her discomfort at his appraisal, she offered the first thing that came into her head. "I heard bellowing, and thought there was something amiss." Maude was nowhere to be seen, and Agatha seemed to have vanished into thin air. No one had seen her since the day before when Cicele had been abducted. Something about Agatha's disappearance niggled at the back of her mind, but like vapor, when she tried to capture it, the impression vanished.

Now Guyon stood staring at her. She wasn't sure why she was so self-conscious, but her cheeks flamed as his eyes traveled over her face, then down her body, in a slow, deliberate sweep, finally coming to rest on her face again.

Growing impatient with his silence as his eyes roved back over her body, she demanded his reason for coming to her chamber.

A sly smile spread across his face. "You are just as comely as I recall, wife."

The emphasis on "wife" was not lost on Cicele. With a huff, she crossed her arms over her chest. "Why. Are. You. Here?" She spoke slowly, trying to conceal her rising anger.

Guyon didn't answer immediately, he continued his leisurely appraisal, which infuriated her.

Blasted man.

When he finally spoke, it was with the arrogance of a man who believed he owned her body and soul. "Apart from the fact that you are now my wife, and I will enter your chamber when I wish, the castle is preparing for our wedding feast," he said as he made his way towards her, "and naturally we are the guests of honor."

She stood rooted to the spot, unable to form a coherent thought.

Some emotion slid across his face, but vanished before she could identify it.

"The expectation will be for us to consummate our vows this eve, but before that noteworthy event I think we need to talk."

She noted his sarcasm, but couldn't speak. A large lump had formed in her throat making speech impossible. She wasn't sure if it was the thought of enduring an evening of feasting and celebrating a marriage she resented, or the inevitability of her marriage being consummated. Both sent chills down her arms and legs, and made her sick to her stomach.

Something in Guyon's expression changed. She didn't know what it was, but the line of his mouth seemed to soften. "I am sorry, Cicele, but we have little choice."

At least he was sensitive enough to see that the prospect of sharing a bed with him was a little daunting.

Before she could reply Maude and Beatrice entered, both carrying clothing and ushering in servants who carried a bathing tub and water.

He didn't bother to acknowledge the other women. "I will be back to escort you to the hall," he said as he continued to look at her. A small smile creased the corners of his mouth.

She nodded her agreement, and he was gone.

It was with a certain amount of trepidation, and not a little chagrin, that she surrendered to Maude and Beatrice's skillful attention.

"Has Agatha been found?" she asked, to no one in particular.

Both Maude and Beatrice shook their heads as they organized the bath and laid out her clothing for the feast to come.

"Did you sleep?" Beatrice asked, concern evident in her voice.

Cicele gave her what she hoped was a cheerful smile. "Yes, but I could still sleep for a week." Cicele hadn't recovered from her ordeal in the woods, or the fact that her new husband was the infamous "le Bête." And if she was honest, she had not expected her own reaction to Guyon's closeness. Everything in her body responded to him. But she would keep that to herself. With a determined effort, she chose not to think of her new husband. Sadly, she had a lifetime to think of him.

When Cicele had finished dressing and Maude left to borrow a gold circlet from Isabeau, Beatrice took the opportunity to speak with Cicele privately. "What happened?" she asked as she took Cicele's hands in hers.

"I was fishing in the weir…"

Beatrice gave a little gasp of censure, but Cicele ignored it.

"I was set upon by six men and taken hostage, but Guyon came and rescued me." She didn't want to elaborate, so kept her account short.

"You were lucky that he was on hand to save you." Beatrice's eyes traveled over Cicele's face, probing for something.

Cicele didn't need Beatrice to expand on her comment. It would not have been the first time a widowed heiress was kidnapped, raped, and forced into a marriage.

Desperate to change the subject Cicele held Beatrice's gaze. "Have you confessed?"

Beatrice averted her eyes and tried to remove her hands from Cicele's grasp.

"Beatrice. You must." Cicele tried to keep her voice even, but she was growing anxious. She didn't want to be embroiled in the deception she was privy to.

Her cousin raised her eyes to meet hers. "I haven't found the courage," she admitted.

Poor Beatrice. She had been living under Isabeau's protection for over four months, first as a wet-nurse, but when Elizabet produced enough milk to feed her twins, Beatrice had become Isabeau's maid. It wasn't until Cicele had arrived, and recognized her cousin masquerading as a servant, that Cicele had insisted the truth must be told. Beatrice refused to share with Cicele why she was hiding, and Cicele hadn't pushed her. Beatrice had pleaded for Cicele to keep her secret, but that was a month ago and still she hadn't confided in Isabeau. Time was running out and she must tell Isabeau the truth.

"What do you fear? I'm sure Isabeau suspects you are not who you profess to be. What was it, oh yes, a miller's widow," she said sarcastically. "Why maintain the ruse?"

Beatrice managed to wriggle her hands free of Cicele's hold and walk towards the bed. "I'll have nowhere to go, and if my father finds me he'll kill E—" she stammered and couldn't finish what she was about to say.

Cicele understood her cousin's dilemma, but she also understood that Beatrice had to trust Isabeau. "You're our cousin; we would never allow anyone to harm you, or young Edward, but you must tell her the truth."

Beatrice was just about to say something when the chamber door opened and Isabeau walked in.

Isabeau must have noted the expression on Beatrice's face, and caught the mood of the chamber. "Have I interrupted something?" she asked, looking at Cicele, then Beatrice.

Cicele didn't reply; instead she continued to stare at Beatrice.

"Oh, my lady," Beatrice murmured. "I have to confess something and I'm afraid you will be disappointed with me." Beatrice's voice quivered with emotion.

Cicele watched as her sister approached Beatrice and held her hand. "I am certain that whatever it is you have to tell me it can't be that bad."

Beatrice gave a small nod and took a deep breath. "I am not who you think I am."

Isabeau looked over at Cicele and gave her a sly smile. Cicele had to turn aside to hide her own grin. Isabeau had probably suspected all along that Beatrice lived a lie.

"And, Beatrice, who do you think I think you are?" She indicated for Beatrice to sit down on the bed next to her. Cicele watched in fascination as Isabeau skillfully drew Beatrice's story from her.

"I'll wager you are exactly who I think you are, kind, caring, and…" She took Beatrice's chin in her fingers and tilted her head up so she could look her in the eye. "And a noble woman who has need to keep her identity secret." Cicele noticed Isabeau give Beatrice a small smile when her breath caught.

"You knew?" Beatrice blurted.

Isabeau gave her another sly smile. "Well, as I'm well versed in keeping secrets, I suspected you had a few of your own. What do you want to tell me?"

Beatrice laughed, relief making her shoulders slump. She took a few moments to gather her composure. Looking at the two women she lowered her eyes. "I can't tell you." Her cheeks flamed red as she looked first at Isabeau, then Cicele. "Please. I beg you." She was beginning to become agitated.

Isabeau took her hands. "Beatrice, look at me." When she did Isabeau continued, "we will keep your secret, but please know that you can trust me. I would never allow you, or Edward, to be placed in danger."

Beatrice swiped at the tears streaming down her face. "Thank you, my lady." Beatrice gave Isabeau small smile.

"Beatrice is our cousin. Her mother was our father's sister," Cicele added. "Beatrice's father betrayed Matilda, so he is not welcome at court. He is not a pleasant man, Isabeau, so we must do all in our power to ensure he knows nothing of her presence here."

Isabeau nodded at Cicele. The delight on Isabeau's face was evident as she gathered Beatrice into her arms. "Well, not only do I have a sister, I have a cousin too," she gushed.

Beatrice sniffled, but didn't say anything as a commotion outside the chamber door caught their attention. Isabeau laughed as she stood and straightened her kirtle. "Your new husband, I presume?" She quirked her eyebrow at Cicele.

Cicele worked to keep her face impassive. "Yes, I suspect he's come to escort me to the hall."

Isabeau nodded, but before she left she turned to Beatrice and Cicele. "We will talk more. There has to be a way to keep you and baby Edward safe, and maintain your secret." She smiled at Beatrice, then gave Cicele a knowing expression. "But now I am required at table." Isabeau turned and kissed Beatrice's tear-stained cheek. Then she was gone.

Cicele didn't have a chance to discuss anything with Beatrice before Guyon strode into the room demanding her attention. Without so much as a "by your leave" she was escorted, none too graciously, to the hall by her husband. It took all Cicele's vast reserves of patience to refrain from complaining about his brutish behavior.

Chapter Nine

As meals went it was perhaps the most disagreeable of her life. No, she remembered one that was more hideous—her marriage feast with Sir Nicholas. Her father and Sir Nicholas seemed unmoved by her peevishness and that had rankled. Realization that she had been betrayed by the man she loved and forced to spend years with a husband as old as her father had only been bearable because she carried a secret. The agony that that dream had been ripped from her was a scar she still carried.

After the heartbreaking loss of her and Guyon's stillborn child, and the time it took to heal, she had allowed Sir Nicholas access to her chamber. But just as the physician had predicted, her womb never quickened again. Not once in the five long years of her marriage had she once missed her menses.

How was it possible to forgive the man who sat beside her now? Humiliation that she had once thought herself loved, only to discover his duplicity, and now to be married to him, was too much to bear. The sad irony was not lost on her; she would be forced to endure his attention with little hope of a child to lighten her days. The realization left her feeling hulled out and empty.

Shaking herself free of her maudlin thoughts she heaved a great sigh and concentrated on the meal she must endure. Pride of place had been given to her and her husband. They sat at the middle of the high table where the choicest cuts from seven courses would be delivered to them first.

Father Ascelin had presided over grace, and blessed the newly married couple, and now the first course was presented. Five dishes were placed before her and Guyon, as honored guests, so they could choose the choicest from each dish. Cicele stared in wonder as delectable dishes of Leche Lombarde, mortrews, venison boiled in almond milk, onions, and rice, and beef and chicken pottages were presented. Guyon cut a slice of Leche Lombarde and placed it on their trencher. "I seem to remember this is one of your favorites," he teased as he served her.

He had remembered. Such a small gesture, and it stung. Why be so considerate now, when he had been a faithless cur all those years ago? Such consideration seemed incongruous with his treacherous character. Unfortunately, her body didn't seem to care about the past. His mischievous smile made her tummy flutter.

"Thank you." She was furious at herself for falling for that smile. Again. Concentrating on the food placed before her, she managed to cut herself a piece while ignoring the man seated next to her.

She did indeed love the dish of pork, with its combination of eggs, pepper, cloves, currants, dates, and sugar all boiled together in a bladder, then sliced and served with a rich sauce. Her mouth watered in anticipation as she inhaled the aromas of the morsel as she drew it into her mouth. She closed her eyes and savored the rich flavors.

She was embarrassed to see that Guyon had not taken his eyes off her. His pupils seemed to consume all the color in his iris until his eyes glowed black as he watched her. The skin on the nape of her neck tingled, and her stomach tightened. He looked as though he was about to devour her. A little thrill skidded down her spine. *Oh, dear God.*

Ignoring him and her body's reaction, she sipped on a delicious Rhenish wine as she ate her food. It was extremely intimate sipping from the same cup and allowing him to cut and offer her portions of food. In fact, it was the first time they had ever sat next to each other and shared a meal together. Their secret liaisons were always rushed; there had never been time to enjoy food and leisure in each other's arms. It was with some difficulty that Cicele managed to drag herself back to her surroundings and away from memories that would only serve to break her heart all over again.

With great fanfare, the second course was delivered. Roasted venison, pork, and other delicacies were presented. She ate sparingly as the meal would last for several hours. It was unusual to have a feast at supper, but it was a diversion she appreciated. When the meal was finished, they would be led to their chamber, where the priest would bless them as they lay in bed.

The thought of consummating their marriage filled her with dread. Thankfully, she was interrupted from her mental meandering by a page who set before them a large roasted trout.

"Do we have you to thank for this?" Guyon asked, raising his eyebrow in question. His eyes were alight with an emotion she couldn't identify.

Her cheeks burned. Oh, blast the man; he had seen her in the weir. *Of course, he had, you goose, he saved you so he must have been close enough to see you fishing.*

There was no point in dissembling, so she raised her chin trying to appear unperturbed at being found out. "Yes, I rather think you do."

Guyon eyed her for several heartbeats. "I will not permit you such freedoms when you live in Alnwick," he said, holding her with dispassionate eyes. "It is not only dangerous, it is foolish in the extreme." A small smile made the corners of his mouth turn up.

"And those delectable legs of yours are too much of a distraction for any poor sot who happens to be passing by."

There was an inflection of humor in his voice but Cicele thought that he didn't find anything amusing about her habit of fishing.

She watched as he placed a piece of the roasted fish on a fresh trencher. So it began. Now that she was once again married her short reprieve at pleasing herself with what she did, and were she went, had come to an end. Well, he might own her body, but by all that was holy he wouldn't own her mind, or her heart. Those he could not have.

Instead of answering him, she bent her head in acknowledgement of his demand. Then she cut a serving of flesh from the piece before her and placed it in her mouth. She chewed it slowly, then when she had swallowed she turned to look at her husband who hadn't taken his eyes off her. "But I shall enjoy the fruits of my labors, my lord, while I can."

His eyes widened for a moment, then he barked a laugh that caused several people close to them to stop talking and turn to look. His smile was devastating. Although, in truth, she didn't know if it could be described as a smile. His lips creased to reveal his teeth, but his eyes didn't crinkle at the corners, nor was there any lift to his cheeks. But somehow his face softened and his dark eyes shone with something altogether dangerous and extremely tempting. Her eyes slid to his lips, and she couldn't seem to drag them away. Her skin tingled and heat surged through her body, even down to her toes. It terrified her to realize her desire for this man was so easily ignited.

While he kept those tantalizing dark eyes on her she was incapable of resisting the pull of attraction. With a start, she realized she had begun to lean towards him. His smell filled her nostrils—clean linen and something masculine that she recognized as uniquely him.

It was with some relief that the moment was interrupted when a cheer went up. Jugglers began entertaining the crowd. Normally, the evening meal was accompanied with musicians playing their instruments on the minstrel's gallery at the far end of the hall, but this eve the entertainment was much more jovial. Soon there would be troubadours singing of courtly love and the chivalry of knights. Although it was all nonsense, Cicele loved to hear the ballads celebrating love and sacrifice.

After the roasted meat course a selection of baked fruits was presented to her. Dragging herself away from the scene of merriment before the dais she chose a small helping of damson in wine and busied herself with the task of eating it.

A wave of mortification hit her when she noticed that she had again begun to lean towards her husband as he made a comment about the entertainment. Furious with herself that he had captured her so easily she hastily straightened in her chair and concentrated on the jugglers in front of her.

To her distress, she heard a chuckle beside her. A low, masculine sound that made her skin prickle, and the hair on her scalp tingle. Saint's bones, he knew he had caught her as easily as a trout in a trap. It was as though the previous six years had not passed, and she was back in Rouen longing for stolen moments when she could be in his arms.

God in heaven, she couldn't let Guyon back into her heart, and she most certainly didn't want him in her bed. But for a moment the thought created a warm tingling in her stomach. What a fool.

THE PRIEST HAD COME and blessed the bed, but Guyon had not been present. Without a word the priest left after the blessing, leaving Cicele alone in her chamber to await her husband. It was well into the night when Cicele heard the quiet knock at her door. It was him, she was sure of it. The air around her seemed to vibrate whenever he was near. Having decided several years ago that she could live without the reaction his closeness produced in her, she was angry with herself for succumbing to him so quickly. Vite was curled in a basket by the fire and raised his head at Guyon's knock, but the dog remained in his small nest of coney fur.

"Come." She didn't exactly bark the order, but it was a close thing.

He entered and walked to where she was sitting by the fire. Refusing to look at him, she stared fixedly at the flames that danced before her. Her heart thumped in her chest and the skin on her arms tingled. Her body's reaction to him was unsettling and alarming. It wouldn't take much for her to succumb to him. But that would be a disaster. She would never allow herself to be so vulnerable again. Her heart had shattered when he failed to return as promised. Everything they had shared had been a lie. No, best to keep herself aloof and wholly disagreeable. She had perfected the art.

"Cicele?"

Her body tingled in recognition of her name upon his lips. The sinking feeling of the inevitable struck her as her body responded to what he offered. But she strove to keep its treacherous inclinations under control. She had no wish to be used again by the man standing in the shadows of her chamber. It had been demoralizing and heartbreaking. She shook her head and refocused on what she must do.

Although he stood in the semidarkness, his presence filled the room. "Cicele, we need to talk, especially if we are to travel to Alnwick tomorrow."

She turned to look at him, but couldn't make out his face, although she felt his gaze upon her.

"Why did you agree to the marriage?" That was not what she had intended to say. Although if she were honest she hadn't been satisfied with his answer to the question back in the forest. It was most likely he wanted what every other man wanted, an available womb to plant an heir, and the wealth her title offered. It was with some resentment that she remembered Guyon had achieved those same things by betraying her with another. She would not be so accommodating. Not again.

He walked over to the fire, and sat in the chair beside her. His gaze was intent on the flames. Watching as their shadows danced over the clean lines of his face, she could see his frown. When he turned to look at her, his eyes held an expression she couldn't interpret.

"Henry ordered it."

There was no emotion in his voice, or his expression. What had she hoped for? Even now, after all her humiliation, there was a small corner of her mind, a kernel of hope in her heart that he had some affection for her. His face told her the truth. God in His heaven, she was an idiot.

Could she put aside her anger and hurt and accept that marriage provided a certain security for her? The ordeal in the forest proved that. In exchange for her security he received her lands and title, and vast wealth, and she no longer had to worry about being abducted and forced to marry someone even more loathsome.

"I see." She wet her lips and tried to keep her roiling emotions under control. "I have no wish to be raped and forced into marriage, but I find I have little appetite for *another* husband." The inflection of her voice was meant to wound, and she could see from his face that she hit her mark.

The tension in his jaw was obvious. He was angry, but she refused to cow. She was the one who had been left ruined, and heartbroken, when he failed to return as promised.

"That was not always the case," he said quietly.

She huffed a small laugh. "I was left with little choice but to marry a man I had never met," she sneered, unable to control her anger. "While the man I had loved, and given myself to, proved to be a worthless cur. Having had his fun, he abandoned me to my fate." She took a shuddering breath. "No, sir, I have not the appetite for marriage." She wanted to say "especially to you", but she held her tongue.

"I will do my duty, Cicele. You have very little choice." He spoke without any hostility, but his eyes were cold and unfeeling. Good. She could live with his displeasure.

She watched him as his jaw clenched. The firelight danced off his skin, making shadows on his face. He was furious, and dangerous. But for all his ferocity she knew he would never hurt her. Not physically anyway. This "beast" that King Henry kept leashed was no threat to her, yet there was something darker, more untamed, about him that gave her pause.

"Of course, with your history you are likely to hie off in the middle of the night to God knows where," he accused, through clenched teeth.

Her head sprang back as though slapped. "You think so little of me?" she asked, hardly crediting her own shock and dismay.

"I speak as I find. You didn't even wait a month before you agreed to marry Sir Nicholas, or am I mistaken?" He spoke the cruel accusation with all the finesse of a marksman.

She couldn't find the words to reply. It was as though the air in the chamber had vanished and she couldn't get any to fill her lungs.

"You toyed with me. Never did you mean those words that I cherished. Then when you didn't return, as you had promised, I had little choice but to marry or be ruined." She shook with pent-up fury. "So don't you dare fling accusations at me when they are not warranted." She scrubbed her hand over her cheeks to wipe away the evidence of her tears. She would not let herself be cast as the villain in this story. God knows, the guilt she bore for her own foolish behavior was enough to destroy her. But she would not accept his censure when he was the one who failed.

"I have no wish to speak of the past. What's done is done."

When she didn't reply, he continued. "It seems to me you take unnecessary risks, putting yourself, and others, in peril. I suspect your former husband was too lenient, but I shall not be so tolerant."

In truth, she did feel responsible for Agatha's disappearance. Whatever had happened to her maid it was because Cicele had refused to heed Agatha's warnings. Still, she wasn't going to confess that to the swine sitting next to her.

She turned to look at him. "Do you suppose that I went fishing knowing that men hid in the woods waiting to abduct me?"

"That, my lady, is the problem. You don't seem to grasp that your behavior is dangerous in the extreme."

"A little fishing in the weir is hardly dangerous."

He didn't respond, but the expression on his face communicated he thought her a lackwit.

She chose to return her gaze to the fire rather than continue to engage in a conversation that had deteriorated into casting insults.

They sat in silence for what seemed an eternity. It wasn't comfortable. Cicele's skin prickled with anticipation, while the remains of her wedding feast sat like a stone in her stomach.

"I have no wish to force myself on you, but we must consummate our marriage. I am sure you, like myself, do not want to have our union contested." He didn't look at her as he spoke, but concentrated his gaze on the fire.

They were quiet for some time.

"I was unable to return to you as promised, and when I did you were married," he said, almost as if talking to himself. There was a pleading expression in his eyes that spoke of pain and regret, but she forced herself to remain unmoved.

"Yes, I was delayed, but you could have waited until I returned, but you did not." It was so easy for him to disregard what had transpired between them, but she refused to let him cast it aside.

"You promised me the stars, and I gave myself to you," she sobbed, despite vowing she wouldn't. "I trusted you, and you deserted me."

He looked at her for a long time. "I am sorry, Cicele, but I didn't for one moment think my delay in returning would mean you would be thrown into the arms of another. I had no choice. I was not able to return to you as quickly as I had promised."

"Ha. Men always have choices," she threw back at him.

"For God's sake, Cicele, don't be so naive. None of us has the freedom to choose." He was silent for a moment. A ragged sigh filled the silence. "We were young and foolish and thought we could outsmart the Fates.

"I was unable to come as promised…"

She didn't let him finish. "I have no interest in hearing your confession," she snapped. "You betrayed me and proved to be a man without honor. Whatever it is you want to say, tell the priest, for I won't hear it." She cast him a withering look. "You may own my body, but you will never have what you so casually threw away." Her heart, her very soul, had been his. What a dullard she had been not to see the lies behind the sweet assurances.

He held her gaze for several agonizing heartbeats. "Very well," he replied. No emotion in his tone. "But mark my words, I take my vows of marriage seriously and will protect you. After we consummate our marriage you may be assured that I will not seek your chamber unless invited."

His dark eyes appeared black in the dim light of the chamber, while his face might have been carved from stone. There was no softness, no compassion, no kindness in his expression.

"There will never be an invitation for you to visit my chamber, my lord husband." She took a moment to calm her racing heart. When she was in control of her emotions she continued, "As we anticipated our marriage vows six years ago, I see no need to do so now." She dared not look at him, so kept her eyes to the flames dancing in the hearth.

A cold silence.

"Very well, I will bid you good-night." He didn't look at her, or bow, he just stood up and walked out.

She was beginning to get her breathing back under control when she heard him reenter the chamber and speak to her. "Make no mistake, Cicele, you *will* be my wife in every aspect except our chamber. I will not tolerate a troublesome wife."

She bristled at the veiled insult, but chose to ignore it. "I took my vows in good conscience, my lord; you will find no fault with my role as your wife," she said in a rush. "Now, if you will excuse me, I am tired." She rose and waited for him to leave.

Slowly, with deliberate restraint, he bowed to her. "I am ever your servant, madam." Then he turned on his heel and walked from the chamber.

She slumped back into her chair. With a desperation she hadn't experienced for six years, Cicele admitted to herself that she was still in love with him. And it threatened to break her heart all over again.

Chapter Ten

Something cool and refreshing lay across his face. Enjoying the sensation Guyon lay still and tried not to think about his confrontation with Cicele the previous night. His head ached and his mouth had the telltale metallic taste that announced the demon had come to him in the night.

"Was it bad?" he asked, his voice a gruff bark.

"One of your worst, my lord." Warin spoke quietly, anticipating the pain his master would be experiencing.

Guyon heard the creak of a chair; someone else was in the room. He sat up with a start and laid his hand on the knife that he always kept beneath his pillow. It wasn't there.

"Where's my knife," he snapped as he took the damp cloth from his face.

The answer was before him.

Thomas, who must have arrived with the rest of Guyon's retinue sometime during the night, sat on a stool while Warin bandaged his arm. "Fear not, it is a mere scratch," Thomas laughed, his light tone at odds with the gravity of the situation.

"I could have killed you," Guyon moaned. Self-loathing curled in his gut. What if it had have been Cicele? He couldn't bear to think of such a monstrous thing.

Thomas fixed him with a gimlet eye. "Even when you are possessed with a legion of hell's demons, you are still not likely to kill me with that puny knife you keep under your thick head." Thomas stood when Warin finished bandaging his arm, and walked to where Guyon sat in bed. He placed his hand on his friend's shoulder. "Just don't think to put a bloody great sword under there." He quirked his eyebrow and exposed his teeth in a parody of a grimace.

Warin gave Guyon a cup full of steaming liquid. He accepted it from his squire, then sniffed it. And gagged. "What the…?" He cursed as he flung the cup away. It landed with a thud on the rushes.

"I'll grant you it smells unpleasant," Warin said, unfazed by his lord's outburst.

"Unpleasant," Guyon roared. "It's vile, get me some wine." The boy calmly retrieved the cup and proceeded to pour another measure of steaming liquid from a jug on the table beside the hearth, and returned to face Guyon as he sat in bed.

Thomas took the cup and raised it to his nose.

Guyon watched with dispassionate interest as his captain screwed up his nose.

"Smells like a cesspit," he announced.

Guyon noticed the humorous glint in his eye. "Then you drink it."

"Ah, I would, but I'm not the one who is possessed of demons. This is sure to kill anything still lurking in that black heart of yours."

Both his squire and his captain stood over him. "God's teeth, give me patience," Guyon grumbled, but he took the cup and gulped down the now warm liquid. When he had drained the cup his body gave an involuntary shudder. "Christ's cross, that is worse than drinking horse piss."

"And when did you drink that?" Warin mumbled under his breath as he took the empty cup from Guyon's hands.

"I heard that, insolent pup." But there was no heat in his voice.

BY THE TIME dawn arrived Guyon was ready to depart Beauforde. He had instructed Thomas to have the men ready to escort him and Cicele to Alnwick. Ranulf had dispatched a large group of men-at-arms to ride out before dawn to scour the countryside to watch for an ambush. There was a good chance Lincoln would have sent more men when he discovered Cicele had been rescued. Guyon wouldn't put it past him to try and ambush them as they traveled to Alnwick. They may, even now, be lurking somewhere in the woods. Hopefully the combined precautions would keep Cicele and himself safe.

Ranulf was lounging on a high-backed chair by the hearth when Guyon entered the hall. "You look like hell," he sniggered. "Difficult night?"

If only you knew. But Guyon kept that thought to himself as he collapsed into a chair next to Ranulf. Exhaustion, the usual companion following a night terror, made his limbs leaden and slow to obey. A page, who had been standing by the table, poured some wine and offered it to Guyon. It was a fine fortifying red that slid down his throat and pooled in his empty stomach. A warm, languorous sensation began to radiate through his body. "I would stay and enjoy your excellent hospitality if I wasn't required to take up my role as sheriff." Guyon sighed as he sipped his wine.

"There have been reports of increased poaching and violence since Odard died."

"He was an inept fool who should have known better than to torture a prisoner with such powerful connections," Guyon noted. It was common knowledge that Odard, the previous high sheriff, had stupidly tried to extort money from a wealthy merchant by torturing his servant, who had been falsely accused of poaching.

"It will be a pleasant change to have a high sheriff who is not stupid, or corrupt," Ranulf commented, as he cast Guyon an inquiring glance.

"You assume I'm not open to bribes," Guyon smiled back at his friend. "But being Lord of Alnwick will require large sums of coin to raise an army when necessary. I shall require deep coffers."

"Well, I suspect those deep coffers have been supplemented by your timely marriage to the lovely Lady Cicele."

"Ha!" Guyon snorted. "As I recall you found her a might too haughty for your tastes."

"God's bones, the girl was a harpy," Ranulf smirked. "But as I recall you found her sharp tongue and claws to your liking for a time."

Guyon shifted in his chair. Guilt over the way he treated Cicele all those years ago still nibbled at his conscience, although he would make the same decision again if required. "Honor, it's a millstone around our necks," he mused.

"Better honor," Ranulf replied, "and when necessary, make the sacrifices it requires, rather than become a man with none."

Guyon turned to look at his friend. Ranulf was one of very few men who knew the truth. Well some of the truth. "I regret that she was so badly hurt by my actions."

"Are you referring to Cicele or Alice?" Ranulf asked.

Guyon huffed. He hadn't shared the depth of his guilt, or his regrets, concerning both women, to another living soul. Perhaps now it was time to unburden himself. "Both," he admitted. "Marrying Alice to save her from ruination, and to legitimize her son, that I will never regret." The guilt he carried over her death still gnawed at his innards. "But I fear Cicele will never believe that I chose Alice only after Cicele married." Guyon didn't look at Ranulf. "She is the only woman I have ever loved." It was good to unburden himself to his old friend.

"Have you told her?"

Guyon barked a hard laugh. "I tried last night, but she would hear none of it."

Ranulf leaned over and placed his hand on Guyon's shoulder. "Give it time, my friend," he encouraged. "And perhaps try to be a little less yourself," he suggested with an expression that was more grimace than grin.

Guyon laughed despite himself. "That's rich. Am I to take the counsel of a man who has a reputation for terrifying maids out of their wits?"

Ranulf slapped Guyon's shoulder. "Yes," he bellowed. "Just ask my delectable wife."

"Speaking of your wife, I suspect it's time to find my own, and be on our way."

Guyon left Ranulf to drink his wine by the fire while he went in search of his wife.

GUYON DECIDED he had better confront Cicele, knowing she was probably thinking how she might renege on their journey after last night's conversation.

The woman infuriated him—headstrong to a fault and altogether too reckless. Was it too much to ask to have a biddable wife? Well perhaps that was asking too much; it was Cicele after all. God help him, she still made his blood race in his veins. Marriage to Lady Cicele was proving to be more complicated than he had expected, and it was only his third day in the woman's company.

As he strode to the tower where her chamber was situated, he made inventory of last night's seizure. If she had been lying abed with him, it would have been her he had knifed, not Thomas. To place her in jeopardy, or for her to find out about his night demons, was too much of a risk. God forbid, if the king, or his enemies, discovered his shameful affliction.

He hated that his body betrayed him. And having no recollection of the episode always made him feel vulnerable and weak. Thomas had said he was often violet, and screamed like an animal before weeping like a babe. But other times his body trembled and he usually pissed himself. Never would he allow Cicele to see him in that condition. It might mean he could never enjoy waking in the morning with her in his arms, but he would be damned if he wouldn't find a way to breach her defenses, and bed the little harpy.

The memory of his own culpability six years ago only added to his guilt, but honor was everything, and Guyon would do the same again if necessary.

Despite his confidence that he could respect his wife's decision to refuse him her bed, he had the nagging suspicion it might prove to be more onerous than he would prefer. In truth, he had no allusions about trying to keep his distance from his infuriating, beguiling wife.

On entering his wife's chamber Guyon had to clench his jaw so tight his ears ached, and he began to see stars. The woman was beyond impossible. Taking a deep breath to try and regain his temper he spoke quietly so as not to offend Lady Beauforde, who stood beside his wife. The comely lady's maid standing beside his wife had a defiant tilt of her chin, and glared at him with eyes the color of wild thyme honey. He recognized her from the day before, although there was nothing of the "maid" about her today. Was it his imagination, or was there something of a familial resemblance between the three women?

He didn't have time to unravel the mystery, for now he required all his wits to deal with his wife. God's bones, she was exasperating.

Looking at the three women standing before him they reminded him of the Moirai, those ancient weavers of fate. And like Zeus, he suspected he had little ability to control their plan. Where was Ranulf when he wanted him? Couldn't he at least control his good lady wife? That thought struck Guyon as somewhat ironic; he himself clearly had very little ability to control his own woman.

By some miracle at that precise moment Ranulf emerged through the chamber door. Laughing, he looked at Guyon with an amused expression. "God's bones man, they look like the Fates. What have you done?" He smiled towards his wife, who returned his with a knowing expression that gave Guyon a pang of envy. He longed for Cicele to look at him with open longing like that. *Addled-brained dolt!* He silently reprimanded himself.

Ranulf turned back to Guyon and clasped his shoulder. "I suggest you agree to their plan, for they have the look of women who shall not be thwarted."

"We have been trying to explain to my husband," Cicele said in a slow condescending tone, which infuriated Guyon, "that without Agatha, who seems to have disappeared, it has taken longer to pack than I anticipated."

Guyon exchanged an exasperated glance with Ranulf, then turned his eyes back to Cicele. "I am not being unreasonable," he countered with impatience. "What I do object to though, is that you delay our departure unnecessarily."

Cicele gave him a demure smile that set his teeth on edge. "I am sorry, my lord husband, but I was unable to ready myself at such short notice. My ordeal has left me tired and ill prepared for such an early start." At least she had the decency to lower her eyes as she spouted such nonsense to him. That, in itself, gave Guyon some satisfaction. He wasn't sure whether her abduction, or their discussion from the previous night, was the "ordeal" she referred to. He wouldn't ask for clarification.

She looked at him under hooded eyes. The little minx was using the oldest trick in the book, and God help him, it was working.

"I am almost ready, my lord," she purred. "I trust I haven't inconvenienced you too much?"

God's splintered cross, she was good.

Like any good warrior Guyon knew when to press an advantage, and when to relinquish ground. On this occasion, a dignified retreat was the best option, but, by all that was holy, he would make the conniving little minx pay for this.

"I shall wait." He slowly cast his gaze to Lady Beauforde, then the "maid," and lastly Ranulf. "Will you please excuse us, I would like a moment alone with my lady wife." It wasn't a request.

When they were alone Guyon continued to hold her with his eyes as he moved towards her, closing the gap until he could smell the lavender soap she used to clean her hair. "You go too far, my lady. Have a care or you may find you exhaust my patience," he growled as he leaned his head towards her, his mouth tantalizing close to hers.

She didn't move. Not her body nor her eyes, which were glued to his lips. His own heartbeat thundered in his chest. It was torture to be this close to her but not touch. Dangerous, but rewarding as he watched her gold-flecked eyes grow wide and the pink tip of her tongue flicked out to moisten her lower lip.

"Be careful, wife, do not push me. I am neither tame nor predictable when cornered." His words stirred the air between them, making the side of her veil flutter.

Guyon was so close he only had to incline his head a fraction and he would be able to kiss her. *Tempting.* Desire surged through him, resulting in a cock-stand that made his balls ache, but now was not the time.

What was it about her that roused such hunger in him? Yes, she was a beauty, but it was her haughty self-possession that intrigued him. The desire to take her against the wall of the chamber was like a living beast within him, prowling, waiting for the opportunity to be unleashed. It had been six long years since he had felt this kind of attraction. He was consumed with a burning desire to possess this woman and bury himself inside her.

With a Herculean force of will he reluctantly took a step back creating enough distance between them. He needed a moment to think. "It is likely to take two or perhaps three days to travel to Alnwick. The wagons are slow and cumbersome," he said looking at her. "I have no wish to delay further. I will expect you within the hour." He gave her a smile that he hoped conveyed his patience with her games was at an end. "I trust that is agreeable with you, my lady?"

She blushed. The tinge of pink that traveled up her neck and into her cheeks almost had him reach out and take possession of her there and then. But he stayed rooted to the spot.

Finally, after several heartbeats she replied. "Yes, my lord."

But the minx refused to look at him when she said it.

The bloody woman was going to be the death of him.

CICELE KNEW she had probably pushed a little too far, but something about baiting him was exhilarating. True, she had been hurt by his high-handed dismissal of his behavior all those years ago. That he thought she would be interested in his excuses almost made her spit. She balked at having to submit to him, yet she would never have been so reckless with her previous husband. Although Nicholas had never hit her, he would never have tolerated her belligerence.

"Well, that went better than I expected," Beatrice said as she reentered the chamber.

Cicele huffed a small laugh, "I think my lord husband, like most men, tolerates such behavior because he is under the misguided assumption that women are prone to less hysteria when they have their needs adequately met."

"And by 'hysteria,' you mean—?"

Cicele held her cousin's gaze for several heartbeats before she answered, "Oh, the usual. Tears, fainting, refusing access to the chamber."

Beatrice choked on a laugh. "You could never be so Janus-faced. Could you?" Beatrice's eyes became round and her mouth fell open as she observed Cicele's sly smile by way of reply.

"Come now, cousin, didn't you play such games with your husband?" Cicele asked.

Beatrice's expression immediately became shuttered. *Oh, sweet Mother Mary, I've gone too far*. It was obvious to Cicele that Beatrice had suffered at her husband's hand. Cicele knew her cousin had married several years ago, but as to her life with him she had no knowledge.

"What did he do to you?"

Beatrice looked to her feet. Cicele thought she might not answer, but she waited in silence to give her cousin a chance. It took several heartbeats before Beatrice raised her gaze to meet Cicele's. "It is of little consequence, as it is in the past."

Cicele saw the fear in her cousin's eyes, and decided not to push. Beatrice would confide in Isabeau, or herself, when she was ready.

Changing the subject, Cicele focused on her own predicament.

"I had better scurry down to my impatient husband before he comes back up here and drags me down himself."

"He can't keep his eyes from you, Cicele, and don't pretend that you haven't noticed, because I watched you last evening as you shared your wedding feast."

Heat flooded Cicele's cheeks. "I have no knowledge of what you say, cousin."

"And I thought I kept secrets."

Trying to avoid her cousin's eagle-eyed inspection, Cicele changed the subject.

"I did notice that Sir Gilbret spent a great deal of time watching you, cousin."

Beatrice surprised her with a bitter laugh. "Now that is a bare-faced lie," she replied.

Cicele knew very little of Beatrice's plight, except that she was terrified for her son's life. That alone was reason enough for Cicele to take pity on her.

Cicele decided not to press her cousin. Instead she walked over and took Beatrice's hands in hers. "Beatrice, look at me." When she did Cicele continued, "You have no reason to fear; Isabeau will ensure you and baby Edward are safe here," Cicele assured her with a smile. "Although I will miss you terribly."

Beatrice nodded, and brought Cicele's hands up to her mouth and kissed them.

Overcome by the gesture, Cicele had to take a few moments to calm her emotions. When she felt more herself she gave Beatrice a sly look. "Now I must hurry or I will find my lord husband's patience exhausted."

Isabeau arrived with her great hound at her side. "All is ready. I will miss you so much," she cried as she hugged Cicele.

Clinging to her sister's hand, and talking about nothing, Cicele allowed herself to be led down the stairs, through the hall, and out into the upper bailey where her husband awaited her.

An elaborately decorated wagon was waiting at the foot of the steps. The carved wooden sides and roof were gilded and inlaid with mother-of-pearl, while the window had a piece of brocade that shimmered in the early morning light. Surprised to see something so exquisite Cicele gasped out loud.

Maude was already seated inside the wagon. Hearing his mistress's voice, Vite's head appeared out of the open window, his pink tongue lolling out of the side of his mouth. Never had Cicele seen anything so luxurious. Was it for her?

Her husband walked towards her, then stopped as she turned her head to meet him. She was speechless.

A smile creased the corners of his mouth. "I hope you will be comfortable on the journey." He inclined his head towards the wagon. When she didn't reply, he continued, "I have a horse ready for you if you want to ride at some stage." A squire brought forward a bay palfrey with a rich brown coat, her legs, mane, and tail all jet-black. Intelligent, deep brown eyes assessed Cicele as she let the horse sniff her gloved hands.

"I can see you will be great friends," her husband said. "Would you prefer to ride her now, or use the wagon?"

From experience Cicele knew that wagons were not all that comfortable over rough roads, but the one before her offered such luxury she was tempted to climb inside. But when she turned to look again at the mare standing before her she decided on riding.

"What's her name?" Cicele asked as her husband led her, and the horse, to the mounting block.

"Nyssa," he answered as he leaned in to speak to her in a conspiratorial tone. "I seem to recall you spoke of a longing to breed palfreys. It was a long time ago now, but I thought she might be the beginning of that desire becoming a reality." He gave Cicele a smile that made her toes curl and her stomach ache in want. "If you still hold that particular ambition."

Cicele was overcome for a moment and couldn't speak. When she had her emotions under control she turned to her husband and gave him a deep curtsy. "I thank you, my lord."

Cicele stroked the mare's head, then trailed her hand over her shoulder. "She is with foal?" The mare's girth was a little rounder than Cicele would have expected.

"Yes, she will foal in May or June."

He had done this for her, while she had been churlish. A hot flush of shame singed her cheeks. "You are generous, my lord, and I thank you."

He didn't answer, but took her gloved hand and helped her climb the mounting block steps, before hoisting her into the saddle.

A shiver of awareness made the small hairs on the back of her neck rise as he leaned in and placed his hands around her waist. She could still feel their imprint on her waist as he walked away.

Her heart beat at a frantic pace and she couldn't quite catch her breath. It was terrifying, her body's reaction to her husband. Everything in her head screamed "No!" But her body didn't obey. When it came to her husband, her body was its own master. The realization made her head ache and her stomach hitch.

Forcing herself to calm down she concentrated on watching Vite make himself comfortable on the pillows next to Maude. The little devil refused to look at her. She had to smile. He did that when he thought he was going to be scolded.

When she had her emotions, and body, back under control she walked Nyssa to where Ranulf and Isabeau were waiting to bid them farewell. Beatrice had taken her place behind Isabeau, Edward in her arms. A sharp pain seared her chest. She would miss them.

Unshed tears pricked at the back of her eyes, and her throat closed tight. Isabeau seemed to understand. "I shall miss you, sister, but you will come when I begin my lying in, won't you?"

Cicele could only give her sister a weak smile and nod. Already silent tears streaked her cheeks. Two months ago, this woman had been a stranger, now she was so much more than a sister. She was her dearest friend.

Once again Isabeau understood. "Go now, before your husband loses what little patience he has left." She smiled and waved as Cicele turned her horse around. She wouldn't look back. Eyes forward, she kept them trained on her husband's back, as he led their retinue out of the bailey and into her future.

Chapter Eleven

FINALLY, AFTER FOUR GRUELING DAYS OF TRAVELING, CICELE WAS eager to reach their destination. The wagons had become bogged down often, making for a slow, tedious journey. But the days had also been free of rain, a small concession that Cicele would accept.

Each evening they found themselves recipients of generous hospitality. It seemed many were eager to court the new high sheriff's favor. Maude had shared her accommodation at an abbey, and two manors. Thankfully, Guyon had been true to his word, and not pushed her to share her bed, instead choosing to bed down with his men.

The first night he had surprised her by escorting her from the abbot's rather fine table, which had been laden with all manner of food, and led her to her room. "I have had Thomas begin to make a search for your maid, Agatha."

Cicele had been so surprised that she had merely stared at him.

"This does not please you?"

"Forgive me, I was momentarily surprised. Thank you."

His eyes traveled over her face, lingering for a moment on her lips. Then he bowed and left. Her legs wobbled as she entered the room and closed the door behind her. She had expected a cold, distant relationship with her husband. But she wasn't prepared for generosity and thoughtfulness. She had no defenses for that.

The next two evenings he had escorted her to her chamber door, but had not lingered as he had the first night.

Just thinking about how he had devoured her with his gaze that first night made her face burn. Oh, lord help her, she thought she might ignite under such a gaze.

By mid-afternoon on the fourth day, Cicele caught her first glimpse of Alnwick. The imposing castle sat atop a hill overlooking the river Aln. Its dark outline was silhouetted against the slate blue sky, creating a striking backdrop for the town nestled at the base of the hill. The road had been busy all day with folk traveling towards the town. There were merchants with wagons carrying wares to sell at the castle's square. Farmers leading their stock to the butcher's hill outside the gates. The atmosphere was that of a fair—voices and shrill laughter filled the air. Her own heart beat in time to the excitement thrumming through her veins.

It wasn't until they got close to the main gate that Cicele reconsidered her initial impression of Alnwick. For there, above the entrance, was a gibbet with the remains of an outlaw. The crows had done their work on the softer parts of his flesh leaving gaping holes where eyes, nose, and mouth had originally been. An involuntary shudder scudded down Cicele's back, and bile rose in her throat. She swallowed convulsively to try and keep her meager morning meal in her stomach, and not over her new riding boots.

Gibbets at crossroads were a common enough sight, but never had she been this close.

"It is disagreeable, but necessary as a deterrent." A deep voice spoke somewhere close to her right shoulder.

Cicele couldn't drag her eyes away from the grisly sight. True enough, she had seen men hanged, even severed limbs and heads of traitors that had been tarred and hung or placed on spikes. Never having lived in a large town, she hadn't expected the sight and it shocked her.

Recovering her composure, she spoke to Guyon. "I hear tell that the last lord of Alnwick was apt to dispense justice with an iron fist."

Guyon cast a cursory glance at the gibbet. "My uncle was a cruel bastard, much like his father." He then looked at Cicele. "I am nothing like my uncle."

Cicele nodded, but her eyes swiveled back to the grisly sight.

"Methinks I should have ordered you into the cart," he laughed. "But we both know how that would have gone." His smile was devastating. His dark eyes had a mischievous glint about them as he quirked his eyebrow in a playful challenge.

Well, she wouldn't disagree. "I would never have wanted to miss this." She swung her arm in an arc. "But in truth, I could have done without seeing that." She shuddered as she nodded to the gibbet that they now rode past. The sickly-sweet stench of rotting flesh coated her tongue and throat. Her stomach heaved and her neck and face became clammy.

A skin of wine was thrust into her face. "Drink!" Came the barked order. "Now."

She got such a fright she obeyed without thinking, her throat opening and swallowing in reflex to the liquid's presence.

"Better?"

Cicele handed the skin back and wiped her lips with the cuff of her mantel. They were past the gibbet and through the main gate before she realized it. The smell was not much better inside the walls, but the vile odor of decomposing flesh was absent.

"Thank you. That was well done, and I appreciate it." She offered him a small smile. "I am not usually so squeamish, but I must confess I did get a shock."

"It is not surprising. It is one thing to see men hanged, it is another to see what time and carrion birds can accomplish."

"The wine has restored my strength." She gave him a small smile.

"Didn't want to see you foul your new clothes." He gave her a wolfish grin. "They are most becoming, wife."

She couldn't help herself. She blushed. The heat spread from her breasts up her neck and scolded her cheeks. Hell's teeth, didn't she have any dignity? One compliment and she was a blushing maid awaiting a tumble in the hayloft.

Before she could answer Guyon had rode ahead of her as he led their retinue through the town towards the castle gates.

Some of the town's people gathered on the sides of the road to watch as the new lord and lady of Alnwick rode past. Most did not lower their eyes. There was a mood among these people and it wasn't one of respect or acceptance. The previous lord of Alnwick was Guyon's estranged uncle, who was rumored to be as oppressive as the last high sheriff. These people had endured years of harsh justice and outrageous taxes. In her heart, she believed Guyon to be honest and reasonable, but she wouldn't allow herself the luxury of trusting it to his care for a second time. It would destroy her.

GUYON HAD BEEN DISTRACTED for the four days it took them to travel from Beauforde to Alnwick. Four long, torturous days where Cicele had been close but not close enough. He could smell her, and if he let himself, he could taste her. Those memories were old, and faded, but he would never forget the sweetness of her mouth, or the salt-sweet taste of her skin on his tongue.

Bringing his thoughts back to the present before it was obvious his mind was not on the man standing in front of him, Guyon scrubbed his hands over his face, feigning weariness.

He had been introduced to the steward and chamberlain, both loyal to his uncle, and wary of their new lord. They would not take kindly to a new master, but he would give them a chance to prove their loyalty. He had sent the chamberlain to settle Cicele, while he followed the steward to his solar.

Sir Robert Morton was perhaps two score years, but his body revealed none of his age. He was fit and well-muscled and looked to be able to handle himself well with a sword. Sharp, intelligent eyes surveyed Guyon as they stood facing each other.

"You wish I was not here?" Guyon decided to get the measure of the man.

"If you prove to be a better man than your uncle, then you will have no trouble from me, my lord."

Guyon strove to keep his face free from the smile that threatened to expose his surprise at the man's insubordination.

"You take a chance speaking so freely, Sir Robert."

Gray eyes, the color of a winter's sky, studied Guyon for a moment. "You are la Bête, and although your reputation is fierce, and probably slightly exaggerated, your character is not. You are a man of honor, and that, my lord, is why I choose to speak so candidly."

Guyon held the steward in a steely gaze. He trusted his gut when it came to assessing men, and his gut told him that Sir Robert Morton was a man that could be trusted.

"Honor, and a strong sword arm are what I want in my vassals. You, it seems, Sir Robert, might just prove to be such a man."

Sir Robert didn't respond, but he bowed and left to organize the noon meal leaving Guyon alone in his solar.

"The mood of the town is worse than an alehouse without ale," Thomas commented as he entered the solar and poured himself some wine from the jug on the table near the fire.

Guyon huffed, but didn't bother answering. He was still trying to drag his mind back from memories of Cicele's pliant body slick with sweat. Deciding movement would help, he walked to where Thomas was standing and poured himself a goblet of wine. He took a deep draft of the rich red wine his estate in Burgundy produced, and immediately felt more in control. Only slightly though, much to his chagrin.

Thomas didn't seem to notice Guyon's inability to contribute to the conversation. "We will have to find a way to win the townsfolk over to us," he suggested. "But I hear the merchant guild is run by a greedy sot who is free with his denouncement of la Bête as Alnwick's new lord."

"A name?"

"Master FitzWallah."

Guyon gave Thomas a sly smile. "Perhaps we should invite him to dine with the 'beast,' and assess his weaknesses. Is it his fear or his avarice that loosens his tongue? Food and wine may work to our advantage." Guyon enjoyed a challenge, and greedy merchants eager to spread pernicious rumors about him were just the kind of challenge he savored almost as much as a good fight.

"My men are already in the alehouses listening to the gossip."

"Ah, Thomas, you are ill-used serving me." Guyon slapped his friend on the back.

"I've needed those spies to keep your head off a spike," he guffawed.

Guyon laughed with his friend. It was true Thomas's network of spies had saved his skin on more than one occasion.

Taking another slow sip of wine, Guyon thought about a strategy for undermining the merchant guild. "We will do nothing until we have proof he is withholding taxes," he said as he walked to a table where a pile of parchments awaited his attention.

"And Thomas," Guyon spoke over his shoulder. "Make certain your men do nothing to aggravate them. I want him unaware of our interest." Guyon had discovered that men whose tongues wagged usually had something to hide, and FitzWallah would be no exception.

Thomas nodded, and walked out of the solar.

"Thomas." Guyon called his friend back, just before he disappeared through the door. "Any word about Agatha?"

Thomas turned. "None, which is strange. It is as though she has vanished, but I'll keep looking." Then he left.

"What do you have?" Guyon beckoned for the cleric who had just entered carrying ledgers to take a seat at a large table. A lad followed carrying a bundle wrapped in linen.

"The ledgers are not as complete as they should be, my lord," the monk replied. A worried scowl creased his forehead.

"Your name?"

"I am Brother Martin, Lord. I served Odard as his cleric for the past year." The little man's eyes darted to Guyon's face, then back down at his hands.

"You fear me, Brother Martin?" Guyon kept his voice low as he moved to stand over the man so he would have to look up.

The cleric didn't answer, or look up, but kept his head bowed and squirmed in his chair.

"Answer me this, are the ledgers of the king's taxes accurate?" Guyon growled.

The man was about to speak but Guyon cut him off. "Before you answer I suggest you take a moment to confer with your God, for if you lie I shall have your head on a spike."

The man whimpered, which gave Guyon no satisfaction. He couldn't abide cowards anymore than he could abide unscrupulous churchmen who fed themselves off the fat of the king's taxes, while honest men toiled and received no justice.

The man surprised Guyon then. He looked up and met Guyon's eye. "Lord Odard kept a second set of ledgers, my lord," he said in a clear voice.

No coward then. Good. "And they are where?"

Brother Martin took the large parcel wrapped in linen from the lad, who then scurried from the chamber. "They are here, my lord; I took the liberty of taking them before Odard died."

Guyon gave the man a slow smile. "I value courage and honesty, but above all, I value loyalty in my servants. Are you such a man, Brother Martin?"

The cleric continued to look at Guyon. "If the man is deserving of it, my lord, then he would have it."

"Then let us pray you decide I am such a man." Guyon walked back to the table where the jug of wine and several goblets lay. He poured wine into his own goblet, and some into another. Then he took both goblets back and faced the monk. "We shall drink to a shared view of loyalty and honesty." Guyon passed the goblet to the cleric. Both men took a sip while eyeing each other.

When the cleric tasted the wine his gaze swung to the jug on the far table, then back up to Guyon's eyes. "My lord, never have I tasted such wine," he said in awe.

"I'm glad you approve. I find life is too short for bad wine, and I am fortunate to have estates in Burgundy," he said with a self-deprecating shrug. "I am a fair master, Brother Martin, and strive to maintain my servants' loyalty. If you work hard and are honest then we shall have a favorable relationship. Yes?"

The monk took a bigger sip of the wine this time. As he savored the liquid in his mouth, Guyon assessed him. He was shrewd, and not easily intimated. That did him credit, but could he be trusted? Only time would tell. He would get Thomas to have one of his "spies" get closer to this unassuming little cleric. If the man had any weaknesses, Thomas was sure to ferret them out.

"Show me the ledgers, explaining the discrepancies so I can make a full report to the Exchequer." Guyon was in for a very long morning, but the sooner he understood the situation the sooner he could make changes that would please the king.

~

THEY HAD ARRIVED mid-morning to Alnwick and Cicele began making herself at home. The chamberlain, a rather surly man who seemed to resent her presence, showed her to the second level of the main tower where she would have her suite of rooms.

"He's as welcoming as a winter frost on chilblains." Maude snorted when the man left them to attend to his other duties.

Cicele chose to ignore the comment for the moment, and instead let Maude organize the chambermaids, who were only now lighting the fire in the hearth.

So, this would be her home? Alnwick comprised one large tower, with several smaller towers spaced around the large inner bailey wall. The outer bailey had a high circular wall with four main towers and a large gatehouse which was used by the guards.

There was a separate hall, bake house, kitchen, and chapel inside the inner bailey, and a large garden nestled against the western side of the wall.

The outer bailey was huge, with a square and market place. Several private dwellings were nestled along the eastern side. That was where the rich merchants and nobles lived.

From her chamber windows Cicele could see a garden on the eastern side of the bailey, with several fruit trees and some hives. It would be a place she would investigate when she had time. For now, she needed to unpack and arrange the household. The steward had been introduced to her on arrival, but he had been absent since.

"I've never seen a more churlish group of men in my life," Maude muttered as she set several servants scurrying to bring Cicele's chests up to her chamber.

"I agree, they are an ill-favored lot, but perhaps they need a woman's touch."

"This is a grand chamber, and the one next door will serve as your solar. The light in there is better."

Cicele agreed, it was a grand room with light colored walls painted with ivy designs halfway up the wall. Tapestries hung on three walls and an alcove with a seat and a window gave her a view over the eastern side of Alnwick.

Cicele walked through the small corridor which led to her solar. It was light, and like her chamber, had painted walls and a large fireplace. An archway led into an adjoining room. It was a small space that would be ideal as her chapel. She could imagine that she might be able to spend almost all day in these rooms without having to spend time with Guyon. It was time to acknowledge her body's reaction to her husband. It was better if she could find some pretext to keep out of his way. It was safer.

They stopped for dinner when Guyon came to escort her to the hall. There were well over fifty men seated waiting to begin eating. Father Orrick, the castle chaplain, blessed the meal, and the new lord and lady of Alnwick. He was a man of few words, which was appreciated by Cicele as her stomach growled in protest at the delay to being fed. The priest heard and gave her a tolerant glance, which she returned with a small apologetic smile.

"Patience, wife, I hear is a rare gift." She could hear the humor in Guyon's voice as he leaned over to whisper, making the skin on her arms and neck prickle.

"Alas, my lord, it is one I am all too aware I do not possess." What was she doing? *No. No. No. Don't start flirting with him.* But she didn't seem to be listening to her own admonition where her husband was concerned. God help her.

"Perhaps you would care to ride with me after our dinner. I would like to view our new home," he purred as he leaned closer, his breath tickling the sensitive skin on the side of her neck.

Not able to answer she gave him a nod while valiantly trying to swallow the lump that had formed in her throat. Saints in heaven, she was doomed.

She ate little with her throat closed, and her stomach in knots. All her resolve to keep him at a distance seemed to have flown south with the swallows.

"How is your accommodation?"

Not wanting to look at him she played with the stem of her wine goblet. "It is comfortable, my lord."

"You are very formal, wife."

God in heaven, his voice did things to her that should be classed as sinful. Schooling her expression into one of disinterest she turned only to be captured by warm brown eyes that spoke of languid summer afternoons.

Wetting her lips, she tried to speak but couldn't.

His eyes immediately slid to her mouth, then slowly back up to meet her eyes. A lazy smile spread across his face making the fine skin around his eyes crinkle.

She was lost. Days, weeks, hours. She didn't know how long she was held in that gaze that set her heart racing, and her toes curling in her slippers.

Guyon, still holding her captive with his eyes, ran a finger over her jaw. "Trust me, wife, when I tell you that no other has captured me so completely as you."

What in all that was holy could she say to that? She couldn't risk her heart to someone who treated her with such disregard. Her affections had meant nothing to him, and she didn't think she had the capacity to trust him a second time.

It was an effort, one that took all her concentration, and no little discipline, to avert her eyes. She would snuff out this intolerable attraction that threatened to destroy her again.

Memories of a younger Guyon riding away from her, not to return as he had promised, had her clenching her jaw. He had promised to return within the week, and ask her father permission to marry her. But he had not returned when promised, and as the days turned into weeks she began to realize that he was not coming back. No missive, nothing. He had abandoned her, and left her to face ruin.

She already suspected that she might be with child and was

desperate for him to return. It was almost a month to the day since he had left that her father had discovered her secret, and within a few days she was married to a stranger who was as old as her father.

"Why didn't you return when you promised?" That wasn't what she had intended to say, but the words fell from her lips before she had a chance to call them back.

If she was honest she wanted to know why he didn't come back for her, but instead had married another. But her pride would not allow her to ask that question.

His eyes widened, then narrowed as he looked at her. "I've already told you I could not." He continued to look at her. "Then when I did return, admittedly later than I had originally intended, you were already married to de Grenville. And heading back to England."

"I had little choice." She wouldn't tell him, she would keep that part of her heart closed. It was all she had of her son, and she wouldn't share it with him.

GUYON WANTED to lean over and kiss those lips that were wet and inviting. He could smell the faint fragrance of lavender and musk that had been Cicele's scent since he first breathed her in.

Take it slowly, fool, he chided himself, but like the half-wit he was he didn't want to heed the advice.

Without thought he lifted his finger to her jaw, savoring the intimacy. Absurd as it was to be sitting on the dais with a hall full of retainers, Guyon imagined himself secluded with his wife in their chamber. "Trust me, wife, when I tell you that no other has captured me so completely as you." It was true, he had not lain with a woman since that fateful day in Rouen.

A battle raged behind her eyes—lust, fear, then resolve. He

recognized it immediately, and although he was not surprised he was disappointed.

"Why didn't you return when you promised."

If she had slapped him across the face his shock would not have been more pronounced.

Deciding to answer as honestly as he could he replied with measured control. "I've already told you I could not. I had assumed you would wait, but when I did return you were already married to de Grenville."

"I had little choice."

Guyon didn't take his eyes from hers, but he did take the time to gather his thoughts. "I have tried to explain, but you give me no opportunity."

That made her eyes snap back to his. "You didn't return when you promised, and neither did you send a missive telling me why you were delayed. It was a month, Guyon, and still you didn't return. What kept you from me?"

"I could not return, it was not my decision, but my liege lord, Geoffrey's." The lie spilled from his lips. He hated himself for it, but it was the only way. Never could he divulge that he had been hit on the head at the tournament, and then the demons had come and rendered him useless for almost three agonizing weeks. "I could not send a message. And then, when I did return, you were married and had left for England."

She looked down at her trencher, her bottom lip quivering. "But you married Alice."

Guyon heard all the sorrow and recriminations in that one small sentence.

Taking a deep breath to calm himself, he thought carefully about how to reply. "I married Alice after I found you were married and gone." That at least was the truth. And, by God, he had regretted his decision to marry Lincoln's pregnant mistress ever since. His honor had demanded it, but that was another secret he was unable to share.

A tear slid down her cheek and something shattered in Guyon's chest. He reached out his hand and brushed it away with his thumb. "Please believe me, Cicele, Alice was not the reason I did not return. Can you not try and trust me again?"

He was pleading now, but he didn't care.

"To trust you is something that will take time, Guyon, and I am not sure my heart is strong enough to take the risk." Her eyes roamed over his face, and then with a small sigh of resignation she turned to speak with Father Orrick on her other side, who sat beside her.

Guyon picked up his goblet and swirled the stem between his thumb and fingers. He could work with that. It wouldn't be easy to earn her trust, but he would do whatever it took to have her back in his life. If the last few days had taught him anything it was that his need for this woman was as strong as it had always been. And the secrets? They would stay hidden, he would make sure of that.

Chapter Twelve

They didn't go riding that afternoon; instead Cicele went back to her chamber and sewed with Maude. Weary from her meal with Guyon, and the gulf that separated them, Cicele didn't want more time in his presence, so had made her excuses. But she found the confines of her solar too restrictive, so she decided to take Vite and Maude and explore the town. The charter for a Thursday market that the king had issued meant the town would be abuzz with merchants. Her mind went back to the festive atmosphere she had seen when they had arrived earlier that morning.

The upper bailey held the tower and the hall that abutted it. A small stone chapel sat on the eastern side of the tower, its small horn windows reflecting the gray sky of mid-afternoon. They walked under the portcullis at the upper bailey's gate and through into the lower bailey where the townspeople had gathered for the market.

The noise was the first thing to attract Cicele, then the chaos of people yelling at each other as they went about their business. It wasn't safe for Vite to run about so Cicele picked him up and held him close to her chest before he darted off.

Buffeted by people as they rushed about, Cicele was about to go back when someone clasped her upper arm.

"It is not safe for you to be out here alone."

Her heart pounded in her chest and her ears blocked out the sound of people yelling as her pulse thundered in her ears.

"Guyon!" It came out as a squeak. "Lord, you gave me a fright."

She turned to see him scowling down at her. "What were you thinking being out here without a guard?"

"I thought you were riding." She tried to put some force behind her tone, but her heart was still frantically beating and she couldn't quite get her breath.

He now had his hand resting on the small of her back directing her towards some stalls on their right. "I needed to spend time going over Odard's ledgers. The man was a corrupt, greedy fool."

"The mood of the people this morning suggested they did not look forward to our arrival."

"Odard, with my uncle's help, ground these people under his foot, but I will not be cast in the same light." He gave her a wolfish grin. "There is an irony that I admit to appreciating."

"And what, pray tell, is that?"

"My uncle, like his father, spurned my mother for marrying my father. Both thought that their sons would inherit Alnwick. But it is I, a lowly wolf catcher's grandson, who has outlived them all." A cold, bitter bark of laughter punctuated his remark, making Cicele's skin crawl. He could be terrifying when he wanted to be, and stupid, stupid woman that she was found his ferocity thrilling.

They made their way through the crowd heading towards a merchant's stall that sold pies.

"What are you doing?" He had led her to a stall that sold sweet pastries, the aroma of cinnamon and honey making her mouth water.

"I have been told these are delicious, and thought you might enjoy one as we examine the stalls."

"Oh." Good lord, was that all she could say? *Maude!* She had forgotten all about her maid. Cicele turned quickly looking for her maid only to discover that she was safe behind her and Guyon. Four guards flanked the little group, their eyes alert for trouble.

Turning her attention back to Guyon, and the pastries, Cicele licked her lips as Guyon offered her a bite.

"You have your hands full, so allow me." His voice rumbled from his chest, his eyes never leaving her lips. Mesmerized she opened her mouth and took a bite from the pastry between his fingers, his eyes never leaving hers as he watched her.

A searing heat traveled up her neck as she watched his expression. Other parts of her body ached with a need she hadn't felt for six years. He looked as though he might devour her, here in front of everyone. Desperate to remove herself from his hungry gaze, and her traitorous body, she turned from him and began walking to the next stall.

"You didn't enjoy the bun?"

She heard the teasing tone, but refused to answer. He was dangerous to her composure. *Dullard.* She chided herself but her pulse again beat at a frantic pace and her stomach hitched. She was in no doubt it was not because of the delicious morsel she had just consumed.

Vite began wriggling in her arms trying to get down and explore.

"Here, give him to me."

Vite was pulled from her arms and settled into the crook of Guyon's arm. "Stay there, you little beast, and I'll see what I can find for you when we get back." Vite gazed adoringly at Guyon as he settled against him.

Cicele quickly looked away so Guyon wouldn't see her smile. Big, gruff Guyon talking to her wee dog caused a surge of pleasure to flood her body.

"Oh, look." One of the stalls was set back from the others and had a canvas cover over the trestle table. Spread on the top of the table were a collection of chessboards of various sizes and materials. Behind the table was another table holding what looked like books. Next to the tables were various pieces of furniture of an unusual shape. Cicele had never seen anything so wonderful.

As she walked towards the table holding the chessboards a dark-skinned man with a mustache and finely trimmed beard greeted her with a smile. "Marhaba, welcome to my humble stall." He gave Cicele a deep bow. His clothing and welcome identified him as a Moor.

Cicele bowed and smiled at the man. York had a sizable Moorish and Jewish population. Most came from the Iberian Peninsula and lived in harmony alongside their Christian neighbors.

"You play the ancient game, my lady?" His dark brown eyes twinkled with mischief as he spoke.

Guyon huffed a laugh. "She is a fierce competitor, who knows the king's game well."

His compliment gave Cicele a thrill. They had only played a few times that summer in Rouen, but Guyon was as competent as she, and she had loved their battles over strategy.

Cicele looked at the items when her eye fell on something partly obscured towards the back.

"That one." She pointed to where she meant.

The seller's eyes widened, but quickly recovered and retrieved the board she had chosen.

The large board was made of a wood so black it shone like polished stone. On the deep sides of the board were intricate designs carved into the wood. The top of the board had a pattern of black and mother-of-pearl squares. It wasn't new. In fact, Cicele could see that the corners of the board were scuffed and the surface was well worn, but its slightly battered condition added to its charm. Running her hand over the surface, her fingers traced the texture of the wood and shell checkered board.

"It's beautiful."

"It has been in my family for generations, but now seldom gets used." There was a sadness to his voice that made Cicele look up at him. His dark brown eyes reflected sorrow. "It was my wife's."

"Your children don't use it?"

"Alas, it is not a man's board, and I have no daughters." He gave a small shrug of his shoulders, "and the pieces are well worn." He handed Cicele a linen bag, which she accepted. Untying the bag, she retrieved what appeared to be the Queen, which was also made from the same black wood as the board. The features on the Queen's face were worn, but the craftsmanship was extraordinary. "She is exquisite."

Guyon had remained by her side as she had spoken, but now he broke the silence. "Would you be inclined to allow my lady wife to purchase your treasured piece?"

The man looked closely at Guyon, then at Cicele. She still held the Queen in her hand, lovingly tracing her finger over the crown as she waited for his reply. The feel of it on her finger filled her with peace. A tear slid down her cheek, but she ignored it.

"My wife's board makes you cry?"

"It is that it has been so loved that makes me cry." She was embarrassed, but didn't flinch under his scrutiny.

"You are new to Alnwick?" he asked her.

"I arrived with my lord husband just this morning."

"You are the new lady of Alnwick?"

Cicele gave him a small smile. "I am."

He put out his hand, palm up, indicating that he wanted the Queen, and the bag of chess pieces back.

Something in Cicele's chest tightened. It was irrational, and Cicele prided herself on being rational, but she was disconsolate as she handed it back.

The man retrieved the bag and the board and placed them in a box that was made of the same dark wood.

Then he handed the box to her. "This is my wedding gift to you; may you love it as my wife did." He glanced at Guyon, then back to Cicele. "And may Allah bless you with a daughter, so your family may cherish it."

A great sob escaped her throat as her tears streamed down her cheeks. "I cannot accept, it is too much."

"Ah, but it is my gift to you."

"I have nothing to give you in return."

He tilted his head to the side and studied her with an expression Cicele could only interpret as roguish. "Perhaps one day you will remedy that, but for now take my gift." He gave her a lavish smile. "I like to see a beautiful bride happy."

Cicele wanted to embrace him, but settled for a nod of her head. "You are most generous. Thank you."

Guyon nodded to him, then steered Cicele away from the stalls and back towards the square.

They walked in silence as she clutched her gift to her chest, Cicele was too overcome to speak, and grateful that Guyon seemed to understand.

As they neared the square several young boys jostled Cicele as they sprinted past.

"Be careful of your purse," Guyon warned. "They will cut it from you without you knowing."

"Fear not, I have no coin, so no purse is necessary."

Guyon stopped and stared at her. "You have no coin?"

Embarrassed, Cicele huffed a laugh. "You possess all, my lord, where would I get coin?"

"But surely your father provided for you?"

Cicele eyed Guyon for several heartbeats before she replied. "Neither Nicholas, nor my father, saw fit to give me a penny. It is something I am used to."

Guyon looked like all the air had been knocked from his lungs as he stood gaping at her. After several moments, he seemed to gather himself together, then led her from the square towards the gate leading back to the upper bailey.

THAT NIGHT, after the meal, Guyon came to her chamber and asked if she would like to play a game of chess with her new board. He had brought some wine and fruit in the hopes they would spend the evening together.

She couldn't refuse, as she longed to play. And besides, Maude was useless, having never learned to play the game.

There was very little conversation as they settled in and concentrated on the game, but for the first time in Guyon's presence, Cicele's heart ceased its panicked beating, and she enjoyed his company.

"I sent Thomas to offer a charter to the Moor who gifted you the board. He will have the freedom to sell his wares throughout Northumbria."

Cicele was astounded at such a magnanimous gesture. Moors, like Jews, struggled against prejudice, and often found their stalls, or themselves, abused and hounded out of a town. "I am sure he will appreciate that."

Guyon eyed her while he sipped his wine. "Interestingly, Thomas saw Father Orrick sitting with the Spaniard sipping tea."

Cicele didn't know what to say. It was unusual for Christians to associate with Moors or Jews, but a priest? That was extraordinary. "I wonder what he wanted?"

"Thomas tells me the priest is interested in the practice of medicine coming from the East. It seems Father Orrick purchased a text from the merchant."

Cicele liked that Father Orrick was a priest who held no prejudice against the Moor.

Returning her thoughts to the board, they continued with their game, letting the conversation end.

When it came time for Guyon to leave he surprised her. "I have something for you."

Cicele watched as he left the chamber, only to return a moment later with a small wooden chest in his hands. "I want you to have this," he said as he placed it on the table beside them.

Intrigued, Cicele stood and went to open the box but found that it was locked.

"Here, you will need this."

She took the key Guyon handed her and opened the box to find that it was full of coins. Confused, and a little shaken, she didn't know what to do.

"I want you to have control of your dowry estates, and this is the income from Redesdale."

"But." Overcome with emotion she couldn't speak. Silent tears slid down her cheeks. Never had she been given her own income.

"You will also have the income from Lesbury and Alnmouth." He was standing beside her, his breath making her veil flutter against her cheek.

"Cicele, please look at me."

She didn't want him to see how much his gesture meant to her, but she couldn't ignore him either.

"I don't know what to say," she whispered, as she struggled to contain her emotions.

Guyon took her chin and tilted it up so he could see her eyes. "I want you to have your own money. I will clothe you, and provide all you may need, but you, my wife, will have the freedom to spend your money as you see fit." He gave her a small smile. "I hope you would do me the honor of helping me manage your estates."

Manage my estates? "You want me to help you manage the estates?"

His smile increased as he ran his thumb over her bottom lip. "I want you to help me, Cicele. To offer advice. To counsel me as I make decisions. Will you do that?"

Simpleton that she was, she couldn't speak, so she nodded as a small sob escaped her throat.

His expression changed in an instant. Gone was the concern, only to be replaced by a roguish grin. "I think that sharp tongue of yours has finally been silenced." His thumb grazed her lips as his eyes searched hers. "I shall bid you good night, wife."

Then he was gone. And still she was speechless.

THE NEXT MORNING Cicele lay in her bed; it was still dark and no one had come to revive the fire, so it was well before dawn. Lying in the warmth of her bed, with Vite curled up beside her, Cicele pondered over her evening with Guyon.

It had been pleasant. That thought, more than any other, was a surprise. But if she were honest it was the gift of independence that had shocked her. Guyon had changed from the man she had loved. Yes, he was older, but he was somehow more confident. More self-assured. Not arrogantly swaggering about like he had in Rouen. She was ashamed to remember that it was his arrogance that had attracted her. Every other male in Rouen had bowed and simpered, but not Guyon. She had wanted to discover what lay behind the arrogant mask, and in the process, she had fallen in love.

But they had never really spent any time with each other. Yes, they had talked of inconsequential things, and ridden in the woods around Rouen. Their attraction had been instant, and it wasn't long before they were snatching moments where they could kiss, and make love, without detection. Looking back, Cicele realized that she didn't really know Guyon.

Heartbreak had been replaced with loathing when he had failed to return. There had always been a suspicion lurking in the back of her mind that he had rejected her in favor of Alice, the woman he had married. Holy Mary, mother of God, that had stung. Guyon was someone else's husband.

Now she had her wish, but had it come too late? Could they be friends? She would not invite him into her bed, but she would suspend her judgment of him until he proved himself. Strangely, that didn't seem as impossible as it had the day before.

All thought of Guyon vanished as her bed-curtain was pulled back and Maude's face appeared in the dull light of the chamber.

"Good morn, child," the maid intoned; then she noticed Vite's head had emerged from his nest of furs to welcome Maude. "And beast."

Cicele ran her hand over Vite as he perched on her chest, his little tail wagging while his tongue lolled from the side of his mouth as she stroked him.

"That beast is altogether too spoiled; he should be in the stables like the rest of God's creatures rather than tucked up in your bed."

"Maude, how could you say such a thing." Cicele held the dog's ears to his head so he would not hear such vile threats. "He is the perfect bed companion."

Maude gave her an astute glance that had Cicele's cheeks burning. "Well I can think of another who would be a satisfactory bed companion, my lady, but you seem disinclined."

Cicele didn't want to discuss Guyon, and the reasons why she refused him her bed, so she ignored her maid, who was more a mother than a servant, and rose from her bed.

The chamber was cold so Cicele washed and allowed Maude to dress her quickly. No sooner had she tied her belt around her kirtle when Guyon walked in, without so much as a knock.

"A knock would be appreciated," Cicele huffed.

Guyon wasn't cowed by her welcome; in truth he seemed amused if she guessed his expression correctly.

"Ah, wife, you look a picture with your hair about you like that." He cast a glance at the bed before returning to meet her eyes. "A pity I was not a fraction earlier." His smile could only be described as wolfish, and Cicele's tummy hitched in response.

Trying not to sound churlish she strove for indifference. "Why, sir, are you here?"

Guyon closed the distance between them, then tilted her chin up so he could see her face. "I would ask your attendance on the dais this morning as the lords from Alnwick are to swear their fealty to me."

Cicele was taken aback for a moment. He wanted her presence?

Seemingly able to read her mind he answered her unspoken question. "As I said last night, I will rely on you to keep my affairs and estates running when I am called away." His expression was intense, all his playfulness gone. "I need you."

It was said simply. The sincerity in his voice and his eyes undid her resolve to remain aloof.

His fingers still held her chin, as he continued to hold her gaze waiting for her answer.

Fighting back the sting of unshed tears she simply nodded. Her throat was so tight she was unable to swallow, and her treacherous tongue, as usual, disobeyed her.

He held her for a heartbeat longer and she thought he might kiss her. Oh, Lord help her, she wanted him to. But he released her and gave her a bow instead. "I will expect you within the hour." Then he was gone.

"Well, we had better get you into another kirtle and surcoat if you are to play the Lady of Alnwick.

Cicele walked as though in a dream. *I need you.* His words played over and over in her head as Maude fussed. She had never been needed before—those three words released something in her heart.

Idiot. He can't be trusted! The warning robbed her of the euphoria she experienced just moments before.

Yes, she couldn't afford to lower her defenses so easily. Her heart could not survive another fracture.

Chapter Thirteen

The hall was full of men milling about talking as they waited their turn to swear their oaths of fealty to him. It would be like this for weeks as Guyon's mesne lords came from all over Northumbria to pay homage to him as their new lord. The town would thrive as men and their retinues arrived wanting accommodation and stabling for their horses. Guyon was now an earl, with over 200 manors spread over three counties. Revenues from the manors in Northumbria alone made his head spin. God's bones, how was he ever going to keep track of it all? Sometimes the magnitude of it threatened to overwhelm him.

Thank God he had Thomas and Cicele. Brother Martin was also proving his worth with his knowledge of the taxes and incomes from his vast estates. Hopefully his lords would prove to be more honorable than his uncle. Instead of concentrating on the men gathered in the hall, waiting to swear their oaths of fealty to him, Guyon's thoughts drifted back to the previous evening.

He'd gone back to his chamber after bidding Cicele good eve. They had played chess, and sipped their wine. It was as he watched her nibble her lower lip as she concentrated on the game that he had decided he would make a habit of coming to her chamber to play chess with his wife after the evening meal.

The image of her face as he gave her the box of coins was seared into his memory. When she had informed him that she had no money he was outraged. That was something he could do for her, and he had, without hesitation.

Smiling at the memory, he was interrupted as the steward of the hall announced his wife. Head held high, she walked through the men, who parted like the Red Sea, as she made her way to the dais. Guyon rose and held out his hand to help her take her seat next to him.

Their eyes met and longing flooded him. His body reacted to her whenever she was close, but it wasn't just her body he longed for. It had hit him as he lay in his bed the night before, he wanted her friendship. He wanted those dancing gold-flecked eyes on him as she laughed and shared her day's events with him. Dragging himself away from his meanderings he forced himself to concentrate on the formalities being played out before him.

When Cicele had settled into her seat, and Father Orrick had prayed a blessing on the formal proceedings, Guyon indicated for a page to pour Cicele a goblet of wine. Guyon and Cicele, as Lord and Lady of Alnwick, toasted each other, then did the same to the men gathered below the dais.

Guyon motioned for Thomas to bring the first of the men who would swear their oaths.

"Sir Robert Morton."

His steward knelt before Guyon with his clasped hands stretched out before him.

Guyon got to his feet and placed his hands over Sir Robert's. When Guyon released his hands Father Orrick held an ornate bible in front of the knight, who, after placing his right hand on the Bible, swore his oath, "I promise on my faith that I will in the future be faithful to my liege lord, never cause him harm, and will observe my homage to him completely against all persons in good faith and without deceit."

Then the knight rose and walked back into the crowd of gathered knights so the next man might give his oath.

It was a long morning, but Guyon studied each man as he came forward, assessing each one. Thomas would be doing the same, as would Cicele.

CICELE'S LIFE began to take on a routine within days of their arrival at Alnwick. The day started at dawn with prayers, then she met with the steward as they supervised the distribution of the precious spices that the castle's cook required for the day's meals. Sir Robert Morton, the castle's steward, was not what he appeared, much to Cicele's relief. Intimidated by his brusque manner she had not looked forward to dealing with him every day, but now she enjoyed their hour together discussing the needs of the castle.

"That man has taken a liking to the wee beast." Maude inclined her head towards Sir Robert as he bent to pat Vite.

"Vite has a talent for warming many a cold heart." Guyon's care of the little dog when he had rescued them both flashed across her mind.

Maude snorted, but Cicele smiled as they walked to the hall for the noon meal. It had been a long morning with more nobles arriving to swear their oaths to her husband.

Her heart skipped a beat as her eyes settled on Guyon, sitting at the dais waiting for her arrival. Seeing her, he stood, his eyes pinning her to the spot. A tingling sensation ran up her back and made her scalp prickle. Her heart was softening. Was that such a bad thing?

The previous evening Guyon had leaned in to kiss her good night after their game of chess but she had pulled away. Why? In truth, she didn't really understand what was happening to her. He had been hurt by her rebuff, she saw it in his eyes. "I want you, Cicele, but I will not force myself on you." He held her chin in his fingers as his eyes met hers. She thought then he might kiss her, but he had released her and walked from her chamber.

The memory had her cheeks burning. She could no longer deny her growing desire for him. But could she take the chance and trust him? She didn't have the answer to that, more's the pity.

"You will ride with me, my lady?" His eyes caressed her face and she couldn't look away. Every fiber of her body, including her toes, felt that caress. The table had been cleared and she was about to excuse herself.

"I can't." It came out as a squeak. God help her, she became a blithering goose when he looked at her like that.

"Can't, or won't?"

Did she detect a slight edge to his voice? Mastering her emotions, she took a breath before she answered. "It has become my custom to distribute alms after the meal, and as lady of Alnwick it is a duty I will not neglect." That was another activity Cicele relished. Every day, after the noon meal, she walked with the castle almoner to the castle gate to distribute alms: the food left over from the midday meal that she personally administered to the poorer townsfolk who milled about at the castle's western gate.

"Your sentiments do you justice, and I for one would not keep you from them." His face changed before her eyes. "But I, madam, will miss you."

If she had been a trout caught in a weir she could not have been more stranded under his seductive gaze. She would have sold her soul in that moment. Then he blinked and broke the spell. *God in heaven, what's wrong with me?* Aware what was wrong with her, she steeled her resolve and refused to be so easily seduced again. He had changed so much, or perhaps he had always been like this, she just hadn't known him well enough in Rouen. Well that wasn't true. She had known his body, but his character had been unknown.

She was falling in love. Ill equipped to steel her emotions against this generous, playful, and caring man was beyond even her calloused heart.

Not saying a word, she rose and gave him a bow, then fled the hall, albeit at a sedate pace. She would not give him the satisfaction of seeing how much he unsettled her. "Goose, one look at you and he sees the effect he has on you." She chided herself quietly as she went to meet the castle almoner.

Surprisingly, it was not the almoner, Brother Jude, who met her but Father Orrick. He gave no explanation, but led Cicele through the bailey and out towards the gate. A heavy gray sky blocked out the sun, making the usually vibrant bailey leached of color.

Maude had insisted Cicele wear her warmest cloak, which Cicele was now most grateful for. Cicele and the priest were almost at the town square when she heard an eerie wail.

Father Orrick didn't hesitate. He immediately led her, with the guards following, to a small cluster of people looking at something on the ground. When they were closer she saw a small boy was lying at the crowd's feet, his little arms and legs flailing wildly. A ball of spittle hung at the corner of his mouth, but it was his eyes, vacant, glassy eyes, that drew a terrified gasp from Cicele's throat.

Crossing herself to ward off the evil before her, she clamped her mouth tight so she didn't wail in her distress. Terror gripped her, threatening to turn her bowels to liquid and her stomach to acid. Bile surged up her throat, burning as it went. Refusing to vomit before the gathered crowd she swallowed her fear, dragging air in through her nose and releasing it in small controlled breaths.

The small crowd of people who had gathered stood in horrified silence. Then a woman, round as she was tall, with a leather apron covering her thick woolen kirtle began cursing the boy and his distraught mother, who was kneeling helplessly by her child.

"Make way," Father Orrick shouted as he strode to the little body convulsing on the ground. When he reached the boy, he knelt in the dirt and began reciting prayers in Latin.

A cold dread washed over Cicele as she remembered a scene she had witnessed many years ago at her father's castle at Redesdale. Running from her nurse, Cicele had hidden behind a curtain in the steward's chamber. What she witnessed terrified her. Sometimes she still had nightmares about it.

Her father's steward had been holding his son down as the young boy was seized with a demon much like the lad before her now. Cicele had been so terrified she never told anyone, but she had prayed nightly that if she was good God would not allow demons to take possession of her like they had the steward's son.

Watching the priest, and rooted to the spot where she stood, Cicele was incapable of helping. All she wanted to do was run. Making herself stay still, she watched as the priest ministered to the child.

An involuntary urge to back away had her gripping her cloak, but she refused to be controlled by her fear. So she waited for the priest to finish his prayers. The boy now lay still on the ground, until his mother quietly gathered him into her arms. Her anxious glances at the crowd reflected terror for her young son.

"He's got a demon!" a woman in the crowd yelled.

"Demon! Demon!" The chant went through the crowd, rising to a panicked crescendo which created imminent danger for the child and his mother.

Cicele's eyes darted back and forth. The scene needed only a spark for it to become violent. Should she get help? Send the guards back for reinforcements? No. She didn't want to be without their protection.

Her eyes darted back to Father Orrick, who stood up and placed his left hand on the woman's shoulder while he raised his right hand to silence the crowd. Almost immediately an eerie silence descended. Cicele's blood turned to ice in her veins. Concern for the boy and his mother now outweighed her own terror.

"God be praised," Father Orrick said in a clear, calm voice. "The Lord has seen fit to heal the child as you can see. Now you must go about your business." He gave the crowd a blessing, then stood silently waiting for them to disperse. For a few moments Cicele feared they wouldn't leave and she would be forced to use her two guards to intervene, but then the woman who began the shouting blessed herself and walked away, urging others to follow her.

When the crowd had gone, the priest turned to the mother and took the child from her arms. "Take me to your dwelling where I may tend to your child."

He cast her a glance, inviting her to accompany him, but Cicele was rooted to the spot. She didn't want to be near the child, or his mother.

"You have nothing to fear, my lady. All will be well." He gave her a solemn smile. "You are in no danger."

Cicele, still holding one of the baskets of food, took a deep breath to calm her nerves, then turned, instructing the guards to accompany her as she followed Father Orrick. The alms would have to wait.

The woman led them towards Shite Creek, the running sewer that ran parallel to the outer bailey wall. In Cicele's experience affluent towns bred filth, and Alnwick was no exception. Thankfully, there was a makeshift bridge of rough-sawn planks lying across the foul-smelling stream, allowing them to walk over the ditch without trudging through the putrescent waste. Cicele's stomach lurched as she inhaled the malodorous brew swirling at her feet.

They continued to trudge out through the small tower gate that finally led them to the village that had grown up outside the walls. The hovels were a little more ramshackle than those inside the walls, but at least they were free of the reeking odor that those fortunate to live inside the walls had to endure. Cicele was tempted to believe that if she had to choose between the safety of living inside the walls or outside where there was scant protection but the air was devoid of the sickening stench, she might choose outside the walls. Everyone knew that odor meant disease.

Finally, they came to the woman's hovel.

"Excuse my humble abode," she said in a timid voice as she led the priest and Cicele inside. The two guards waited outside.

Cicele immediately looked to the woman who wore an expression she interpreted as shame. Embarrassed that her own discomfort had been so obvious, Cicele gave a small nod and walked to where Father Orrick had laid the lad on the rough woolen blanket covering the bed. His calm, compassionate presence stilled her own anxiety.

"What do you do after one of his attacks?" he asked in a quiet, authoritative voice.

"He sleeps," she said. "I give him tea when he wakes. He complains of a pain in his head so I keep feverfew for him."

The woman walked to a shelf that held several objects and when she returned she showed the priest a small wooden box that contained a scant amount of tea. To Cicele's eyes there seemed to be more dust than plant matter.

As the woman and priest talked, Cicele ran her eyes over the interior of the dwelling. The hovel was small, but Cicele was surprised that it was cleaner than she expected. As her eyes grew accustomed to the dim light inside she glanced at a parchment lying on the table. *Could the woman read?*

When the murmur of conversation stilled Cicele asked the woman. "Do you read?"

She looked at Cicele, then to the parchment on the table. "Yes, my lady," she replied, but avoided looking back at Cicele.

"What's your name?"

"Ebeta, my lady."

"And where is your man?"

The woman had been looking to the floor, but at Cicele's question she raised her eyes to meet Cicele's gaze. "He died on St. Martin's day, along with my infant daughter." Her voice broke on the last word, and Cicele had no hesitation, her panic over the boy's condition momentarily forgotten as she enfolded the woman in her arms. Her own eyes burned with unshed tears as she remembered her own agony at the loss of her son.

Some moments passed before the woman separated herself from Cicele's embrace. "My husband was a scholar and scrivener. My family did not approve of our marriage, so when my Moise died, and I came back here, they cast me aside."

"Who was your husband?" It was Father Orrick's turn to ask the question.

"Moise of London," she answered.

"I knew of this Moise of London; he was the Archbishop of Canterbury's favored cleric."

A small smile creased the corners of the woman's mouth. "Aye, he was until he met me and decided to leave his service."

Cicele had to know who would be so callous as to refuse to help a grieving daughter, and her son. "Who is your father?"

Ebeta bit her lower lip and wrung her hands. Cicele thought that perhaps she would not answer.

"Master FitzWallah."

Cicele had heard of him. Guyon had mentioned that Thomas was making enquiries about the merchant guild that Master Fitz-Wallah was head of.

"Mamma." A frail voice interrupted whatever Father Orrick was about to say.

The woman responded to her child's plaintive cry, and Cicele nodded to Father Orrick that it was time to leave.

Before she stepped out of the door Cicele placed some of the alms she was to distribute on the table, then left, eager to get away from the woman and her child.

"YOU FEAR what you have just witnessed?" Father Orrick didn't look at her as they strode back through the inner bailey's gate. They had left Ebeta's hovel, then distributed the alms, and now they were returning to the safety of the castle. Cicele was eager to return to her chamber, and wash the filth from her skin. Then she would pray for God to protect her. The image of the child writhing on the ground tormented her, and would do so for days.

Not wanting to lie to the priest, she confessed her fear. "Did God truly heal the child?"

The priest stopped suddenly, forcing Cicele to stop as well. His bright, intelligent eyes examined her. "That child suffers from what many call the 'falling sickness.' He is neither demon-possessed or evil, but rather has a disease." There was a note of impatience in his tone, which surprised her. Cicele liked Father Orrick. He was intelligent, balanced in his views regarding church law, and perhaps most importantly in Cicele's mind, he possessed a great deal of common sense.

"I have always believed that what we witnessed today was the result of demon possession." She shuddered as she remembered her terror. It was well known that demons could jump from one person to the next.

She flinched when the priest placed a gentle hand on her shoulder. "That child is no more demon-possessed than you or I."

That didn't calm her fears, rather they increased tenfold. The priest must have seen her anxiety. "You fear what you do not know, child," the priest said softly. "The church teaches what it believes, but sometimes even we," he pointed to his chest, "are fearful of what we do not understand."

He fixed her with a gimlet eye. "Come, I shall share what I

know of this disease, then perhaps you will not be ruled by fear and ignorance."

Cicele bristled at his assertion that she was ignorant, but chose not to comment; instead she followed him quietly as he led her to the small chamber and solar next to the chapel.

The chapel bells began to peel, interrupting what Father Orrick was saying.

It couldn't be Vespers already?

"You must go and prepare for the evening meal, my lady, and I must be about my prayers." He gave her a gentle smile.

She had spent all afternoon with him as he explained about the falling sickness. It was difficult to readjust her thinking on the subject, and she wasn't sure she could accept it all in one afternoon, but she was now sure that what afflicted Ebeta's boy was not demonic.

"Thank you, Father, for your patience." She was humbled that he had taken the time to explain some of what he knew of the disease.

"You are an intelligent woman; use what God gave you for good. Now go, before your lord husband finds you, and scolds me for keeping you from his table."

With a final word of farewell Cicele made her way back to her own chamber, where Maude would be waiting to dress her for supper.

Chapter Fourteen

Two days later Cicele, with Maude grumbling beside her, made her way back to Ebeta's hovel. Cicele had told Maude about her experience with Ebeta's child, and her afternoon with Father Orrick. Unsurprisingly, Maude was inclined to agree with Father Orrick. Cicele's maid was a woman who had very definite ideas about all manner of topics, not least the church's propensity to engender fear in the ignorant masses. Cicele bristled that Maude would condemn her as ignorant and superstitious, but she held her tongue. Ingrained beliefs, so it seemed to Cicele, took some time to change, but she was adamant that she would continue to visit with Father Orrick and learn more about the falling sickness.

They arrived at Ebeta's door with a basket of food and clothing. Ebeta took some time before she answered their knock.

One look, and Cicele drew the woman into an embrace. "Ebeta, what has happened?" Thoughts raced through Cicele's mind as she waited for Ebeta's sobs to stop and answer. Relief coursed through Cicele's chest when she spied little Moise playing with knuckle bones on the dirt floor.

"Come now." Maude gently peeled Ebeta away from Cicele's embrace and led her to the only chair in the hovel.

Cicele cast her eyes over the room and noticed that all Ebeta's possessions were packed. She was leaving.

Ebeta dried her tears, while Cicele introduced her to Maude. It was Maude's motherly presence that had Ebeta tell her story of woe.

"The townswomen have been calling me a witch, and threatening to have me dragged before the bailiff if I do not leave."

Cicele was horrified at the townspeople's cruelty, but she understood their fear, even if she did not condone it.

"What of your father, child?" Maude asked.

A racking sob escaped her shivering frame. "He will not offer us his protection."

Maude took a heaving breath, but Cicele placed her hand on her maid's arm. Maude's outrage was not what was needed.

"Where were you going?"

Ebeta sniffed, but wouldn't meet Cicele's eye. "I don't know, but away from here."

Desperation drove people to make foolish decisions, but Cicele would not stand by and let this gentle, brave woman, and her child, face their future alone.

"You will come with us."

Ebeta's mouth dropped open, but no sound emerged.

"Yes, an excellent solution to the problem you were discussing with me just this morning, my lady."

Cicele had no idea what Maude was talking about, but didn't contradict her maid.

"Lady Cicele was just saying that she required a companion who could read and keep her company on the long lonely days of winter." Maude cast Cicele a withering look as Cicele opened her mouth to speak.

She knew that look, and as she had done most of her life, she ignored it. "Yes, Maude is right, you would be an excellent companion."

"Me, my lady? No!"

"And, pray tell, why not. You read, it is reasonable to assume your education included sewing and playing an instrument." Cicele quirked her eyebrow to emphasize her question.

"Yes, but…"

The pale face of the young woman before her made something in Cicele's chest tighten. This could have been Beatrice, alone and without support. Whatever her cousin was running from, she had been fortunate enough to find Isabeau, who had offered her protection without hesitation. Cicele could do no different, and would not abandon Ebeta to a fate that would surely have her and her young son dead within the month.

Allowing no further arguments Maude organized the guards that were Cicele's constant shadows when she left the castle to carry Ebeta's belongings, while Maude carried little Moise. Cicele led her little entourage back through the town and into the castle.

After showing Ebeta the chamber she would share with Maude, Cicele settled Ebeta into a chair by the fire in her solar when Moise fell to the floor and began shaking and foaming at the mouth.

"Maude, quickly, fetch Father Orrick."

It seemed like forever before the priest and a young cleric arrived. Father Orrick opened the box the young cleric held and retrieved a glass vial. The priest poured a few drops from the vial into a cup of watered wine, and when the child had recovered he helped him to his mother's lap. Slowly, with infinite care, he dribbled the contents of the cup into the child's mouth.

It was so distressing to see the child's suffering. The fear that had gripped Cicele when she had first seen Moise on the ground in town was no longer there. In its place was deep compassion and concern for the little boy whose face was a mask of fear and confusion. Maude came and stood beside Cicele, taking her hand in a silent demonstration of concern.

When Father Orrick had finished, he stood and placed the cup on the tray. "How long has the child suffered?"

Ebeta stroked her son's head. "When he was taken with the fever that took his father and sister."

Ebeta had said that her husband and daughter had died on St. Martin's day, which was celebrated in autumn, so that was only a few months ago.

"This year?" The priest asked

"No, Father, last year."

My God, how had she survived for so long with a frail child and no husband to support her?

"And how often does the falling sickness take him?" The priest asked, his voice soothing the distraught mother.

Ebeta looked down at the child lying in her lap. "Sometimes every day, but then he can have none for a month."

The child's face was pale, and his little body frail and thin. Cicele had originally thought him to be three summers old, but now she wondered if his body was small because of the cruel sickness that tormented his little body.

"Keep him quiet, and reduce his exposure to bright sunlight. Also, it would be beneficial if you incorporated meat in his diet."

When Father Orrick and his assistant left, Cicele urged Ebeta to take little Moise back to the chamber she shared with Maude, and rest. Maude offered to go with her, but Ebeta declined.

"That was terrifying," Maude whispered as she sat in the chair by the hearth that Ebeta had just vacated. Cicele looked at her old maid as she poured them both some wine. "If anyone discovers that little Moise has the falling sickness she will be forced to face Father Markus. I'm sure he will not be as enlightened as Father Orrick."

Cicele had been pondering how she was going to keep Moise's

sickness a secret. As yet, she had not come up with a viable solution.

"The abbot of Alnwick Abbey is a vocal opponent of Father Orrick's methods. He prefers superstitious zeal over compassion and science." Maude's tone mirrored her own disquiet over the abbot's enforcement of the strict rules of the church.

"Then we must do our best to make sure he never finds out," Cicele snapped. She was immediately sorry for her harsh reply and offered her apology. "I'm sorry, Maude, I didn't mean to bark at you."

Maude accepted the wine Cicele handed to her. "Ha! If I trembled every time you voiced your strong opinions I'd be permanently groveling on the floor." She smiled as she took a sip of wine. "I'll leave that to others who don't know you as well as I."

"I'm not that bad," Cicele huffed.

Maude rose from the chair and kissed Cicele's cheek. "Yes, you are."

"Well, it's a shame I can't make Father Markus tremble," she said as she drank from her own cup. She would also like to make her husband tremble. God in heaven, where had that come from?

"At least we should be able to keep it from your husband… although he seems keen to continue his uncle's legacy of endowing the abbey," Maude mused, as she resettled herself in a chair and looked at Cicele. "Your husband seeks the abbot's approval in his new role as sheriff. It would not go well if the abbot was to find out the new sheriff was harboring a 'demon-possessed' child under the castle roof."

"True." The last thing Cicele needed was to clash with Guyon over Ebeta and her child. Hopefully their secret would be just that. Their secret.

It didn't even take a day for the "secret" to be revealed to her husband. The castle had ears and eyes everywhere. The next afternoon Cicele found herself standing before Guyon. She was tempted to shift from foot to foot as the evidence of his barely suppressed fury caused involuntary shivers to streak up and down her spine. Refusing to be cowed, she faced his disapproval with characteristic defiance. Head high, she looked him in the eye and willed herself to stand tall. Stomach in knots, and perspiration beading on her upper lip, she refused to show him how anxious she really was. It took all her willpower not to move her hand to wipe the moisture away from her upper lip.

"What were you thinking?" His scowl was something to behold. She had never seen him so angry. And dangerous. The telltale tremor in her legs threatened to have her knees crumble under the weight of his rage.

Gathering her strength, she fought for control of her lower limbs.

"Well?" he bellowed.

She jumped.

Now he was out of the lord's high seat and advancing on her.

Terrified, she was tempted to run but her legs wouldn't move. She was trapped. Convinced he was about to hit her she cringed when he stopped in front of her—his breath fanning her face. Her father had struck her when he found out about her pregnancy, but he hadn't been as angry as the man towering over her now. His rapid breathing suggested his fury was barely contained.

When he didn't strike, she raised her eyes to look at him, expecting to see a raised hand ready to inflict what she knew in her heart was justified.

Horror. His eyes reflected a horror that took her by surprise. "I would never hit you, Cicele," he said in such a quiet voice she almost missed it.

"I only wanted to help." She was angry that her voice betrayed her fear. "Ebeta, and her child were…"

Interrupting, Guyon continued, "You have shamed the most important man in the town, and God knows he's likely to make my life a living hell." He took a shuddering breath, "Why, in God's name, didn't you think to ask me before you embarked on such a scheme?"

Thinking he had paused to give her a chance to explain herself she opened her mouth, but before she had time to form the words he continued his tirade.

"FitzWallah is demanding that I remove his daughter from Alnwick immediately."

Horrified that Ebeta would be left to fend for herself, Cicele responded with little thought. "The man's a brute." Although shouting, she managed to regain some sense of her surroundings before she continued in a calmer voice. "Perhaps we should continue this in your solar, my lord." She wasn't going to let him continue to berate her in front of the men gathered in the hall.

"To defy such a powerful man by bringing his disgraced daughter into my castle is an action I cannot—" He caught his breath. "I will not condone." He spat the words at her as if to inflict upon her what he claimed his fist would not do.

Defiant, Cicele glared back at her husband. "You hypocrite, she has done nothing disgraceful except marry a man she loved." Cicele was shouting again. The arrogance of her husband, and Ebeta's father, drove her beyond caution.

"She is his daughter, and therefore must submit to him."

It was too much. She wouldn't stand here and argue fruitlessly any longer.

"When you have calmed yourself enough to speak to me, and not beat me with your shouting, I will explain myself." Without another word Cicele spun, turning her back on her enraged husband, and with all the dignity she could muster, walked from the hall. In the moment it took for her to turn she had the satisfaction of seeing Guyon standing, where he had been towering over her, with his mouth agape and wide disbelieving eyes staring at her. Her insolence had shocked him into silence.

She kept walking, not bothering to acknowledge the men gathered in the hall. Her cheeks blazed with mortification that her altercation with Guyon had been witnessed. Even Vite was ignored. Perhaps deciding it was better to stay where he was, she noticed the dog had slunk back to sit by the hearth next to a dozing mastiff who was too old to take offense.

Over the draw that connected the inner bailey to the outer compound she trod, not bothering to stop. Through the outer bailey she trudged, then over the great draw straddling the moat. She continued through the main road that led past the assortment of hovels and on into the fields that were full of winter crops. Only when she reached the orchard wall at the eastern side of the castle did she slow her pace.

Never had she been exposed to such public humiliation. A deep seething rage thrummed through her limbs. She continued to walk, fearing if she stopped she would do violence to herself. She had once been so angry with her father that she kicked her clothes chest. Her toes had pained her for weeks.

Finally, she came to a clearing where she could hear the gurgle of a creek. Following the noise, she eventually came upon its source. The area was a small glade at the far end of the orchard that offered protection from the cold northerly wind that was always present in winter. Soft moss and leaf litter welcomed her as she sank to her knees.

Her whole body began to tremble. With shuddering sobs she succumbed to her shame and wept. She'd only wanted to help, but once again her actions had attracted derision rather than praise. She gave her emotions free rein as sobs wracked her aching chest. Anger gave way to humiliation.

All her life Cicele had wanted to be needed. To feel her life was of some use. But her father, then her first husband, Nicholas, had made it clear she was of no value save as a path to enrichment. What had she expected from Guyon? In truth, she had suspected that this would be his reaction if he found out about Ebeta. *Fool. You stupid, ignorant fool.*

Ignoring the tears that streaked her cheeks she lay back, her cloak protecting her from on the cold carpet of leaves, and considered her actions. She would do it all over again. Ebeta, and her son, needed protection, not to be abandoned and left to fend for themselves.

Here in the quiet of the creek bed, with the distant cawing of crows squabbling over the sprouting winter barley, Cicele had to accept that her marriage was an unmitigated disaster.

Chapter Fifteen

FRANTIC NOW WITH WORRY OVER THE EFFECT HIS OUTBURST HAD ON Cicele, Guyon began to realize he may have gone too far. He had wrestled with the desire to call her back, but in the end decided to let her go. It took him several minutes to calm himself after his verbal attack. Running his hand through his hair he began to pace the length of the hearth. *God's teeth, she drives me to distraction.* It was not his custom to question his motives, but since marrying he had become increasingly aware that her presence disturbed him.

Everything about her aroused his passion, and like a simpleton he still clung to the belief that she would relent and take him to her bed. But she had not.

Yet, it was her face, and the allure of her hair falling through his fingers that jolted him awake most nights. He was uncomfortable with the notion that she could affect him so in such a short period of time.

Guyon had never wanted for the company of women. They seemed drawn to him, and since a young squire of one and five he had not questioned their desire for his company.

For the past two weeks, it had been Cicele who had visited him in his dreams. No, that wasn't true. She had invaded his dreams, both waking and sleeping, for six long years.

Perhaps, he reasoned, it was because he had been without a woman for so long that this troublesome vixen, with shards of copper in her hair, and golden eyes had invaded his sleep. No, it was more than that. Guyon knew himself well enough to be honest. She was like no woman he had ever encountered. Every fiber of his being longed for her.

"So why the long face?" Thomas's voice startled Guyon.

He didn't bother to reply.

Thomas, with his ability to slice through to the bone of any given situation, put words where Guyon would have preferred silence.

"I thought you would be pleased to have some distance." His penetrating gaze gave Guyon no escape.

Heaving a groan birthed of confusion, and something else he didn't care to name, Guyon answered honestly, "So did I."

"FitzWallah seems to have come to his senses."

"The bastard thinks more of silver than honor." Guyon despised men who would barter their family for wealth and position. He had been so angry with Cicele for not telling him what she had done, that he had not informed her that he had already dealt with Fitz-Wallah regarding his daughter. Nothing in the castle escaped Thomas's notice, including Cicele's care of a young widow and her son.

"It seems he has been awarded a charter to transport woolen cloth from Alnmouth's port." Thomas smiled at Guyon.

Guyon had sent Thomas to offer the inducement as a bribe. His instinct had been rewarded, as he suspected it would be. The head of the merchant guild was only too happy to drop his complaint about his daughter's new found security with Lady Cicele in return for the lucrative trade that entered Alnmouth's port.

Why in God's name hadn't Guyon explained the situation

instead of losing his temper with his wife? He knew the answer—frustration that he could never have what his heart longed for from his wife.

Thomas cleared his throat.

"What?"

"There are reports of poachers near Lesbury."

Guyon cocked his head to one side and eyed his friend, "What has the steward done about it?" He had inherited Lesbury's beleaguered castle on his marriage to Cicele. It protected the town, and the port of Alnmouth, which sat at the mouth of the River Aln, and as he had been granted a charter to establish a port, he didn't want poachers getting in the way of his plans.

Any number of mercenaries or displaced villagers probably sought refuge and easy food from the forests surrounding the area.

Guyon would begin work on enlarging the castle. If he failed to control the eastern coastline Henry would find another to replace him. And that was never going to happen. Guyon had fought too hard and too long to fail now.

He would travel to Lesbury and inspect the stone fortifications and hopefully dispose of a few poachers while he was there. As sheriff he was entitled to hang poachers where they were caught, rather than bring them back to be tried.

"We will ride at first light tomorrow with a small retinue of ten mounted men. And, Thomas, bring the coroner so we can dispatch the culprits on sight." Guyon watched his friend as he nodded and turned to leave. "Thomas!"

"Yes, my lord."

"Where is she?"

Raising his eyebrows Thomas took a moment to assess Guyon. "She was seen heading over the draw and into the orchard."

Guyon didn't appreciate his friend's scrutiny, but he had little option if he was to find Cicele before he lost the light.

"I can have one of the guards fetch her back?" Thomas suggested. His tone betrayed a hint of humor.

Not bothering to rise to the bait Guyon decided he, and he alone, was responsible for retrieving the woman who sent his pulse racing and his anger surging. "I'll fetch the wench myself."

Guyon ignored the wry smile that slid across his friend's face as he turned and walked through the hall.

Guyon was unprepared for the sight of Cicele lying among the leaves beside the small creek. He stood under the skeletal branches of a barren apple tree, not wanting to disturb her. In truth, he wanted time to look at her without fear of being observed. She had taken her veil off and lay with her hair spread over the leaf litter. A beautiful woodland sprite come to torment him and his ordered existence.

Enough! Scolding himself for his weakness he strode towards her, making sure he made as much noise as possible. When he stood over her he stared down into her face. Her eyes were settled upon him, although she made no effort to move. Ensnared, he couldn't move.

Smiling, as though she read his thoughts, she goaded him.

"Knowing how much you like to control, I thought you might prefer a passive victim."

Without warning Guyon scooped her up and folded her in his arms.

Pulse pounding in his ears he held her against him. His body screamed its desire for the woman in his arms. "You dice with danger, my lady," he growled, barely able to contain himself.

Eyes as wide as an owl's on a moonlit night, Cicele could only gape. Her throat bobbed as she swallowed what he imagined was fear. "Shall I show you how much control I can exert upon you, lady wife?"

She didn't reply. Holding her face in his hands so she continued to look at him, he drank from a well of beauty and vulnerability that almost unmanned him. His frantic heart beat like a wild animal fighting for escape from its cage within his chest. He drove himself to the edge of recklessness. Memories of his mouth on hers. Memories of her skin, her touch. They drove him beyond caution.

Lowering his head, he skimmed his lips over her mouth and felt her body tremble in response. They held each other's gaze. Torturous moments. Then slowly, and with deliberate care, he lowered his mouth to her lips and savored her taste. She didn't resist, so he skimmed his tongue over the seam of her mouth. His heart thudded as she parted her lips and allowed him entrance. Their tongues sparred in a deadly game of desire, but he didn't have the will to do what he knew was right. Until he heard her soft moan. Instantly, it brought him to his senses.

Lifting his head, he captured her gaze. Her eyes had darkened, the inner black almost obscuring the outer color of golden brown.

"This, my lady, is control," he growled, "and if you had any sense you would rejoice in it."

"I did what I thought best for Ebeta and her son."

"I know." Guyon had to apologize to the woman before him, although his pride took a toll he hadn't expected.

"I'm sorry, Cicele. I should have told you that I had taken steps to mollify FitzWallah." He gave her a weak smile. "Ebeta and her son are safe."

"Then why so angry?" She huffed, but didn't move away from him. That small fact gave him hope. She didn't trust him, but she wasn't afraid of his anger. He could work with that.

"I found that I did not like you keeping secrets from me." *Janus-faced bastard, you have secrets you have no wish to share.* Ignoring his conscience, he looked into her eyes. The attraction was potent, but so was the mistrust he discerned behind their golden hue. He couldn't look away.

She broke their unspoken contact and gave him a curt nod. "Don't ever think to bully me again."

Taking her in his arms had been one of the most reckless things he'd done in a long while. He could hear his ragged breathing. If he didn't leave now he would do something that could destroy any chance he had of earning her trust.

"It's time to go!" He heard the hard edge in his voice, but could do nothing about it. His body was so tense his muscles quivered with the strain it took to control them.

She didn't acknowledge him as she strode past him, but she was close enough for him to reach out and grab her arm. He hated that she could block him out so easily. She surrounded herself with an impenetrable wall. Too late he realized it was a mistake to seize hold of her. He'd been too rough, too unwilling to have her leave him.

She lashed out as he took her arm, slapping him across the face. "Keep your hands off me," she spat.

Such was his surprise he released her. Only to be left standing like a dolt as he watched her walk back to the castle. He had to admire her. She possessed all the dignity of a queen.

Walking behind her, all the while savoring the gentle sway of her very shapely bottom, Guyon cursed under his breath. Taking Cicele to wife had become the distraction he had vowed would never happen. "God's teeth," he grumbled under his breath.

CICELE DECIDED to have her supper brought to her room, where Ebeta joined her. Little Moise lay asleep in his mother's arms. The sight of Ebeta with her young son cradled in her arms caused an ache so deep in Cicele's chest she couldn't breathe.

"Are you well, my lady?" Ebeta's tone reflected the look of concern on her face.

"Yes, I am well," Cicele lied. She looked to the table that contained the last of her evening's meal so she could avoid Ebeta's hawklike gaze.

Ebeta snorted, "Excuse me, my lady, but a blind man could see that all is not well with you." Then more gently she continued. "Pray, tell me what ails you."

Cicele turned to face the woman who was fast becoming more than a maid. In truth, it was unusual for Cicele to lower her guard so quickly, but with Ebeta she felt comfortable. It seemed Ebeta felt the same way.

Apart from Maude, Cicele had not confided in anyone about her past with Guyon, or the tragic events of her first few months of marriage to Nicholas. Was it possible to seek peace after so long? She didn't think so, but perhaps it was better to share some of her heartbreak with the woman sitting next to her now. Ebeta was no stranger to suffering and loss.

Cicele made her decision. "I lost a babe, a boy, early in my first marriage." A tight band constricted her throat as she spoke. Tears rolled down her cheeks as she remembered the agony of loss. "And, for my sins, God has cursed me with an infertile womb."

Ebeta placed the sleeping child on the small pallet at her feet and went to Cicele. Kneeling before her she took Cicele's hands in hers. "God is not so cruel, my lady." She spoke quietly, never letting her eyes stray from Cicele's face. "Whatever you think you have done to deserve such ire, methinks it is overstated in your conscience."

Cicele looked at the woman kneeling before her for several moments before she had the strength to answer. "I wish with all my heart you were right, but my womb never quickened. Not in the five years of my marriage, and I fear I will never know the joy of having a child of my own." Before she could stop herself, she wept. Ebeta took her into her arms and rocked her until the sobs subsided. When Cicele was again quiet, Ebeta released her and sat back on her heels.

With a gentle finger she brushed away a strand of hair that had become stuck to Cicele's cheek. "Perhaps after your child's death, God granted you time to heal. Perhaps now you will find joy with your new husband."

Cicele couldn't bring herself to confide in her new maid, so she did what she had always done. She hid her true feelings and pretended to be another creature altogether. She pasted a smile on her face and said what she knew Ebeta wanted to hear. "Yes, you are surely right."

Then she stood and walked to the table and poured two cups of wine, bringing one to Ebeta who still knelt on the floor. "A little wine, then I shall retire."

Before Ebeta could reply the door to the chamber opened and Maude came in with a young page following behind.

The old maid took one look at Cicele and stopped. Cicele had known this woman all her life. It was Maude who had been Cicele's wet nurse when her mother had died giving her birth. And it had been Maude who had been her constant companion ever since. The woman could read Cicele like a book, so Cicele did the only thing she could think of so she wouldn't have to face Maude's questions.

"Ah, Maude, I'm tired and wish to retire."

Maude and Ebeta glanced at each other, but neither argued with Cicele as she began to pace before the fire.

Never one to be cowed by her noble mistress, Maude took Cicele by the shoulders and drew her to a seat by the fire, where she knelt before Cicele and asked her to explain why she was distressed.

Cicele watched as the older woman's usually austere mouth creased in a knowing smile. "What did that great brute of a man do to you, child?"

Immediately Cicele turned her stricken gaze upon the woman who had been the only mother she had ever known. "He kissed me." She gulped as more tears threatened to run down her face.

"Ah," she said knowingly. "And what did you do?"

Despite her best intentions at self-preservation Cicele admitted what she didn't want to. "I let him." Hiccupping as she struggled to contain her emotions. "Then I slapped his face." Cicele's eyes beseeched the older, wiser woman to offer some solace.

Maude's eyes ran over Cicele's face as though deciding whether she should reveal what she thought. Finally, she must have decided to share what was on her mind. "I've watched your husband over the past week and noticed the man's gaze often falls upon you."

Cicele had sensed his gaze. Although she was unsure exactly what his guarded, even furtive glances meant, she was sure Guyon would be agreeable to consummate their marriage.

"I see an open longing settle upon the man's face when he looks at you, child, but you flinch from his gaze. Why?"

Tilting Cicele's chin so she could look at her, Maude inclined her head to the side and purred, "Did you not like his advance then?" Her eyebrows arched in question.

Cicele watched as her nurse arranged her features into a passive mask. In truth, her nurse knew her too well.

A chest-shuddering sigh escaped Cicele's lips. "I did like it." Cicele refused to meet the older woman's gaze, "But I swore I would never succumb to him again."

"My dear, sweet girl, you have endured several years without love; either from your father or Nicholas." Maude patted Cicele's knee.

Nicholas had not been a bad man, but he was unable to give Cicele the love she craved. She had given her heart to another, and Nicholas was wise enough to acknowledge his young wife could offer him little affection.

"I am convinced that your husband would welcome you into his bed, and perchance his heart, if you gave him some encouragement." Maude stroked Cicele's flushed, tear-stained cheek, "You have been cooped up in that fortress of yours so long you forget to what the good lord created you." Maude didn't try to hide her sorrow at the brutal loss of her own husband, and son, as she continued, "It is well past time you welcomed the marriage, and found joy beneath the cover of a husband."

Cicele's cheeks burned as she listened to her maid's candid comments. She suspected her cheeks turned a greater shade of crimson than the rich red of her cloak hanging on the wall. She remembered back to a time when life with Guyon had been the happiest moments she had ever experienced. Shaking her head to dislodge the images, she once again focused on the old woman kneeling in front of her.

Was it possible that something could come from the attraction? Cicele wondered if God in his mercy saw fit to knit her heart back into one piece. Alas, she wasn't sure even heaven could arrange such a future from the marriage she had been forced to accept. The scars were too deep.

Sighing, Maude helped Cicele undress, bidding her sleep off her misery. "Things always have a way of sorting themselves out come morning."

Ebeta had been sitting quietly on the edge of the bed listening to the conversation. "I shall leave you also." She bent down and kissed Cicele's cheek. She spoke so quietly so that only Cicele could hear. "I, like you, keep my secrets, but I am convinced that there is always hope if you but truly desire it." Then she picked up her sleeping son from the pallet and walked out of the chamber.

"You must make some decisions about how you wish to live out your life. Hiding behind walls of your own making is not going to solve anything," Maude counseled.

When Cicele refused to comment, Maude muttered as she handed Cicele's discarded garments to a young maid who placed them in the clothing chest in the corner of the chamber.

When the girl had finished, she gave a quick bob of her nut-brown head and fled the chamber. Vite had been lying in front of the hearth but now he looked to where his mistress sat and decided it was time to offer his own contribution to the conversation. He trotted towards the chair where Cicele sat, nudged her leg to be picked up, then squirmed with delight when she kissed his head and placed him on her lap.

Maude bade her good eve and left Cicele to her turbulent thoughts.

Chapter Sixteen

SHE KNEW SHE SHOULD GAIN HER BED, BUT THE THOUGHT OF LYING down in the dark brought back memories of the past. She didn't have the fortitude to deal with those memories, or their associated fears, tonight. No, it was better to sit by the fire and shut out the longings one kiss had kindled deep within her.

Unfortunately, sitting proved less appealing than Cicele first thought. Deciding, she bent and kissed Vite's head. "You stay here and keep an eye on my bed." She smiled at the little dog, who would make himself at home on her pillow as soon as she was gone. Cicele gathered her mantle about her shoulders and left. Vite's soft whimper followed her as she closed the door and walked down the stairs and through the hall.

The burning sconces on the walls gave her enough light to navigate through the hall without stepping on any sleeping figures. There was a small alcove to the right of the main doors that led to the bailey. Thankfully the door was well greased and gave no hint of her exit. Slowly she walked through the bailey towards the portcullis that led to the outer ward. The men-at-arms patrolling the wall-walk nodded in recognition, but didn't challenge her.

Quietly she entered the long single story building that lay against the inside wall of the outer bailey. There was a small lantern hanging from a peg at the entrance to the stables that offered sufficient light for her to see where she was going, although she was forced to wait for her eyes to adjust to the surroundings. Warmth and quiet embraced her in a soft blanket that soothed her jagged emotions. The aroma of horse sweat, manure, and hay reminded her that she was of the earth. No masks necessary here. In this place she could be herself. The stalls were to her right, and as her eyes adjusted she could see the horses as they rested their heads over the stall gates.

Calm, soulful eyes followed her as she made her way towards the last stall. She stopped for a moment to scratch Nyssa's head before moving on to her destination. As she neared she heard a soft nicker.

Standing before the stall barrier Cicele waited for the huge stallion to come to her. It was difficult to make out his shape; black as night, the beast blended with the shadows making it impossible for Cicele to discern between horse and shadow. With her hands at her sides, she waited. Forcing herself to breathe in slow deliberate breaths, she watched. Another nicker. She smiled. She knew this game. She turned her back and made to leave, but before she took a step a warm breath stirred the hair beside her cheek.

It had been during the first day of her arrival at Alnwick that Cicele had discovered Guyon's greatest treasure—his magnificent war horse, Notus. She was warned not to get too close in case the huge destrier, with a fierce nature, might decide to bite. She smiled again as she considered the beast that stood before her. Doleful eyes studied her, their intelligence evident for any who cared to look. She had been surprised that so many of the stable boys were frightened of him, but she had seen something in his eyes that had assured her he would not hurt her.

Even so, she approached with caution, conscious that she placed herself in harm's way. Swallowing her fear, she moved to where the god of the south wind's namesake stood. "You are a beautiful boy," she crooned, "you make your mother so proud, you mighty beast." The great black head nudged her as if seeking more affection.

Cicele lay her head against his forehead and stroked his muzzle. Releasing a shuddering breath, she let all her confusion drain away. If only she could find the peace she sought. Guyon's kiss had awakened sensations and longings that she had sworn to never revisit. It had been years, six to be exact, since she had experienced the frisson of desire that the kiss had awakened.

Nicholas, God rest her dead husband, had never been a brutish lover, but never in their five years of marriage had he kissed her. He would come to her chamber, squeeze her breasts, and then stick himself into her and release his seed. Then he would thank her, and return to his own chamber. Even thinking about it caused heat to scorch her cheeks in mortification. After the passion she had shared with Guyon, her marriage had been a hideous reminder of what she should expect from marital relations with her husband.

But now her body quivered as she remembered her response to Guyon's kiss. She recognized her body's reaction for what it was. Desire. "Ah, Lord, what a goose I am to hunger for that which I cannot have," she sighed. Unshed tears burned the back of her eyes. Only a simple-minded maid would think there could be love and affection in a marriage where betrayal had marred any hope of true intimacy.

Her first marriage had been bearable only because Nicholas rarely sought her out. He was so often away at his other estates that Cicele spent much of her time alone. And when he did visit her chamber, she learned to lie still beneath his body waiting for the ordeal to be over.

Deciding to waste no more time thinking of a future that was beyond her, she settled into the joy of this moment. In a dark stable, she allowed her confused emotions time to settle.

GUYON ENTERED the stables hoping to find a quiet, dark place to think. He hadn't been able to concentrate since he had kissed Cicele. Damn the woman, she had him in knots. Best to plow the wench and get it out of his system. But he wouldn't force her. God knows he had never forced a woman in his life, and he wasn't about to start with his wife. And, in truth, he wanted more than sex. What he wanted was her friendship. *God's teeth, he was an idiot.*

Guyon snatched the small horn lamp hanging from the peg and stalked towards the far stall. There was a shape at the far end of the stable next to Notus's stall that he recognized immediately. She had her forehead on the horse's neck and was mumbling something to him. An unreasonable jealousy surged through his body. He wanted to be his horse and have Cicele whisper to him, but deep in his heart he knew that she would never again trust him with such vulnerability.

"You take the most extraordinary risks, wife." He wanted to lay claim to her; even here in a stable she was his.

Cicele didn't move away from the horse, but she did lift her head to look in Guyon's direction as he approached.

"The beast is fearsome, and likely to take a great chunk out of your arm," he warned as he arrived in front of the stall. His reached out his hand and stroked the horse's head.

She huffed a laugh. "I am inclined to think that the beast is all bark and no bite." He couldn't see her face clearly, but he did detect her impudent tone.

"You underestimate him at your peril."

She turned her eyes upon him and examined his face, their golden flecks shimmering in the glow of the lamp. He couldn't look away. Nor did he want to.

"Perhaps," she said as she smiled. "But then again, maybe it is he who underestimates others."

Guyon suspected she wasn't talking about his horse anymore, if indeed she ever was.

He placed the lamp on the half post beside the stall and moved closer to his wife. Her back was against the stall door, with Notus's head over her shoulder. When the horse realized he was being ignored, he retreated back into his stall. *Good lad.*

Guyon stood so close to Cicele he could feel her heat through his clothing. Her eyes lowered to his lips. The invitation was obvious, and never one to reject such an invitation, he obliged.

Bending his head, he skimmed her lips with his, then took her bottom lip between his teeth and gave a little tug. A soft moan was all the encouragement he needed. He nipped her lip again so he could salve the bite with his tongue. Slowly, he raised his head to watch her reaction. Her wide-eyed expression told him what he wanted to know.

Wanting to tease her he asked in a serious tone. "Does my kiss meet with your approval, madam?"

She looked away, took a breath, then glanced back at him. "I have not enough experience to offer an accurate evaluation."

Guyon took a moment for her reply to penetrate his foggy brain. He was a little confused. But that was probably the kiss addling his thoughts. They had kissed each other breathless on several occasions during the summer in Rouen. His pride demanded that she not forget, but something in her tone suggested she was not thinking about their shared past.

"Did your husband mistreat you?" A sinking feeling in the pit of his stomach was the response to her expression.

He took her chin in his hand as she looked away. "Answer me," he whispered.

"Nicholas never kissed me. My experience with him is limited to the marital act." She refused to look at him.

So the oaf was inept, lazy, or an idiot not to take more care of his wife.

"Well, my lady, I am inclined to reacquaint you with the exquisite torture of the kiss," he teased.

She looked confused. "Exquisite torture?"

Oh God, he didn't know if he would get through the next few minutes.

"It is, I assure you," he ground out. "As, by your own decree, our kisses will not lead to more enjoyable activities, it becomes a delicious form of torment." He leaned forward and kissed her again, this time running his tongue over the sensitive skin on the inside of her bottom lip. "Are you ready for your first lesson?"

He rather thought she was. Her breathing was shallow and fast, while her eyes had a slightly glazed look. This was indeed going to kill him. Hell's teeth, he couldn't think of a better way to die.

IT WAS reckless to welcome his kiss but it seemed her body knew what it wanted while her mind spun in confusion. It had been years since she had felt anything save bitterness and regret, but as his lips caressed hers she was powerless to resist the pull of something long forgotten.

Desire.

The only time she had felt alive in the past six years had been when she discarded her noble garb and donned a servant's clothing and hunted in the forest, or fished in the weir. The exhilaration of doing something so reckless would grow until her heart almost burst from her chest. Tingling with anticipation as she reached for her bow and arrow and sighted her quarry, she knew what it was to live without regret and the constant knowledge that her wretched existence would never change.

But now, as she leaned into him, everything she felt in the hunt was insignificant compared to the euphoria flowing through her. The pleasure as her heart beat in frantic time with her need made her skin tingle and her toes curl in her slippers.

It was madness to let him past her carefully erected defenses, but for the first time in six long, grueling years she relished the closeness of his body close to hers. She couldn't trust him, and she couldn't forgive him, but, God in His glorious heaven, the moment was too wonderful to resist. His taste, his scent, his warmth overwhelmed her. Those precious snatched moments in that long-lost summer came rushing back to her. Powerless to prevent her body from responding to him, she flattened herself against his chest as her arms curled around his neck, drawing his mouth closer as her tongue battled with his. The empty shell of the woman she had become began to bloom under the intensity of their passion.

How she had dreamed for this in the dark of her chamber, but now the joy she experienced put those forbidden dreams to shame.

This was life. This was hope. This was a mistake.

Taking charge of her senses she drew back from the delicious mouth that offered oblivion, and let her arms fall to her sides.

Sensing her change, he immediately stepped back. As she knew he would. His breathing was as ragged as hers, and in the faint light of the lamp his eyes were the color of night. It should have given her a sense of satisfaction to see the effect she had on him, but the familiar pang of regret stole her pleasure.

It was torture, and there was nothing exquisite in the shallow feeling that she was left with. All trust had been lost, and she didn't think her heart would ever be whole enough to give it to this man again. Without a word, she turned from him and began walking away, desperate for the solitude of her chamber. She could weep for the longing his kisses ignited in the cold barren places of her heart, but she couldn't allow him there again. Of that she was sure.

"Don't go."

It was a plea that she should ignore, but she couldn't. Her body ached for his touch. Why deny herself? She knew why, yet she couldn't seem to make her body stop itself from turning back towards the voice that had always called to her.

Slowly, with deliberate steps, she walked back to where he stood waiting.

Without a word, he pulled her to him and covered her mouth in his. Hungry, demanding lips urged her to respond.

She let herself feel the full force of her passion for the first time in over six years. The sensations of his warm mouth on her lips sent shivers down her body making her breasts ache and her nipples pebble. She had forgotten that her mouth was connected in some delicious way with her breasts. Sighing she parted her lips in response to his tongue's insistent prodding.

Need. Raw, primal need sang through every vein. She was lost and for once she didn't care.

"Cicele." A moan laced with all the passion of long forbidden memories caressed her neck.

Dragging herself away from his embrace, Cicele caught her breath. Lips burning with the memory of what he offered, she forced herself to take a step back. What had she done? One kiss and she was prepared to forget all the pain and despair. She would not welcome him back into her body, and worst of all, her heart. *Stupid, foolish woman!*

Her lips throbbed and her body ached with unspent passion. She had been so close to forgetting. It wouldn't happen again.

It took several moments before she felt she could look at him and when she did she wished she hadn't.

A smile creased his lips and his eyes burned with lust. "I did say it was an exquisite torture," he whispered, his voice a sensuous purr.

"I can't, Guyon," she replied.

His self-satisfied expression didn't change, but the skin around his eyes tightened. He was angry and frustrated.

Good.

He didn't reply but stood facing her, eyes boring into hers. She couldn't face his anger, coward that she was. She had wanted to hurt him as he had hurt her, but she found she didn't have the stomach for it anymore.

She was tired. Tired of longing for vengeance. Tired of hoping for a different life. Tired of the nagging sense of loss that had wrapped around her heart all those years ago.

"My body may respond to you, but make no mistake, I remember the callous way you abandoned me. I know what you told me, but I cannot trust you, Guyon. I will never allow you into my heart again." She took a shuddering breath. "And this." She waved her trembling hand about. "Will never happen again."

He still didn't say anything, but stood watching her under hooded eyes. It was dark in the stables, but the light from the small lantern was sufficient to see his face as she stood close to him. Too close. She took another step back.

That small movement seemed to bring him to his senses. His eyes narrowed and he shook his head as if dispelling water. "I leave for Lesbury in the morning; I thought you might like to come with me."

What? It took her a moment to gather her thoughts.

"Lesbury?"

He didn't speak, just nodded. His jaw was clenched so tight she noticed the muscles rippled with the strain.

"I would like that, thank you."

"There are rumors of poachers in the area," he said in a hard voice. "It will not be a pleasant visit if they are apprehended."

She nodded her understanding. "I am sure you will administer justice." Of that she was convinced. "Now, my lord, if you will excuse me I shall return to my chamber." Not waiting for his reply, she turned and walked away. She had to get some distance between herself and those eyes that continued to bore into her. Her resolve was wavering.

A pox on her stupid, irresolute heart. Marriage to Guyon was not what she had imagined. God help her.

Chapter Seventeen

CICELE DIDN'T SLEEP WELL AND WOKE FEELING EXHAUSTED AND out of sorts. It was her own fault. Maude pulled back the curtains around her bed and announced that Guyon had sent a message to say they would be leaving within the hour.

Cursing under her breath, Cicele dressed and, as was her custom, she spent a few moments in prayer before pronouncing that she was ready.

"Maude, you will accompany me, but Ebeta can stay here."

At the mention of her name Ebeta walked into the chamber, "Did I hear my name?" she inquired; Moise walked at her side.

"Yes, you did," Cicele answered. "My husband has asked me to accompany him to Lesbury, but I think it would be best if you stay here, inside the castle walls. I'm not sure it's wise to venture further." She gave Ebeta an apologetic smile. "Maude will accompany me, and you may stay here and rest." And keep away from your odious father, but she kept that thought to herself.

Ebeta's shoulders sagged. "I am grateful, thank you. In truth, I am exhausted and Moise seems to be more demanding than usual this morning." She ruffled her son's hair. "As his strength improves, so do his demands."

"Ha! Men are always demanding when they want food or sex," Maude proclaimed, as she watched Moise play.

"Well, it must be the former," Ebeta laughed, although it sounded brittle, "for he is too young for the latter."

The child paid them no mind; he was too busy playing with Vite who was scampering across the bed while the boy chased him.

"Thank the saints. It is enough that we have one man prowling around, and I am sure it is not food he craves." Maude shot a look at Cicele which suggested she knew more than Cicele had shared. It was uncomfortable to live with a woman who seldom missed details.

Cicele felt her cheeks burning, but chose to ignore it, and steered the conversation in another direction.

"If you are quite finished, I think it is time we were gone." She walked over to Ebeta and kissed her cheek. "Vite, come."

The little dog jumped off the bed and walked in front of her. Tail high. At least *he* was happy to be taking the journey, Cicele thought sourly.

It was only a few miles to Lesbury from Alnwick, and the journey was uneventful. Guyon made it his mission to be as attentive to Cicele as he possibly could. Something about her disapproval delighted him. Of course, it was a game. She knew it, and so did he.

He hadn't been able to sleep the previous night. Images of her filled his dreams, but like the early morning mist that swirled about them as they rode this morning, his dreams vanished and he was left with a sense of dread that had seeped deep into his bones. It still lingered even now as they rode towards Lesbury.

If he was honest he knew why the fear stalked his dreams. He had lost her once, and he couldn't bear to lose her again. His foolish male pride, and a great dollop of honor, had made him stay away all those years ago. He wouldn't do it again.

She responded to him, and that's why he continued to pursue her. If she had shown any disinclination towards him he would have given her her freedom. He huffed a small laugh. God, she had a tongue on her, but her words didn't match her response to him. He needed to be careful not to overwhelm her. Yes, he would work on breaking down her formidable defenses, and in time she would accept him.

Turning his mind back to their encounter in the stables the previous evening, there were glimpses of the unbridled passion they had shared all those years ago. But the nagging truth remained, he had betrayed her trust and it was not going to be easy for her to give him a second chance.

He would have to tell her the truth, but now was not the right time. She had stated that she didn't want to know, but he believed her pride had been hurt, and that underneath that pride was a heart that longed to know the truth. He had never stopped loving her, and never would. All he had to do was convince her that he would never hurt her again.

Yet that was precisely what dogged his dreams. He was sure to lose her when she found out about Alice—the mere thought of his dead wife caused his skin to turn clammy, and his chest to tighten to the point that he couldn't breathe.

Guilt and shame stalked his dreams. If he was to tell Cicele the truth, which he knew he must, he had better make sure she loved him enough to accept him for who he was. He huffed another bitter laugh. In truth, no one could love the vile thing that lurked under his skin, but he was fool enough to hope.

It wasn't in his nature to accept defeat, so he would win her heart, again. And when she was his, totally and completely his, he would tell her the real reason he called himself la Bête.

GUYON LED them into the bailey where they were met by Lesbury's steward. Cicele's heart rose at the sight of the familiar face. This was the place she had spent most of her childhood. Lesbury Castle held many memories, most good, but a few that were too painful to think about now, although they would occupy her mind during her visit; she was sure of it.

It had been almost a year since she had been at Lesbury, and she had missed her childhood home. In that year she had lost a husband, a brother, and a father. But she had gained a sister and a cousin. And another husband. Warmth filled her chest as she thought of Isabeau and Beatrice. The warm glow of the affection that settled in her chest for the two women didn't last when she shot a glance at her husband.

Joy had been the overriding emotion during the past few months since hearing she had a sister. However, guilt wasn't far away. She hadn't loved Nicholas, nor him her, but they had had a reasonable, albeit distant, marriage. But her father and brother she did not mourn. What a simpleton she had been to think they would ever love and respect her.

Although young, it hadn't taken her much time to realize that she was nothing to them but currency. A pawn to enlarge their own esteem and wealth. She looked around as she took in her home.

No memories of her family soured her homecoming. Her father never visited the castle, nor had Roland. Lesbury was too small and insignificant, but it had been her mother's, and it was where Cicele had been born, and where her mother had died. This was a castle that was more Cicele's than all the estates she inherited from her mother. And she loved it.

Glancing over at Guyon as he dismounted it struck her that there would now be memories of this man here. Surprisingly, she was warmed by the idea. Her heart was being drawn back to him, and she was honest enough to accept that the claim he had on her heart was still there. *You already love him, you are just too stubborn to admit it.*

That thought was interrupted by hands clasped around her waist. She looked down to see Guyon beside her. "My lady."

She leaned into him and allowed herself to be hoisted out of the saddle and placed on her feet next to her husband. He offered her his arm as they walked into the great hall.

Wine and fruit were set on a table by the hearth in the middle of the hall. Too early for the tables to be set for the midday dinner, the space seemed deserted. It was a small hall in comparison to Alnwick, but as a child Cicele had thought it cavernous.

"I am leaving to travel to Alnmouth to announce the king's charter for a port and check the port's defenses," Guyon said as he handed her a goblet of wine. "You will stay here."

She bristled at his tone.

"Peace, wife," he whispered as he leaned into her. "I am not ordering you, merely making a suggestion. I thought you might appreciate a rest." He looked at her, his eyes assessing her with unveiled lust. "I did not sleep a wink last night, and I suspect by the look of you that sleep eluded you also." It was the playful tilt of his eyebrows that made her smile before she had the sense to control her expression.

Clearing her throat, she replied, "thank you, my lord, but I must own I slept the sleep of the dead last eve." She gave him her most innocent smile. "In your absence, I shall reacquaint myself with *my* home," she said, emphasizing the "my." Guyon might be her husband, but by all that was holy, Lesbury was hers.

He wasn't fooled. "That, my lady wife, is a lie," he teased as his gloved finger traced a line across her chin.

His gaze lingered for too long. *Damn the man's eyes.* Heat spread up her neck only confirming that she had indeed had a fitful night's sleep thinking about their kiss in the stable.

A small, smug smile creased the corners of his mouth, then he turned and spoke to the steward. Sir Nigel de Bass had been the steward of Lesbury for years. He was competent, and loyal, if a little old. He had two sons, both of whom had died during the wars between Stephen and Matilda. Cicele hoped she could convince Guyon to keep him on as steward. She owed him for his loyalty and his kindness over the years.

It was his wife, Lady Rosalie, who had taken on the task of educating Cicele. Her father's voice echoed in her head. "A daughter's ability to run a household and produce heirs is all that was necessary." Lady Rosalie, God bless her, had ignored her father's directive, and along with Maude and Jabbe, had made Cicele's childhood bearable. Cicele would be forever grateful to the woman who introduced her to the only escapism she had ever known—stories of heroes and their pursuit of love and honor.

Lady Rosalie had also taught her how to read Norman French, and English, much to her father and brother's disgust. "Latin is the language of your class!" She could still hear her father's voice reverberating around the small solar in his castle at Redesdale when he had discovered that Cicele was not reading some austere author from antiquity, but a romance from an unknown author who wrote in the vernacular of the poorer classes. Cicele had savored that small rebellion.

She was brought back to the present with a tap to her arm. Shaking herself free of her memories, she looked in the direction of her husband who had touched her.

"I was informing Sir Nigel that he will accompany me to Alnmouth," Guyon said quietly as he looked at Cicele. "We will be back before sunset. I trust you will keep yourself inside the walls?"

Cicele wanted to object, but considered it a waste of time. Guyon was imposing his will on her in her own castle, and now was not the time to take issue with him. She would please herself what she did, but he didn't need to know.

"Yes, my lord, I have much to do." She smiled sweetly and nodded to Sir Nigel who stood at a distance to give Guyon and her some privacy.

"Sir Nigel, might I inquire of Lady Rosalie; she was not here to meet us."

A sad expression slid across the old steward's features. "My good wife has gone to the priory of St. Mary's, in Bridlington, to pray to the Blessed Virgin, my lady," he replied in a tone that spoke of worry and something else Cicele could not identify. "My wife has felt the loss of our two sons greatly, and has found the need to seek peace, but I shall call her back."

Cicele nodded. She understood the allure of a quiet cloister to soothe a broken heart. Such a luxury was not hers to enjoy, but she would not deny Lady Rosalie. "There is no need, Sir Nigel, let her seek solace." Cicele glanced at Guyon, who gave her a small nod.

The strained silence was broken by Guyon who bid her farewell and led Sir Nigel to the waiting men gathered in the bailey. When the hall was empty Cicele was about to go in search of Maude, who she expected to be waiting in the lord's chamber, when she heard a familiar sound.

Vite was busying himself snuffling among the rushes on the floor in the hopes of finding a morsel of food. "You think of nothing but your stomach," she laughed as the little dog looked up at her with an indignant expression. It was the ears that gave him such a look. Taking pity on him she walked over and scooped him up and offered him a piece of apple that had been sliced. The dog sniffed the proffered treat tentatively, but declined to accept it. "You are too fussy. I should starve you so you become more appreciative," she growled, but kissed his head. "Let's go and find Maude, shall we?" She put the dog back down on the floor and walked towards the far end of the hall to where the stairs led to the chamber above.

∽

CICELE PRESIDED over the noon meal, which was much diminished by Guyon and Sir Nigel's absence. Even Thomas, with his ready smile and relaxed banter, was missing. Cicele would admit to no one, save herself, that she missed her husband's presence at table.

When they had finished, she met with Cuthbert, the castle's chamberlain, to discuss arrangements for the next few days. Cuthbert had organized Guyon to sleep in the lord's chamber, while she was to sleep in the lady's chamber next to it. After settling into the familiar chamber she wanted to go outside and enjoy a beautiful winter's afternoon.

What she didn't expect was Maude's censure.

"What are you doing?" Her maid demanded, in a tone that reminded Cicele of her childhood.

"I am going for a walk to the river and hopefully forage for something to add to the table," she replied with a tone she hoped would communicate she was not to be defied.

Maude heard it, and as usual, ignored it. "It is foolish to venture out without a guard if there are poachers about."

"That's why I shall dress as a servant and then no one will take any notice of me." She didn't bother adding *a male servant*.

"Your husband forbade it, as I recall." Maude crossed her arms across her chest and fixed Cicele with a gimlet eye.

"This is my home, Maude, and you of all people know it will be safe if I stay close to the walls." Cicele took her maid by the shoulders. "I shall be careful, and..." she gave the older woman a sly smile. "If you are lucky I might find some late season berries that grow in the thicket by the old weir. The ones you are particularly fond of."

Cicele waited until Maude released her breath, signaling her acquiescence.

Bussing a kiss on her maid's cheek Cicele began to gather clothing from the bottom of her clothes chest. "Now help me change so I can be on my way."

. . .

It was glorious to be out of doors and in the woods. Vite ran about sniffing every tree before raising his hind leg and marking it. "Where does it all come from?" she asked him as he lifted his leg again to spray urine on an aged ash tree. The dog glanced at her but didn't bother to acknowledge the question. He was too busy making sure every creature in the vicinity knew he was back, and proclaiming himself lord and master of the area.

Cicele sat by the river's edge and watched the water flow. She would not fish or hunt. Deeper, sadder tasks called her to this spot. Eyeing her basket, she would collect berries, if the winter had not claimed them first, and some wild herbs that grew in the small meadow through the trees by the river. But that was for later.

For as long as she could remember this spot had held a special fascination for her. The "small meadow," as it was called, was a lush space covered in grass and wild flowers. The glade lay like a green mat sprinkled with color from the various wild flowers growing in profusion in the center of the woods. Sweet violet, yellow sorrel, and snowdrops all swayed in the slight breeze creating something so beautiful Cicele could only stare in wonder.

Once she had seen a doe with her fawn grazing the grass, and had sat watching them for the longest time before Jabbe had discovered her. He didn't scold her, but sat quietly beside her as they watched the deer. It was a precious memory, and one Cicele cherished as she thought back to her childhood.

On the far right of the glade she spied the small cairn. Walking slowly, she made her way to a place that threatened to break her heart all over again.

Sitting beside the small pile of stones Cicele let her grief bubble up until great wracking sobs shook her body. Always coming here brought back memories that she both cherished and hated in equal measure. With a sense of loss that never seemed to dissipate, Cicele lay next to her son and let the tears run their course. When the storm of emotion passed, she was left with a sense of peace that caressed her wounded heart. Blanketed in the serenity of the meadow she sat. How long she sat there she didn't know, but reluctantly she roused herself. It was time to go.

When would the tears stop? She had cried enough to fill her bathtub, and yet still they flowed. Once, years ago now, she had been terrified that if she started crying she would never stop. Maude had assured her that she would, but that her pain would be a constant companion. It was true. Her fractured soul would never recover.

Having Guyon so close, yet forcing herself to remain distant, had become torturous. She didn't think she could bear to share this place with him. The pain was still too sharp, too intense.

The sun had already begun to dip in her tiny little part of the meadow, but she had time to collect some yarrow that grew on the verges of the meadow. It would be helpful for treating the colds and fevers that always accompanied the long winter months.

Increasing her step, she hoped to get back to the castle with Guyon being none the wiser that she had defied his order to stay within the walls.

Tucking her sorrows back to where they belonged, deep in her heart, she whistled for Vite to come as she began to walk back towards the castle. She remembered to stop and look for the berries she had promised Maude. Alas, the winter had claimed them.

Out of the corner of her eye she could see the dog scampering through the long grass of the meadow when suddenly he froze. Cicele immediately crouched down and surveyed the woods to her right. It was uncannily quiet, which alerted her to danger. Vite slunk to where she crouched and they both waited to see where the danger lay. Blood coursed through her veins as the sound of her heart thundered in her ears. The familiar sense of danger surged through her limbs, making her skin tingle. She didn't want to think about the last time she felt this terrified. Surely to God, she would not be abducted again.

A slight movement to her left caught her eye. Carefully she crawled towards the shelter of a tree on the border of the meadow. Vite followed.

They waited.

There. A movement caught her eye.

The dog whined. "Hush." Vite immediately obeyed.

She counted her heartbeats as they thundered in her head. Then, without warning movement exploded a few yards in front of her. A small group of boys ran in desperation towards the river. The thundering of hooves drowned out any noise the boys made.

They were panicked. And they were young. The smallest, a child of no more than two, tripped and cried out. The tallest boy must have heard because he stopped and looked behind to see the child sprawled on the ground. Cicele watched with fascination as the older boy wrestled with a decision. Stop to save the youngster, or keep running.

Everything seemed to happen very slowly. Cicele saw a group of horsemen through the trees galloping towards the boys. The low hanging branches made their pursuit slower, but they would be upon the boys before they reached the river.

Without conscious thought, Cicele sprang from her hiding place and ran to the little boy who still lay crying on the forest floor. She got to him first and picked him up. The other boys had stopped and were following the tallest boy, who was running to save the child Cicele held.

The panic she saw on his face tore her heart. They were young and desperate. She had to save them.

"Stay behind me," she yelled over the sound of the approaching horses.

The boys immediately did as bid, huddling behind her.

Through the trees a horse, and its rider, crashed closer until they were almost on top of her. She stood her ground. No one would harm them while she had power to protect them. They would not hang. This was her land, and these boys were her responsibility.

⌒

GUYON PRIDED himself on many things, but keeping his temper in check when confronted with a willfully disobedient wife was not one of them.

He reined in his horse before he trampled the bloody woman who stood before him. She had darted out from nowhere to protect a motley collection of children who had been poaching on his land.

Trying to compose himself, and failing, he roared, "What, in God's name, are you doing?"

Refusing to answer, she held her arms out to the side to protect the boys, and raised her chin at a defiant angle that almost made him laugh. The minx had no fear of him. He should be furious, but all his anger had evaporated. With that small display of rebellion Guyon realized that she trusted him more than she was willing to admit. A warm sensation flowed through his veins, and almost had him smiling like an addle-pated loon.

Schooling his face into a scowl, he walked his horse forward until it was beside her, then he leaned over its neck and spoke quietly so his men couldn't hear.

"I am going to give an order, my lady, and I suggest you oblige me with the compliance that I would expect from an obedient wife." She would meet his challenge, and he wasn't disappointed.

Slowly she raised her head to meet his eye. "I will not, unless you give me your word that you will not hang them from yonder tree." She nodded her head towards a tree with a low hanging limb where one of Guyon's men was already throwing a rope over the branch.

Guyon rested his forearms on the pommel of his saddle and

190

glared at her. "I will think nothing of dragging you up and over my saddle if you insist on giving me trouble," he snarled, desperate to keep his amusement and lust in check. Standing defiant, and dressed in men's clothing, she was magnificent.

She flinched at the venom in his voice, but almost immediately she straightened her shoulders and spat back, "You are an oaf and a beast, and I will do no such thing. I am the lady of Lesbury, and my word is law here."

What he wanted to do was leap from his horse and take her there on the forest floor. *God's bones, man, think!*

Watching her, he took a moment to gather his thoughts. "You forget, madam, but it is I who am lord now." He stood up in his stirrups to get a better view of the boys cowering in terror behind her. They were a sorry lot, and in need of help, not punishment.

With a resigned sigh, he sat back in the saddle and called out to Sir Nigel. "There will be no hanging today." Was it his imagination or could he hear Thomas's guffaw somewhere behind him? Shit. Shit. And shit.

Then he turned back to face his wife. "You," he snapped. "Come with me."

"I have promised to protect the boys," she argued back.

"God's blood, lady, do as I bid before I shed their precious blood where they stand." Pitching his tone low, he hoped the quietness of his voice would win him the small concession of her compliance.

She squared her shoulders, and instead of accepting his outstretched hand to assist her into the saddle, she marched past his horse and headed back towards the castle. The boys followed behind her like ducklings after their mother.

God, give me patience.

Chapter Eighteen

CICELE LED GUYON AND HIS MEN INTO THE HALL, INSTRUCTING ALE
and viands to be made available. Although the daylight was fading,
the evening meal would not be served for some time. She watched
from the corner of her eye as Guyon made his way to the lord's
chair. It galled to give up her authority, but as he was her husband, it
was his right, not hers.

As he took his seat with an arrogant swagger designed to show
her he was in charge, he indicated for her to sit on his right. Another
irritation. She didn't want to be sitting next to him. She needed
distance from her husband, whose hooded eyes watched her as
though she was prey. A young page came and offered them a basin
and pitcher to wash their hands. Guyon dried his on a cloth, then
cast her a sideways glance.

She would look worse than the poorest villein. It took all her
resolve to resist the impulse to touch her hair, which was surely in
disarray. Her hood had fallen when she had rushed to save the
little boy.

She chose to ignore her filthy and tattered clothing, and her
husband's lingering gaze, and proceeded to wash her hands.

When the silence became unbearable she stole a glance at Guyon, who hadn't uttered a word since their confrontation in the forest. His eyes held an emotion that she had never seen before, and it almost made her cringe. Almost.

It had been foolish to defy him, but a perverse sense of recklessness had possessed her. She could have waited to visit her son's tiny grave, but she hated being caged, especially in her own home. No, it was too much.

A small rebellious smile flickered at the corners of her mouth. God knows what he thought seeing his wife dressed as a man. Tilting her chin a fraction she returned his scowl with one of her own.

The sound of a scuffle drew her attention to the guards who now escorted the small group of boys to the middle of the floor where they cowered in front of the dais.

She watched as Guyon's impassive gaze settled on the captives. A sorry lot. Hair matted and lice ridden no doubt. Their clothes were rags. But it was their eyes that stabbed at her heart, and conscience. They were too large for their gaunt faces. Haunted with hunger and despair. No doubt the previous sheriff, a pox on his dead, blighted liver, was responsible for the so-called purging that had become a plague on the land.

"What have you to say in your defense?" There was an edge to Guyon's tone which Cicele didn't care for.

The boys were focused on the rushes at their feet. No one dared speak. But as is the way of things, the smallest of the group began to whimper. It was a pathetic mewling sound that had Cicele out of her chair and moving towards the small boy before she realized what she was doing.

"What do you think you are about?" Her husband roared. Everyone jumped at the noise—well, almost everyone. His men seemed impervious to the sound.

She refused to answer and kept walking until she reached the child. As she had initially thought, he would have been no more than two years of age. She gathered him into her chest and soothed his crying, "Hush now, little one, all will be well."

The little boy gulped and began sucking on his thumb, as he continued to snuggle against her breast.

Cicele turned towards the dais and scowled at the man who possessed the power of life and death over these children. Typhon, with all his fiery serpents, could not have looked more deadly, yet she refused to quail beneath his glare.

"These boys are no threat, my lord. Their only crime is hunger, and perhaps odor befitting a swine herd." She screwed up her nose at the offensive smell. "And while they are in *my* hall, I shall see to their needs."

GUYON COULDN'T HELP HIMSELF, he smiled. Like a great lackwit, he grinned as he watched her nose crinkle at the offending odor. What in Hades was he smiling for? He was in charge here.

Bewitched, he had to physically shake himself before he could form a coherent sentence. "You forget, my lady, but, in truth, the hall is *mine*." Now he sounded churlish. Gathering his resolve, he took a mouthful of wine, while letting his eyes bore into her. *Careful, madam, I have claws.*

His wife flinched. A tiny, almost imperceptible movement, but he had seen it. Good, she had read his expression and understood.

His eyes slid to the child she held, then to the other boys that stood trembling next to her. They were no threat, but he couldn't let them go either. What the hell was he to do with them?

Rising from the lord's chair he leaned on the table before him. His weight resting on his knuckled fists. "I grant you leave to feed them." He gave her what he hoped was a dispassionate glance.

"And methinks a bath, for them and yourself." He was about to return to the chair he had vacated, but turned as an extremely enjoyable thought occurred to him. "You will do me the honor of presenting yourself to me in the lord's solar before supper." He gave a slight nod of his head. "My lady." Then he took his seat.

Thankfully, she had gone by the time he turned back to face the hall.

"Thomas, bring the steward and the constable to my solar." He needed to find out what had been going on at Lesbury and Alnmouth over the past five months since Odard, the previous sheriff, had died.

God's bones, he was fit to spit. The woman had the audacity to defy him at every turn.

Cicele, you will be the death of us both. If one of his men defied him he could take a fist, or a sword, to him. But his wife? He wanted to do things to her that would leave them both sated and breathless, but, God help him, that seemed unlikely.

Frustrated, he slouched in moody silence and drank his ale. The image of his wife's mouth, curled in defiance, made his blood boil, and his balls ache.

It was an exhausting process. She and Maude had decided the only way to rid the boys of vermin was to shave every hair off their heads, then burn the shanks of lice-infested hair, and flea ridden rags. Deciding they didn't want lice or fleas in the hall or kitchen, they had taken them to the small infirmary next to the castle's chapel.

Now that they were shorn and clean, Cicele sent Maude to search out Cuthbert, Lesbury's chamberlain, to get clothing, while a page was sent to get gruel, bread, and milk from the kitchens. They would stay in the infirmary until Guyon decided their fate. She had the sinking feeling that her lord husband would not agree with her assessment of the boys, or their future at Lesbury. Still, she was determined to make her feelings clear. Lesbury was hers; surely she had the right to decide on the boys' fate.

Now back in her chamber, Cicele had refused to attend supper; instead she took a leisurely bath, then dressed in a clean chemise and bliaut. Maude arrived as Cicele poked her head through the neck of her woolen garment.

"I see you are hoping to make an impression." Maude cast her eyebrows skyward.

Cicele laughed, "There is no reason to hide my talents under a bushel." In point of fact, Cicele knew full well that her gown was designed to show off her figure. If it got her what she wanted, she was happy to flaunt her curves. She still didn't trust her husband, but by God in His holy heaven, he had awoken appetites that she had kept well-hidden for years. It was shameful to want his eyes on her, but Cicele craved the appreciation she saw reflected in their depths when he looked at her. Sometimes the desire to be held was so strong that her body trembled as she struggled to keep her emotions and longing hidden.

After securing the ceinture around her waist, she sat at a stool so Maude could dress her hair. Finally, draping a sheer veil over her head, and securing it with a thin gold circlet, she was ready to meet her husband.

He had sent a message to come to her solar, which was on the second floor of the castle's keep, one floor below her chamber. It was a room where she had spent time sewing and reading, and playing board games with Maude, or teaching Agatha her letters. She missed the young maid and wondered where she was. Guyon still had no word of her whereabouts. It had been three weeks since Agatha had vanished and she herself had been abducted. Cicele had prayed every day that her young maid was well and safe.

· · ·

ALTHOUGH SHE HAD NOT SPENT MORE than a few weeks at Lesbury since her first husband's death, she had missed her home, especially the solar. Now, she stood on the threshold and surveyed the space.

It was a pleasant room, one she had made her own. The wooden floor was covered with large rush mats woven with squares of thin strips of colored leather to make designs that resembled tiles. The walls were plastered and painted a soft yellow, and hung with tapestries depicting scenes from the Bible. It was essentially a lady's room. The furniture was comfortable, and painted in soft greens that were pleasing to the eye.

Cicele suspected Guyon would dislike such a feminine room in which to conduct his business with her. In a perverse way she would enjoy seeing his discomfort in *her* solar. It had been years since she had been in the lord's solar, as Sir Nigel had used the space, but Guyon would take it while he was here.

There he was, sitting on the only chair in the solar that had a back. She would have liked longer to watch him unobserved, but alas it was not to be, for he rose as soon as he heard her gown swish about her legs. He had been gazing into the fire when she entered, but now stood allowing her to choose where she might sit. She chose a folding chair to the left of the hearth, leaving the more comfortable curule seat free. It would not do to become too comfortable with this man. Idiot that she was, she had allowed her guard to slip. *Tonight I shall keep my distance*, she silently vowed as she took her seat.

Cicele was not disappointed when she saw his eyes travel from her face down her body to her toes, then slowly up to settle once again on her face. A little thrill skidded down her stomach as his eyes lingered upon her. She forced her own gaze back to her hands. It wouldn't do to be drawn in by his seductive dark eyes that reflected her own hidden desire.

The silence stretched between them until it was almost unbearable. Sadly, as she raised her eyes to look at him, the cool, hard indifference on his face was back.

Perhaps she had overreached with her choice of attire. Well, she wasn't about to turn tail and scamper back to her chamber. She would meet his eye, and stand her ground. At least that's what she hoped.

Refusing to speak, she waited for him to break the silence that had enveloped them. It was not comfortable, but she forced herself to keep her eyes on the fire as thoughts and excuses tumbled through her mind.

Finally, with a great heave of his breath, he turned to face her. "What were you thinking?"

His voice was calm and quiet, but she could see his jaw was clenched. He was furious.

Deciding defiance was her best option, she raised her chin and looked him in the eye. "I have lived at Lesbury almost all of my life. Its woods are where I learned to hunt and gather herbs as a child. For you to deny one of my few pleasures is cruel in the extreme."

Determined to deflect his anger at her defiance she changed the subject.

"What of the boys?" Cicele didn't look at him, but continued to search the fire for answers they couldn't provide.

"They shall be punished."

She was about to object, but he raised his hand to silence her. "I am unwilling to allow poachers free rein on my lands. They will be dealt with according to the law." His tone defied her to argue.

The sting of unshed tears bit behind her eyes. The king's justice was harsh, but some small part of her had hoped her husband had the resolve to administer compassion along with justice. What did it serve to sever hands or brand cheeks? Memories of the mutilated body in the gibbet hanging on the walls of Alnwick castle returned.

Any criminal, young or old, could be assured that they would receive no mercy. Her heart lurched as she realized the boys might suffer a similar fate.

She didn't trust her voice, so she remained silent.

"I will deal with them tomorrow," he said as he glared at her. "For now, it is my wife that I must deal with." He emphasized the word "deal" as though she were a trial he must endure. That stung.

"You will want to begin arrangements for your journey, so I grant you leave, my lady."

"We are leaving?"

He didn't even bother to look at her, but threw some cheese at Vite who sat by the hearth. "I will have Thomas escort you back to Alnwick on the morrow."

Not only was he excusing her from her own solar, he was punishing her by removing her from her beloved Lesbury. Tired of the animosity between them she realized she would have to make some concessions if she were to remain married, and not be at odds with her husband for the rest of their lives. Was it her pride? she wasn't quite sure, but she wanted some answers if she was ever to have a life with Guyon.

"You chose Alice over me. Why?" She had never had the courage to ask him before, but if she was going to be banished, she would not be denied an answer.

He shrugged his shoulders. "You were married and gone back to England when I returned to Rouen. I could hardly chase after you."

She barked an unladylike laugh. She would not allow him to cast her as the villain. "You professed love for me. Yet you married another." She heard the heartbreak in her own voice, but didn't care to hide it.

Dark, relentless eyes probed her face. "It seems to me, madam, that you are Janus-faced. You waited less than a month before you spread your delectable legs for another."

Malicious words. Cutting words. A hard, callous slap across the face would have had less effect on her. His words were so brutal, and crude, that she flinched.

As soon as the words were out of his mouth he wanted to bite off his tongue. She had recoiled as though slapped. And he had never condoned violence towards women, or those weaker than himself. But his words had been a vicious blow.

"I am sorry, Cicele, that was cruel, and I didn't mean it." He rose from his seat and walked to where she sat, then crouched down so their heads were level. "I was angry, and those words were my pride speaking."

She sat as though stunned, neither seeing nor hearing.

"Cicele, please," he pleaded for her to look at him.

Slowly, she turned her eyes upon him. The pain and anguish in them tore at the very fiber of his soul.

"I was with child," she sobbed. "Rumors had already begun to spread that I had a lover. My father found out I was with child, and when I refused to tell him who the father was, he forced me to marry Nicholas."

She looked so small and broken that Guyon picked her up and sat with her cradled on his knee. He began rocking her in his arms, desperately trying to soothe the damage he had caused. Was he able to assuage so much pain and suffering? He wasn't sure, but he wanted to believe it was possible.

A lump had formed in his throat, but he had to ask. "The babe?"

"I told Nicholas on our wedding night, and we struck a bargain. He would not touch me, banishing me to Lesbury, till the child was born. Then, if I delivered a boy, he would accept it as his own."

Guyon didn't want to think about the outcome if it had been a girl child, so he didn't ask.

Guyon suspected Nicholas's reasoning, but he needed to ask. "Why would he do that?"

She turned and looked up at his face. "Because he needed an heir, and I offered him one. And he didn't want to lose my lands and title." She nestled back into his arms. "My father had paid him a huge sum, and he didn't want to give it back." A small sob escaped as she continued her sorry tale. "My time came early, and I lost the child a month before he was to be born." She broke off as sobs wracked her body.

Guyon held her close and continued to rock her. Finally, the sobbing stopped and she continued. "When I was healed, I left Lesbury and returned to Nicholas. He was not unkind, although there was never real affection between us." She took a breath. "Finally, after four years of marriage, and no other child, God took pity on me. Nicholas had a brain fever and never fully recovered. After that, if he visited my bed it was for warmth and comfort." She released a deep sigh. "God punished me for my sins, and my penance was to become my husband's nurse. Sometimes he wept in his sleep and I would gather him into my arms as I would a child."

She straightened and turned to face Guyon. "What kind of God would take away my child, and replace him with a child in an old man's body?"

Guyon was incapable of speech. His head throbbed, while his stomach heaved. He swallowed convulsively to prevent himself from vomiting. A cold shiver skated across his skin, yet his face felt hot.

Cicele had moved off his knee and was standing by the hearth gazing into the flames. He wanted to go to her, but his legs wouldn't hold him.

What had he done? He had made decisions based on honor, but in truth he had dishonored the only women he had ever loved.

How could he make it right, all the suffering and death he had caused?

To distract himself he walked to the table and poured two goblets of wine. He handed her one, before moving to the opposite side of the hearth. Now for the truth. Or at least part of the truth.

Taking a fortifying sip of wine, he began. "Cicele, the reason I didn't come back was because I had fallen in the tournament and succumbed to a fever. I lingered close to death for weeks." He couldn't tell her the whole truth, but this was close enough.

"When I discovered you were married and gone to England, I came back to Rouen and pretended my heart was not cleaved in two. In truth, I convinced myself that if you had truly loved me then you would have refused your marriage."

She gave him a look that might have felled him had he not been leaning against the hearth.

"I deluded myself that you were better off without me." Now for the easy part.

"Remeys, as he was then, and not the great Earl Lincoln he is now, had secretly taken Matilda's ward, Alice de Percy, as his mistress. But when he was banished for his assault on you, Matilda refused to let him marry Alice. Then when Matilda found out Alice was carrying Remeys's child she made Alice choose: either she was to go to an abbey where she would take the veil and abandon the child, if it survived. Or, she could marry someone of Matilda's choosing."

Guyon drank from his cup, pleased to see that Cicele had taken a seat and was listening to him. "When you had gone, beyond my reach completely, I made a decision. I couldn't stand by and watch Alice's life ruined, so I offered to marry her. And Matilda agreed."

Cicele almost dropped her goblet. With shaking hands, she put it on the table beside her and clasped her hands in her lap.

"To this day, I believe Lincoln hates me for my interference in both you and Alice's lives. I think he believes I had cheated him out of the lands he desperately wanted." Guyon huffed a digressive laugh. "I didn't care one whit about Remeys, but my father believed that I had raped Alice to get her lands. He never spoke to me again." A pain shot through his chest and began radiating down his arms and legs. "I never got the chance to tell him the truth. He died of shame a few months later."

Guyon couldn't stay still any longer, so he began pacing the floor. "We had only been married a few months when Alice fell down the stairs. She delivered a boy, but neither Alice nor Gervaise, the son she named after my father, survived." Guilt, deep, raw, and uncompromising, swamped him, but he continued.

"What was I to do? In the eyes of most of Matilda's court I had dishonored Alice to gain her lands. Then she was dead. And my reputation was sealed as a beast who would do anything for land. Some even suspected that I had pushed her."

Cicele didn't say anything, but sat staring at him as he sat down again.

"Matilda was the only other person who knew the truth. I am certain that Lincoln won't stop until he possesses you, and sees me destroyed."

Cicele stood up and walked to where he sat. She held out her hands to him. When he took them, she settled herself on his knee and turned her body so she could look at his face. "We were so young and naive to believe that we could tempt fate and marry for love." She gave him a small, sad smile, before cupping his cheek in her hand. "I too named my son."

"You did?"

"His name is Guy, after his father. He was denied a grave in the chapel grounds, so Maude and I buried him in the meadow where I went today."

Guyon tried to make sense of what she said but he couldn't. "He's buried here, at Lesbury?"

"Yes. He was unshriven and denied a consecrated grave, so I buried his little body in the one place I love more than anywhere else on earth."

"You were visiting him when you came across the boys?"

Cicele nodded as tears began sliding down her face.

With the pad of his thumb Guyon wiped her cheek. "I am so sorry, Cicele, can you forgive me?" He had never wanted, no needed, absolution more. If she could not forgive him he would defy the king and release her from the marriage. He knew in his heart that to live with her, but not have her love, would destroy them both. He had to offer her this.

When she didn't answer, but continued to look into his eyes, as though assessing his soul, he made a decision.

"I will release you from the marriage, Cicele." He spoke with a conviction he had never before possessed. "I have caused you so much pain and do not wish to inflict more."

"And who will protect me from Lincoln?" she asked, as a small smile creased her beautiful, sensuous mouth.

He was about to speak but she hushed him with a finger to his lips. "Perhaps we can find comfort in each other again."

He wanted to hold her, to forget all the pain and lies, but he needed to know about his son. "Will you take me to see him?" Guyon didn't dare hope that she would, but he ached to see where his son rested.

A small smile teased the corners of her mouth, but it didn't reach her eyes. "Yes, when you and I have made our peace."

Guyon nodded. It was more than he hoped for.

Cicele reached up to trace her finger along his jaw. "I have never forgotten our time together." She searched his face, a question behind her golden eyes.

Cupping the back of her head, he gently pulled her towards him. She needed to make the move, for he would not force her.

When she lay her lips against his, his heart stopped. He dared not breathe. Her lips warm and soft against his as she spoke. "Make me yours again, Guyon."

He wouldn't think about the half-truths he told. The things left unsaid. Or that he had abandoned her and his son. But he could show her with his body how much he loved her.

Chapter Nineteen

THE KISS SEARED HER SOUL. SHE HAD LONGED FOR THIS SO OFTEN, but also feared it. Not anymore. They had both suffered so much. Neither was more guilty than the other. Cicele realized that now. Her instincts told her to trust this man, a man she had never stopped loving. True, she had hated him for what he had done, and the lie he continued to tell, but she had never stopped loving him. A man who made her cry out in passion when he had brought her to exquisite release.

Denial was something she had cultivated most of her life, but with Guyon she could be the woman she longed to be—free to express herself and marvel in their shared passion. She was his equal both mentally and physically when they made love. She would not deny herself any longer.

"Are you sure?"

Cicele pulled out of his embrace and took a step back.

"Come." Holding out her hand, which he took, she led him from the solar, up the stairs and into her chamber.

They arrived to find Maude supervising a servant who was folding Cicele's clothing. "Leave us." Maude didn't even look up, but shooed the girl and Vite from the room, closing the chamber door behind her.

Cicele released Guyon's hand and stepped away from him.

Without taking her eyes off his, she began to unlace the ties at the side of her gown.

"Let me do that."

She didn't reply, but turned towards him and raised her arm to give him access to the ties on the side of the gown.

"I have dreamed of this for so long, I fear I may wake and find this too is but a dream."

She didn't reply, but let him talk as he unlaced her gown and drew it over her head.

His sure, steady fingers brushed against her ribs making her skin tingle and the hairs on her arms rise in anticipation. It had been years since she had felt the caress of a lover and she was a little afraid.

Her kirtle was next to be removed. The fabric pooled on the floor where Guyon had thrown it in his haste.

All too soon she was facing him in her chemise.

"I am not the girl I was in Rouen."

His eyebrow rose in question, his eyes blazing with desire.

She couldn't hold his gaze. "My body…"

Strong, gentle hands cupped her face. "You are the most beautiful woman I have ever beheld," he whispered, his eyes never leaving hers. "And I long to discover the woman you have become."

What could she say to that? Accepting him at his word, she nodded.

Warm, gentle fingers lifted her chin. "Cicele, look at me."

She did, and what she saw nearly robbed her of breath. Smoldering eyes bore into her. Such desire, such passion, and all for her. It gave her the confidence she needed. Leaning forward she kissed him, not a gentle kiss. Not a chaste kiss. But a kiss that contained all the longing, all the desire she had secretly harbored for this man for years. It seared her soul, dispelling all the shame and frustration that had held her captive for so long.

She bit his lip, drove her tongue into his mouth and waged war with his. She couldn't get enough of his hot, demanding mouth. He responded with as much passion as she did, but he never overpowered her. He was allowing her to take, and she marveled in it.

Finally, breathless, she pulled back, dragging gulps of air into her lungs as she began tugging at his belt.

Frantic, she tore at his clothing. She wanted to feel his skin next to hers. Wanted to feel his strength embrace her. Wanted to be filled with something that she couldn't put into words. Her mind was feverish with need. Every part of her body ached with a need more primal and savage than anything she had ever experienced.

He laughed as he took her hands in his. "I think I like such eagerness in my wife."

"Don't tease me, just take your bloody clothes off."

"As you wish."

Finally, he was naked and standing before her. His body held scars she did not remember, but his body. Dear God. His body was more muscled, more powerful than she remembered. Before her was a male in his prime, and he wanted her. Something urgent and deeply feminine simmered at the core of her being. All this power, all this beauty was hers. She ran her hands over the plane of his stomach, taking delight in his moan as her fingers touched his skin. She stepped back, but he didn't let her escape. His arms engulfed her as he drew her to his chest where he held her tight. Her nipples ached as they brushed against the linen of her chemise as he pulled her into a hard embrace. Her limbs were like melted wax, but it wasn't enough.

"Guyon, please."

He understood.

Scooping her into his arms he walked the few feet to the bed and laid her down. Her body immediately reacted to the loss of contact. But before she could complain he was there, his body covering hers as his mouth devoured her.

Hot. God in heaven, she was so hot.

"Too hot," she gasped.

A tearing sound, then a sudden rush of cool air hit her skin. He had ripped her chemise open to expose her breasts, but before she could comment she was lost in a wave of sensuality that had her writhing on the bed. The heat of his mouth over her breast as he took it into his mouth had her arching towards him for more. His tongue swirled over her nipple, pulling at the ache in her womb. He pulled the torn fabric apart to expose her body. His hands were everywhere—caressing, exploring.

She couldn't think. She couldn't talk. But oh, mercy, she felt and it was glorious.

His mouth crashed over hers as he took her in one swift, powerful thrust. And her body responded with the force of it. Driving her hips up to meet his. It wasn't enough. She wanted more contact, more of him. She wanted to be filled with all that she had lost.

"More." She moaned, trying desperately to gather him into her.

Guyon hooked her leg up and held it over his hip as he plunged into her. Cicele gasped as a wave of pleasure crashed over her. It was fierce, carnal and savage, but she thrilled in the sensation of having her body reach a release that had her seeing stars behind her closed eyes.

A feral groan filled the chamber as Guyon found his own release. Her inner muscles clenched him as he shuddered, spending himself inside her.

They lay together in silence. Their bodies were covered in sweat, but never had she felt so alive. So, invigorated. So fully sated.

Running her hand through his hair she savored the feel of it.

Soft and fine, it slid through her fingers as through water. Releasing a deep breath, she savored the weight of his body over hers.

He lay still, resting his head on her shoulder, enjoying her touch. It reminded her of Vite when she stroked his ears. She huffed a small laugh. "You are as shameless as Vite."

Then his mouth was on hers. Neither demanding or searing, but an affectionate, gentle kiss that spoke of tenderness and love.

Did she dare hope for love? Once perhaps, but now she wasn't so sure. Physical attraction and affection were more than she had hoped when she was told she would marry again. It had to be enough.

When he raised his head as his eyes searched her face. "What is it?"

Forcing herself to smile, she lied, as she reached up and stroked his cheek. "Just thinking when we might do that again."

He rolled onto his side and drew her to him. "That, wife, was merely the first course, but I need a moment before we begin the second."

A few hours later, and true to his word, she felt his growing arousal against her bottom as she nestled into him.

Every inch of her body began to tingle as she rubbed herself against stomach and hips, the hard length of his arousal creating a delicious pool of desire as her own arousal grew. A ferocious hunger began to consume her. Did that make her wanton? Probably, but she didn't care.

Chapter Twenty

CICELE WOKE TO FIND HERSELF IN HER BED. ALONE. A LOVELY languid feeling over her body reminded her of the passion they had shared. Somewhat disappointed to find that she was by herself, she nestled into the warmth waiting for Maude, who would take great delight in rousing her. Cicele allowed herself a satisfied smile as she thought about the look on Maude's face as she was unceremoniously evicted from the chamber the previous night.

She would have to wait as it must still be early. No noise came from the room beyond her curtained bed.

Cicele had gone to sleep in Guyon's arms and had expected to wake with him beside her. They had never spent a night together, and now that she had invited him to her bed she had assumed he would be with her in the morning.

A whimper from behind her curtains told her that Vite was on the other side and would like entrance to his favored spot on her bed. Guyon must have let him in when he left. She fumbled in the dark to pull the bed-curtain back to let him jump up. There he was sitting on the step waiting. Cicele barely had time to draw the curtain before he jumped up onto the bed and gave her a quick lick.

Instead of moving over to lie on the furs at the foot of the huge bed, he began sniffing, his little nose twitching as he investigated the area next to Cicele. "He is not here so you can relax," she chided the dog. "But I suggest you get used to having another male share me."

Vite stopped sniffing, raised his head and looked at her with what she imagined was a look of incredulity. "Yes, a monstrous notion, I agree, but one we will both have to get used to."

"I'm not gone but a few minutes and you have someone else in your bed?" A rumble of laughter followed that ridiculous question.

Cicele was about to grab the curtain but Guyon beat her to it. He was fully dressed.

Disappointment turned her previous joyous mood a little sour, but she strove not to show it. "I was just explaining to his lordship here," she pointed to the dog now sitting by her knees, "that he would have to share me." Cicele watched as Guyon cast a sideways look at the dog. *Males!*

"Is that going to be a problem?"

Cicele laughed when the dog rose from his position and walked over her to get to Guyon. Then he promptly licked Guyon's outstretched hand.

"I should have known you had already won him over," she announced, a slight petulant note to her voice.

Guyon leaned over and kissed her on the mouth. "I rescued him, remember." He kissed her again. "Now, I must go and see to the boys."

With a start Cicele sat up. "What is your decision regarding them?" She had forgotten about the boys. Obviously, sex had addled her brain.

Guyon met her eyes; there was just enough light to discern he was scowling. "I haven't decided, but I shall do nothing till I have had their story from them."

Relief flooded Cicele. They would not lose their lives, or hands. Not today. But she had to make certain they would be safe.

He was about to turn away when she called him back.

"Guyon."

He turned to face her.

"Please show them mercy, they are only children."

He reached over and ran his finger over her lips. "I may be a beast, wife, but never would I harm children." He leaned forward and brushed her lips with a kiss. "Trust me." Then he was gone.

Satisfied that the boys would not be harmed, Cicele lay back down but before she closed her eyes Maude pulled back the curtains. "Good morn, my lady, shall I have a bath prepared near the fire?"

Cicele groaned. She didn't want to face Maude and her questions, but the thought of a bath was too tempting to refuse. She would soak in the bath relishing the warmth on the deliciously tender parts of her body.

"I will endure your questions," Cicele stated. "But not before a bath and something to eat." She was famished.

"Have an appetite, do you?" Maude smirked.

But before Cicele could reply Maude had walked away to organize viands and prepare a bath.

Cicele wrapped her cloak around her naked body and walked to where a fire was roaring in the hearth. While she sat waiting for Maude's return, she thought about her future with Guyon and perhaps, just perhaps, she could begin to trust him again.

THOMAS MET Guyon as he entered the hall. "You didn't tell her, did you?"

Guyon was in no mood to have this discussion, so he walked past Thomas without a word. Guyon didn't want to think about anything, especially the fact that he lay with his wife, but had not told her the truth. Hell's teeth, what was he thinking? If she found out that he continued to lie, then she would surely leave him. Last night had been incredible. His memories of their time together in Rouen paled in comparison to the reality of last night. Never had he had such a deep, teeth-clenching climax before. Every fiber of his body hummed with the awareness of his wife, and she was two floors away in her chamber. Naked.

Not one to be easily thwarted, Thomas interrupted his thoughts and continued to speak his mind. "You must tell her before she finds out."

"Where is Warin," Guyon asked, trying to deflect Thomas's unsolicited counsel.

"He is with the boys," Thomas replied. But as was his way he started again where he had left off. "Guyon, you must—"

"Enough!" Guyon growled. Then he thought better of his outburst. "I know what I must do, but first things first," he said as he gave Thomas a conspiratorial wink. "I have to punish some poachers."

Sir Nigel approached as they walked through the hall. "My lord, do you wish me to deal with the poachers?"

"No, I shall deal with them myself, but join us."

The three men strode through the hall and out into the bailey. Warin was leaning against the stone wall of the chapel waiting for them.

"Have they eaten?"

"Aye, my lord."

"All of you, follow me."

Guyon swung open the door to the infirmary and walked into the semidarkness of the hut. The four boys were seated around a table eating some bread and fruit. As soon as they saw him they fled to the furthest wall and huddled together.

Guyon stood by the table resting his gloved knuckles on it as he glowered at the boys.

The littlest boy began whimpering. It was a plaintive sound, but Guyon ignored it. The largest of the boys, who was probably the oldest brother, tried to keep him quiet, but to no avail.

"You." Guyon spoke to the eldest boy. "What were you doing in my forest?"

The boy was physically trembling. He wore clothing that was too big for him, but at least it was clean. His head had been shaved and looked too big for his skinny body. It seemed he didn't have the wit to answer.

"You scare him, lord," Warin whispered behind Guyon.

"Of course I scare him; they are poachers, and I hang poachers."

Another little boy began whimpering. What a pitiful lot they were. Guyon walked to where the oldest boy stood trying to protect his smaller, terrified siblings. "What is your name," Guyon asked in a more patient voice.

The boy was brave, Guyon would give him that. He was probably only ten or eleven summers old, but he squared his shoulders, not in defiance, but in resolution. "My name is Harry, lord. Harry of Alnmouth."

"And what were you doing in my forest, Harry of Alnmouth?"

Harry turned to look at his brothers. "We were hungry."

Guyon had expected that. "Where are your parents?" Guyon prodded. "But, Harry of Alnmouth, don't lie to me." It was not uncommon for parents to send their children out to poach, reasoning they would not incur the wrath of the lord they were poaching from. Guyon would set them straight if that were the case.

"No, lord." He wet his trembling lips but continued to meet Guyon's eye. "Dead, lord, the last full moon."

The boy looked at the bread and milk on the table.

"You may sit, all of you, and eat."

When they had settled at the table Guyon motioned for Harry to continue.

"The sickness came." Harry swiped the back of his hand over his eyes. "When Ma got sick, and the babe, she told me to take them," he said, jerking his head towards the three other boys. "And run to the woods. She said she would fetch us." A single tear glistened on his cheek. "But she never came."

Guyon turned and looked at Thomas, who understood the unspoken message and left the hut with Sir Nigel. There had been sickness throughout the region, but it paid to check Harry's story. Thomas would check with Sir Nigel and the village alderman at Alnmouth. That was, if Sir Nigel wasn't already aware that sickness had decimated the village of Alnmouth. And if he had, and had not done anything about it, Guyon would be having words with the steward. It was unacceptable to have villagers resort to poaching to survive.

Guyon turned back to Harry and his brothers. He wondered at the boy's ability to keep his younger brothers safe, and fed, for so long.

"Who was your father?" Guyon was beginning to piece this story together with another story he had heard from Brother Martin.

"Harold of Alnmouth, lord."

"When did you last see your father?"

"The bailiff came and took him to Alnwick, lord, but he didn't come back." Harry broke down in tears then. Guyon took the boy and held him against his chest, letting the lad weep for all his suffering and loss.

When Harry was once again in control and sitting with his brothers at the table Guyon continued to question him.

"When did the bailiff come?" Guyon suspected it was towards the end of Odard's tenure as sheriff that Harry's father, like so many others, had been arrested. That was almost a year ago.

Guyon had to wait until Harry had finished chewing the food in his mouth before the boy replied. "They came two days after All Saints day."

"When he didn't return what happened?" Guyon asked.

The lad gave him a forlorn look. "My ma did what she could, but when she got sick I were told to watch the boys." Harry took a deep breath. "That's where you found us."

"Did your father have a trade?"

Harry puffed out he skinny chest. "My father was a plowman, he worked as a day laborer, lord," he announced with great pride. So, they were free, not villeins.

"What happened to your father's plow and oxen?"

Harry swallowed his mouthful of food. "The bailiff took 'em when he took my da."

Guyon would have Thomas check with Sir Nigel to ensure Harry did indeed speak the truth, although Guyon believed him.

Anger, hot and seething, erupted in his gut. Odard was a fucking disgrace. If he wasn't already dead, Guyon would rip his black heart out and shove it down his throat.

He watched the boys eat as he tried to calm his breathing.

When his anger was again under control he spoke. "Do you or your brothers have any skills, besides poaching my coney?" Harry's eyes slid to the floor, his teeth worrying at his lower lip.

A movement behind him alerted Guyon to Cicele's presence. The fragrance of lavender she brought with her was unmistakable. Ignoring his wife, Guyon made a decision. "Warin, take the boys to the stables, they can assist the grooms until I decide what to do with them."

Cicele stopped Guyon with her arm across his chest as he went to leave the infirmary. "The two smallest are too young to work; perhaps they can be fostered by one of the men who has family willing to take them in?" She spoke quietly so Warin and the boys wouldn't hear what she said.

Guyon kept his expression neutral, but he wasn't surprised she had suggested just that. His wife was a rare woman. Her rank and wealth were beyond equal, yet she was neither arrogant nor self-absorbed. When it came to dealing with those in need she was like a she-wolf protecting her cubs. He recalled Ebeta, and the furor Cicele's actions caused. He huffed a small laugh; she was bloody proud when she wanted to be, and a might haughty, but that was usually only with him. In truth, he admired her willingness to become involved with those in need.

He made a pretense at looking at the boys, especially the littlest ones. "Very well. Warin, ask Sir Nigel to make the necessary arrangements to have the boys fostered. They are Lesbury's responsibility now."

Guyon took Cicele's arm and led her out the door and around to the side of the small hut. "A word."

She looked at his hand around her arm before meeting his eye. "My lord?" Her eyes flared with annoyance. Instinctively he released her. They had shared a bed and reacquainted themselves with each other, yet she was not as biddable as he hoped. That wasn't true. He didn't want her biddable and simpering. He loved her sharp tongue and her defiance. *You are a clot, Guyon le Loup.*

"I would have you stay, if that is your wish." He couldn't quite bring himself to apologize for his order to have her return to Alnwick. She had disobeyed him, and his worry for her safety made him react with anger. But now he couldn't bear to see her go. It had to be her choice, and he would abide by it. She had given him her body, but he wasn't stupid enough to think she had forgiven him.

Golden eyes searched his face, probing. Without thinking, he cupped her cheek, wanting, needing, to touch her. To reassure her.

Cicele took his hand from her cheek and pressed a kiss on the tips of his fingers. Even through the thick nap of his gloves Guyon felt the press of her lips on his fingertips. "Then, my lord husband, I wish to stay."

She was about to turn and walk away but again he reached out to claim her arm. "Cicele."

She turned. "My lord." A knowing smile danced about her lips.

"Minx," Guyon growled as he drew her none too gently against his chest and claimed her mouth.

THE KISS LEFT her a little lightheaded. She could get used to this as she melted against his chest.

"Come, I have something I want to show you."

They walked through the bailey and back into the hall and up the stairs to Guyon's solar. She had never intruded on Sir Nigel's solar, but as Guyon was now Lesbury's lord, the solar was his.

They entered a door that led into a small receiving chamber. Guyon led her through the door on the left and into a large chamber which was dominated by a huge table that had various parchments spread on its surface. Instead of offering her a chair he stopped beside the table, and pointed to what looked like drawings of a building.

"This is a plan for stables. What do you think?" His eyes were burning with something she didn't recognize.

"Stables?" She was confused.

"Yes, for Nyssa, and the other mares you will need if you want to start breeding palfreys."

All the air seemed to leave the room. She couldn't quite catch her breath, and her lungs began to tingle from lack of air.

"Cicele, are you well?"

There was a note of panic in his voice, but she couldn't answer.

He led her to a chair by the fire and then poured her a cup of wine. "Drink this."

Obediently she sipped her wine, but her mind refused to work. It wasn't just words. He had been thinking about her dream of breeding palfreys, and had designed stables.

Tears rolled down her cheeks as she looked upon his handsome face. His eyes were worried as he watched her. She loved that face.

Fierce, dark brown eyes roved over her face. "Cicele?"

"I am well, Guyon, just overcome with surprise that you would do such a thing."

He looked at her blankly. Reaching up to cup his face she giggled. "I am happy, just overcome. Thank you."

Recovering from his momentary confusion he smiled. "Well you haven't seen it yet, and you might want to add some changes."

He was like a small boy in his excitement. And that excitement was contagious.

Rising, she walked back to the table and studied the plans, but she couldn't really understand what she was looking at. "Show me."

They spent the rest of the morning discussing the plans the seneschal, Sir Roderick, and Guyon had made. The stables would be built on the large flat meadow on the southwest side of the castle. A small tower and a stone wall would enclose the stables and protect the mares and foals from the weather until they were old enough to be out in the larger paddocks.

"I have the stonemason and his men arriving the day after the feast day of the Purification of the Virgin. They will have enough stone ready to begin construction in spring." The Virgin's feast day was on the second of February. A week away. That meant that they would start to build in less than three months. She could hardly contain her excitement. Her dream was going to become a reality. And it was all due to her husband. Love for him surged through her heart, making her catch her breath.

"Oh, Guyon, I don't know what to say."

"'Thank you' would be a good start." He gave her a mischievous grin. He seemed as delighted as she was, which gave her a warm glow.

"When can we buy a stallion and more mares?"

Guyon shifted his gaze from Cicele back to the plans on the

table. That small evasion had her on alert. All the warmth of a moment ago evaporated, until only the familiar mistrust, from years of disappointment, remained.

"I have a contract for a stallion and four mares. I expect them to arrive mid-June."

"Then why do you look so guilty?"

He bristled, but instead of barking at her, he took a breath and spoke quietly. "I thought you might have been disappointed that you didn't get to choose the stallion and mares yourself. I'm sorry."

She wanted to laugh, but didn't. "You great lump of a man, of course I'm not upset. Do you have details of the horses you purchased? I'm keen to see what you have chosen." She took his face in her hands and stood on tiptoes to kiss him.

She had never remembered a time when her heart was so full.

IN THE TWO days since the boys had been caught, life at Lesbury passed in a whirl of activity. Guyon now came to her chamber after the evening meal, and they played chess and talked of the plans for the stables, and the horses that would be arriving in the summer. Last night it had become a game to see who could disrobe the fastest, before they fell upon each other in their desperation to sate their hunger. Even now, Cicele's cheeks burned with embarrassment at her wanton behavior.

Lincoln was never spoken of, but he was never far from Cicele's thoughts. Guyon had mentioned only that morning that Thomas still had no news of Agatha. But more worrying was his report that Sir Ingram Rainecourt, the steward of Edlington Castle, had sent a messenger to say that Lincoln, along with his snake, Eustace de Sayre, had been seen close to the hills surrounding the castle. Edlington Castle protected the western route to Alnwick. If Lincoln laid siege to Edlington, then Alnwick would be in danger. Guyon had sent extra men to protect Edlington and the road, but Cicele was sure Lincoln was preparing for an attack. Guyon listened to her fears, then he soothed her worries with a passionate kiss as they sat in his solar talking about the plans for the stables. "Fear not, wife, Lincoln will not harm you. That, I vow."

She had accepted his word, but still the fear niggled at her resolve to believe that Lincoln was not a threat.

As she was walking through the deserted bailey after seeing Nyssa in the stables, she heard grunting, then laughter, coming from the tilt yard.

Investigating, she walked to the gate and peered in the direction of the noise. Guyon was holding a wooden training sword and trying to deflect the blows Thomas was raining down on him. Careful not to alert them to her presence Cicele moved closer, but stayed behind a small group of men who had gathered to watch.

Guyon and Thomas were not alone, Warin and another boy also held wooden training swords, mimicking their lord's movements. It seemed the lord and his captain were demonstrating various fighting positions. A high-pitched squeal of delight made her look closer. There, sitting like a row of swallows on a bench beside the wall of the gatehouse, were the boys who had been caught in the woods poaching. Three of them were watching their older brother whack Warin's sword. Cicele was no expert, but she could see Harry had absolutely no idea what he was doing.

Stifling her own laughter, she moved back into the shadows and watched as Guyon stopped what he was doing and walked to where Harry was gallantly trying to protect himself from Warin's merciless onslaught.

Guyon forced his own wooden sword in between the two boys and called a halt to the farce. "You have heart, lad, I will grant you that," he said to Harry.

That's when Cicele saw that Harry's left eye was almost closed, the fragile skin swelling and already turning an angry purple.

"First rule of swordplay is to protect yourself. Like so." Guyon drove his sword up and into a defensive position from which he could counterattack. "And to keep your feet in the right place," he instructed as he demonstrated.

"Now, your turn."

Cicele decided not to stay, but crept away hoping none of the men would alert Guyon to her presence. Guyon was taking the time to show the boys that this was their home, and that they would have a role in the life, and defense, of the castle. Each man, whether knight, man-at-arms, or cook were all trained to fight to protect their lord, and his property.

A deep, searing pain shot through Cicele's chest and up into her throat. Guyon would never know the joy of teaching his own son such important skills, and it almost threatened to bring Cicele to her knees right there in the bailey.

Forcing herself to walk slowly, she made her way through the bailey and into the hall, and up the stone stairs into her chamber. When she was safely behind closed doors she crumpled to the floor and wept for what would never be.

And for the first time she realized that she was not only grieving for her own loss, she was also grieving for Guyon and what she could never give him—a son to bear his name.

Chapter Twenty-One

As she lay in her bed Cicele pondered her growing love for Guyon. The scene in the tilt yard the previous day ran through her mind; however, a nagging doubt continued to whisper, no matter how much she tried to ignore it. *He will leave you; be careful.* Just when it seemed happiness was within her grasp her fears doubled. Try as she might to deny it, the fear was real, and easy to believe. He had done it before.

This war between happiness and a sense of foreboding plagued her. Unrelenting, it discolored the very fabric of their relationship. There were precious moments when she was aware of his eyes devouring her as she sat at the dais eating their meals or playing chess. She gave a little shudder recollecting their time together last night, branding her with his touch. His mouth. Yet the fear that it would all turn to dust stalked her waking moments.

It didn't help that Guyon never seemed to stay in bed. Every morning when she woke he was gone. Perhaps he rose early? But last night she had woken in the hours before dawn to find he was not in their bed. She had waited for what seemed an eternity, but fell back to sleep before he returned. But he hadn't—the bed was cold to the touch as she slid her hand towards where she expected him to be lying.

Where was he? Didn't he enjoy their time together? Sometimes she caught a shadow behind his eyes when he thought she wasn't looking. He was hiding something. She was sure of it. To confront him would surely jeopardize the nascent trust they were rebuilding together. Accustomed to living with the gnawing fear that she would once again be rejected, Cicele had lived her life never daring to confront those who held the emotional power in her relationships.

Maude interrupted her thoughts when she entered the chamber and began chatting to Vite. The dog had chosen to leave the bed and claim his favored spot by the hearth when he had heard a servant come in earlier and rekindle the fire.

"Is your mistress awake, or is she wasting the day away in bed with that great lump of a man?" Maude spoke quietly, but Cicele could hear her.

"I'm here, Maude, and alone," Cicele moaned.

The bed-curtains were ripped back, letting the light from the chamber illuminate the bed. "He's not here?" Maude asked as she inspected the empty space next to Cicele.

It was too embarrassing, so Cicele avoided Maude's eyes and slid from the bed and walked to the garderobe.

When she returned, Maude had her clothing spread out on the bed, which was being made by another young servant.

Cicele didn't want to discuss her husband's absence with a servant present so she remained silent.

Thankfully, Maude must have understood her hesitance to speak so freely when servants were about, so she also remained quiet. That, in itself, was a miracle. Maude was never silent.

Cicele was dressed and her hair braided when the servant left and Maude began her questioning. "He arises early."

It was not a question. It was a statement and Maude wanted

details, but for some reason Cicele didn't want to share. Shame at her inability to keep her husband in her bed burned in her cheeks.

"It is his way," Cicele huffed, hoping Maude would get the hint that she didn't want to discuss it.

Maude swung Cicele's head around and held her chin in her hand. Wanting to squirm out from under her maid's intense gaze, Cicele tried to move her chin, but Maude wouldn't let it go.

"What is it, child?" Maude's expression was one of love and concern. Cicele had no defenses from such a look.

"He never stays with me," she cried as she slung her arms around Maude's waist. "Oh, Maude, perhaps I don't please him," she sobbed into her maid's apron. Her nerves couldn't sustain another day of doubt and anxiety.

Her worst fear rose unbidden—she was not the young girl she had been when they had been lovers in Rouen. She was now almost three and twenty. An old woman who was unable to give her husband an heir. Cicele was all too aware that her body bore the ugly scars of her ill-fated pregnancy. Who could desire a woman whose body was a constant reminder that she was defective? Their time in bed was passionate, but held none of the leisurely affection she remembered from their shared summer in Rouen.

Maude remained silent, which was more telling than anything. Cicele pulled herself back from her maid's embrace and looked up into her eyes.

"What?" Cicele didn't like what she saw in her maid's expression. A pitying look that made Cicele's blood run cold and her stomach hitch. *She knows something and isn't going to tell me.* Oh, sweet Jesu, it was like last time! Cicele had been the last to know that Guyon had been married. Of course, she reasoned, why would she be told. Their time together had been a secret. Cicele tried not to panic, but her skin became clammy and her head felt fit to burst as her heartbeat thundered in her ears.

"Tell me," she whimpered.

Maude stood completely still. Vite came and stretched himself up on Cicele's knee wanting to check that she was well. Cicele flicked his ears, but didn't pick him up. She wanted answers, but Maude seemed to be struck dumb.

"Maude, please," Cicele pleaded, as she took her maid's hands in hers. "What do you know, but are not telling me?"

Cicele's touch must have shaken Maude out of her stupor, for she gave her head a little shake, and took a deep breath. "I couldn't sleep so went for some wine and when I was coming back I saw him go to his solar, but I thought he came back to you." Her voice was little more than a whisper. "Are you telling me that he didn't come back?"

He never comes back, but Cicele couldn't make her tongue move, it was stuck to the roof of her mouth, so she nodded instead.

Always one to be practical, Maude came up with a suggestion before Cicele had even drawn breath. "Well then, child, I suggest you talk to the man."

It sounded so simple. *Guyon, why don't you stay with me?* Or maybe something a little more confrontational. *Guyon, where are you sleeping, and with whom?* Cicele wanted to cry, but forced herself to stand and straighten her kirtle. "I will not pry into my husband's sleeping arrangements. It is not uncommon for the lord to sleep in another chamber," Cicele said emphatically, but one look at Maude and she knew she didn't sound convincing.

With a sinking heart Cicele walked over to the little alcove where her prie-dieu stood. She took the elaborately decorated psalter—the one that had belonged to her mother—from the sloping shelf, and tried to turn her mind to God, but her emotions were in too much turmoil to devote herself to prayer.

She had taken the risk to trust Guyon and let him back into her heart, but perhaps she had been too hasty. He was not the same man she had loved all those years ago. There was a darkness, a ruthlessness, to him that hadn't been there before. It frightened her, but clot that she was, it also tempted her. She needed to remind herself there was also a kindness, and a generosity that balanced his darker nature. She wanted to soothe his brow when she caught glimpses of him scowling. There was a weight that burdened him and she was sure it wasn't connected to the king or Lincoln. Something dogged him.

Well, she would find out before she made herself sick with fear that he would cast her aside again. It was all too easy to believe that she was unworthy of his affection, but she would not give up on her future with him without a fight.

Resolved to confront him, Cicele finished reading the psalm she had chosen. Then she stood and walked through her chamber, calling for Vite to come. Guyon would be with his men in the tilt yard practicing. So that's where she would go.

He wasn't there. Deflated, Cicele decided to go for a ride. It had rained during the night and although the ground was wet, the sun shone. As she walked to the stables a cold wind had her shivering inside her cloak. Summoning a groom, she asked for Nyssa to be saddled. The mare was a docile creature who seemed to understand Cicele's moods. She would be able to ride her until they went back to Alnwick. Guyon had not said when that would be, but Cicele thought it might be soon.

Not wanting a confrontation like last time, Cicele decided she wouldn't go far, and Vite could run with her. They had been at the castle six days, and still she had not ridden out with Guyon. Biting back the disappointment that she had not been able to show him her favorite spots where she had hunted or fished as a child, she decided she would venture to the river. It would be safe to ride out alone.

It was a bit churlish of her to be so upset, but she was a little nettled that he had left without saying farewell. There was so much he seemed to hide from her, and she didn't like it. The joy of their passion the previous evening was a distant memory now. She couldn't shift her growing sense of disquiet over her husband's absence from her bed.

While she waited for her horse to be readied, she asked a stable boy to fetch her bow and arrow. She might find something to hunt while out riding. She fingered her belt, where the knives were concealed in a slim slit on the inside of her belt. Isabeau had given it to her as a Christmas gift, and Cicele cherished it. She could have done with it when she had been abducted. Well, perhaps not. It would probably have been stolen.

A small thrill skidded down her spine when a page came with her bow and a quiver of arrows. Guyon would be furious, but what harm could come from riding in the woods so close to the castle? Guyon was being overprotective to forbid her. She would be fine.

Convincing herself that she was in the right, she rode through the main gate and turned onto the road that led through the fields and towards the woods and the river. Vite ran beside her as she trotted Nyssa past fields where men were plowing the soil in preparation for sowing the barley, wheat, and rye. None of the men paid her any attention, but the small children, whose task it was to remove the stones from the soil as the plow tilled the rich dark earth, waved. Smiling, she waved back.

The sounds and smell of the castle grew fainter the further she rode. Slowing to allow Vite to catch his breath, Cicele breathed in the fresh winter air. It was cold and crisp and burned her lungs as she breathed it in.

A red squirrel with a glorious tail scurried up a tree, scolding her as she rode by. It was too dangerous to gallop through the trees, so she walked Nyssa, with Vite trotting behind.

Tying Nyssa to a low branch so she could crop the grass, Cicele walked to the river's edge. The Aln was narrow at this point, but began to widen the further east it flowed. In the distance she could see the river wending its way towards Alnwick. Lesbury was a tiny village, but now that a charter had been issued for Alnmouth to have a port, Lesbury would grow and prosper. All the trade from the port would be barged up the Aln to Lesbury and on to Alnwick. The tolls would pay for the new stables.

Cicele was just about to walk along the riverbank when Vite growled. Turning, she saw a man step out from behind the trees and into the light.

"Should you be here by yourself, my lady?" he purred as he strode towards her.

Immediately, Cicele knew she was in trouble. He was too close for her to make a dash to her horse and get away. Where were his men hiding? Without conscious thought she slid her bow from her shoulder and notched an arrow.

"I am alone," he said as he raised his hands in the air to assure her he was no threat.

Surprised by his unexpected appearance she said the first thing that came into her head. "I'm surprised." It wouldn't pay to antagonize him, but she was too angry to heed her own advice. "Your master has sent his dog to do his bidding. Again pulling the arrow back she sighted it to his neck. Fifteen paces separated them, just enough for an arrow to do some damage.

A sly smile slid across his weasel-like features, but it was his eyes that made Cicele's skin crawl. They were completely devoid of emotion. If they weren't so green, she could almost believe she was looking into the eyes of a serpent.

He took a step towards her, but Vite barked and stood in front of her. "I see that creature has no sense, much like his mistress," he drawled.

"He is discerning, and finds your presence as distasteful as I do." She stood to her full height, which admittedly wasn't much, but she would never cow before this man. The memory of his rough handling when he captured her outside Beauforde's walls still made her gorge rise. Her arm began to shake under the pressure of holding the arrow taut against her cheek.

He placed his hands before him, palms up. "Calm yourself."

How did he know she would be here? A sickening thought popped into her head. He must have spies in the castle. That gave her pause. She and Guyon were being watched.

Cicele hitched her chin fractionally higher than was natural, but she wanted to give the impression she was not intimated by him.

"I merely wish to talk with you. Please, can we at least be civil?"

"You abducted me, and would have aided your master in raping me and then forcing me into a godless marriage," she spat. "Whatever you have to say I have no wish to hear it." She would not show him the fear that clawed up her spine and soured her stomach, robbing her mouth of moisture.

She took the chance to back away from him and move towards her horse, but he stepped in between her and Nyssa. She stopped and glared at him. "Get out of my way or I will let my arrow fly," she demanded, but she didn't move. He could easily catch her if she tried to run.

He took a step towards her. No! She would never let him capture her. She released the arrow, her bowstring quivering under the strain.

He spat a curse as his hand went to his ear, which was red with blood.

"You stupid little whore, I will fuck you senseless myself, then send you back to that cur you call a husband," he snarled as his hand cupped his ruined ear. Small droplets of blood dripped on his surcoat, but instead of lunging at her he took a step back.

Cicele dropped her bow, opting for her knife instead. She withdrew it from her belt and aimed at his right eye, just as Jabbe had taught her. "You will never touch me, and if you don't leave, you will never see out of that eye again." A small smile danced at the corners of her mouth as her threat seemed to give him pause.

"Your husband is a dead man, and after Lincoln is finished with you, I will have you." He gave her a sickening smile. "And when I'm finished, you will wish to God you never blooded me."

The cruelty in his voice turned her blood to ice, but she didn't relax her arm, although her muscles burned from holding her arm steady.

A distant thundering sound coming from the direction of the castle broke the deadly silence. For one terrible moment Cicele thought it might be more of Lincoln's men, but a look of panic slid behind the cruel eyes of the man that stood in front of her. If she hadn't been concentrating on his face she might have missed it. "So, you *are* by yourself," she mocked.

Relief and something close to shock almost made her lose her concentration. Even now he could still abduct her before Guyon's men arrived.

Straightening her back she steadied her arm, flexing her fingers against the cold steel of her knife. "If you value your life, I suggest you scurry back to the hole from which you crawled before my husband guts you from your balls to your nose." She had never spoken so crudely to anyone in her life, but the man standing before her was nothing but a viper. She would never pity him.

The sound of approaching horses became a little louder.

"Did he tell you what he did to Lady Alice?" His snarl making his lips curl. An ugly parody of a smile.

A shiver of revulsion crawled up her neck, but she didn't answer; all her concentration was reserved for keeping her aim true.

"Your gallant husband covets land." He gave her another sickening smile. "And he has always coveted yours."

"You lie. It was your master who defiled Alice, then sought to do the same to me." A cold calmness descended upon her. "You serve the devil." Hate. Deep, unrelenting hate, surged through her veins. She would never allow him to take her. Not again.

Without warning, he lunged.

In an instant she adjusted her stance and let the knife fly. Thin and deadly, it struck true. Sir Eustace de Sayre, the Earl of Lincoln's henchman, howled as the knife pierced his eye. Blood sprayed as the blade punched through the eye socket, coming to a quivering halt as it lodged in his brain.

De Sayre fell to his knees, then as though drunk, he fell on his side. Dead.

Cicele stood her ground, but her legs began to tremble. She couldn't stop her body shaking. She dare not move, for her legs wouldn't hold her if she did.

The horses were so close now she could hear their snorting as they raced towards her.

A little drunk with shock from having survived the ordeal, Cicele could do nothing but stand and stare vacantly at the body that lay on the ground in front of her.

On seeing the blood seep from his ruined face her legs, weak as warmed wax, folded beneath her. Retching, she vomited bile so bitter it burned her throat.

Strong hands clasped her shoulders. "My lady?"

Wiping her mouth, she turned her head to see Thomas standing beside her. Reaching over her shoulder she followed his hand to see she gripped another knife in her left hand. Her fingers wouldn't obey her brain to release it.

"That, my lady, was a magnificent throw."

Hysterical laughter bubbled up her seared throat. Shrieking like the mad woman she had seen as a child, Cicele sat and laughed for what seemed an eternity.

Finally, the panic receded, but still lurked just beneath the surface.

"Come, lady." Thomas spoke gently, but with an authority that Cicele appreciated.

"I killed him."

A smile akin to a snarl revealed white teeth. "Mayhap you could show your lord husband how to use a blade." Thomas's expression relaxed into a genuine smile. "God knows, he needs the help."

She nodded. His humor seemed to relax her. How absurd, but her relief was palpable as she took his outstretched hand as he helped her stand.

Her horse was brought to her. Thomas knelt to let her stand on his knee so she could mount Nyssa. "Thank you, Thomas."

A roguish smile again appeared on his expressive face. "Can I be present when you tell him?"

Oh God. Guyon.

Chapter Twenty-Two

Cicele sat, too stunned to do more than that. Maude had prepared a bath, undressed her, and tried to coax her into the tub that sat in front of the hearth, but Cicele wanted to be alone.

God knows how long she sat staring into the flames, but she couldn't seem to make her body obey her.

Without warning the door banged open and Guyon stormed in.

"Is it true?" he barked as he stood over her. Instead of relief she reacted with something matching his own truculence.

"You march in here like some rutting bull bellowing something I have neither the wit nor the patience to discern."

That response seemed to stall his temper. "I apologize, but I have just been informed that de Sayre had been seen by the river," he replied in a quieter voice, but his expression was hard as flint. "As you are the only woman with a horse, and were seen riding towards the river, I was worried."

Thomas must not have given Guyon the full account. She eyed him for several heartbeats, her own temper frayed, but she managed to take a calming breath before she answered.

"I will talk to you when you are calmer, and I am assured you won't resume bellowing at me." Although seated and at a disadvantage, she tried for an imperious tone.

With a dramatic huff Guyon slumped into a chair by the fire and gazed at it for several moments. Vite had come over to sniff a welcome and Guyon bent over and scooped the dog up onto his lap. Like her, Guyon had also learned that petting Vite was a sure way to regain one's composure.

She waited.

Finally, he turned his head to look at her. There was a desolate expression on his face that Cicele had never seen before.

"What?"

"I was riding out to oversee the planting on the southern edge of my estate at High Buston when we surprised a group of armed men. We gave chase but they eluded capture. I recognized one of Lincoln's men, so when I returned and one of the guards said he had seen you ride towards the river I almost lost my wits." The words came out in a rush. "I was terrified that he had taken you."

"Have you spoken to Thomas?"

A confused look settled on his face. "No, not since this morning when I left."

Cicele stood and came over to where Guyon sat. She tilted his chin up so he would look at her. "I have something to tell you, but please do not interrupt me," she asked as she offered him a weak smile.

"Cicele—"

"Please, Guyon."

When he nodded and remained quiet she walked back to where she had been sitting, but when she got there she didn't want to sit. Anxiety and something she didn't recognize nibbled at her frayed nerves. "I rode out to the river." She gave him a contrite look. "I took my hunting bow with me, and de Sayre was there."

"Did he touch you?"

She almost lost patience then but managed to hold her temper in check. "Of course not!" she snapped. "He didn't defile me if that's what you meant."

"I meant." He released a slow breath blown between clenched teeth. "Did he hurt you." His self-control was hanging by a thread, as was her own.

"No, he didn't hurt me, but I killed him." Saying it out loud only increased her apprehension. She had killed a knight of the realm. A pox-ridden cur of a knight. But Lincoln would see her hang for it.

Guyon raised his eyebrow in silent question.

"I grazed his ear with an arrow, but when he tried to grab me, I threw my knife which went through the eye." Feeling almost overcome with exhaustion she slumped to the floor. "I—" She couldn't finish. The tiny spark of self-control she had been nursing all morning finally evaporated, and she didn't have the energy to pretend a courage she didn't possess.

Guyon rose and came to crouch before her, placing his hands on her cheek. "Look at me, Cicele." His voice was warm and comforting.

When she did, he smiled. "To kill someone is a fearful thing. But God knows, the man would have abducted you and taken you back to Lincoln." He bussed a kiss on her tear-streaked cheek. "You did well to protect yourself."

"Am I to stand trial?" She could imagine Lincoln would do whatever he could to try and get her away from Guyon. And it terrified her.

Shaking his head Guyon reassured her that all would be well. "I am the Lord High Sheriff, and de Sayre was seen poaching on my land." He raised his hand to stop her when she was about to correct him. "And, as Lord High Sheriff, I have the right to execute poachers on sight." The memory of the boys flooded Cicele's mind.

"You would lie for me?"

"I would storm the very gates of Hell, and challenge Lucifer himself, if it meant I could protect you."

He turned and seemed to notice the tub for the first time. "Come." He lifted her to her feet, then slowly, with infinite care he removed her cloak and her chemise, then led her to the tub. When she had settled into the hot water, he knelt beside her.

Picking up the wash rag, he plunged it into the water and began to drizzle hot water over her shoulders and arms. It immediately relaxed her, so she sank down deeper letting the hot water embrace her.

"Close your eyes."

She obeyed without objection. Strong fingers massaged her head, moving down to her shoulders, kneading her tense muscles until they felt like liquid.

He didn't say anything as he took the washcloth and washed the terror and filth of the morning off her body.

She couldn't think. Couldn't concentrate, so she submitted to his care.

When he had finished, and the water was too cool for her to remain in the tub, he held up a towel, which she stepped into as his arms wrapped around her body.

Taking her in his arms he walked to the fire and sat, resting her on his knee. Then he dried her hair, her back, and her arms.

"Stand up."

She obeyed. Her mind numb, she had not the energy to think, only to obey his directions.

He stood before her, and began to dry her neck, her breasts, her stomach. Gentle strokes. Not seductive, but protective. Cicele was transported back to a time when she was a child standing before the fire as Maude dried her after her bath. A sense of safety and contentment settled into her as she stood and let her husband see to her needs. Finally, he lifted her leg and placed her foot on his bended knee so he could dry it. First the right, then the left.

When she was dry, he dressed her in a fresh chemise that Maude had laid out on the bed. Then he wrapped her in her cloak and sat her on the chair by the fire.

He poured a goblet of wine and handed it to her. "Drink."

She could barely hold the goblet she was so tired and weak. Sensing she struggled, he took the cup and held it to her lips. "Drink, my love."

When she had taken several sips, he picked her up and laid her on the bed.

"Sleep, then when you are rested, we will talk."

Cicele didn't want to sleep. Fear that she would replay the scene over and over in her head plagued her. "I can't."

Guyon gave her a devastating smile. "I'll help." He lay beside her and held her to his chest. "I'm here, Cicele, now rest. You are safe."

She closed her eyes as his fingers trailed tiny circles up and down her arm. Never had she felt so loved, so cherished. It almost broke her heart.

SHE MUST HAVE SLEPT because when she woke she could see it was dark outside. Turning her head from the pillow, she saw Guyon sitting by the fire. The bathtub had been taken and a tray of food lay on the table.

Sitting up in bed she stretched and claimed her cloak, then padded on silent feet to join Guyon by the fire.

When he saw her, he rose. His eyes, the color of darkest night searched her face in an unspoken question.

She smiled and leaned in to kiss him. "Thank you," she whispered against his lips.

Guyon clasped her to his chest and returned the kiss. His was neither gentle, or chaste, but demanding and urgent. "I don't know what I would have done if he had taken you," he growled against the crown of her head. He had released her from his kiss, but not his arms. "Lincoln won't rest till he has you. Which would destroy me." Guyon ran a hand through her hair.

"De Sayre said you only wanted my land."

"And you believed him?" There was a resigned note to his voice that spoke of his disappointment, and probably regret. Men like Lincoln and Guyon took what they wanted. Even the king was weary of their power. Lincoln was powerful, but he was also cruel. She looked at her husband and understood his claim on her heart. He was not cruel, but he was dangerous. God help her.

"No, I did not believe him. His word, like his master's, is a poison to the mind."

"Are you well, Cicele?"

A weary sigh escaped her. Yes, she was well, and to her shame, she had no regret for what she had done. She would confess, and hopefully Father William, Lesbury's chaplain, would absolve her. "Yes, I am well."

Guyon scanned her face, waiting to see if she was telling the truth. Satisfied, he returned to his seat. "We found your maid Agatha."

She spun her head around to look at him. "What do you mean?" She was barely able to keep the dread from her voice.

Guyon smiled. "We didn't apprehend the men, but we did manage to capture their hostage." He gave her one of those rare smiles that made his face appear so young and free. The way he had looked during that summer in Rouen. Cicele's breath hitched at the sheer joy of encountering it again.

Guyon must have misread her reaction because he stood and came to her. Clasping her cheek, he ran the calloused pad of his thumb over her eyebrow. "Don't frown, Agatha is well. Maude is seeing to her."

Cicele was so relieved she nestled her cheek into his palm and closed her eyes. They had recovered Agatha. It had never occurred to Cicele that Lincoln might have captured her maid. What had she endured at their hands?

"Is she hurt?" She didn't want to think what might have happened to her.

"No, they didn't harm her, just held her as possible ransom I suspect."

Yes, she would have paid a great deal to gain the release of her maid.

Lincoln would be more dangerous now that he had lost both his hostage and his butcher.

Dragging her thoughts back to her encounter with de Sayre, and his ability to find her, she voiced her concerns about spies in the castle. "He knew where I was, Guyon. How is that possible?"

Guyon walked over to the table and poured two goblets of wine. When he came back to stand by the hearth, he handed her one.

"Thomas is questioning someone."

Cicele's gorge rose. She understood what "questioning" involved.

"Have no fear, wife, he is not to be tortured."

Cicele was pleased Guyon wasn't so barbaric, but she was worried that there may be more spies.

Guyon must have thought the same thing because he answered her unspoken question. "I am hoping he will incriminate others to save himself a painful death." Guyon sounded resigned, and weary.

He cast her a distraught look. "I will have de Sayre's body taken to the hanging tree at Lesbury bridge and put in the gibbet. He will serve as a deterrent to others who might think to defy the lord of Alnwick."

She nodded her assent. It was a gruesome reminder that for some death afforded no dignity, or peace. The hanging tree at Lesbury bridge was on the main road that led north to Alnwick. She refused to feel anything save loathing for de Sayre.

They sat in silence for some time, each occupied with their own thoughts. Conscious of her own need, Cicele wanted to lead Guyon to the bed, and help ease the sickening reality of Lincoln and his schemes, but she was too self-conscious to make the first move, so she sat and gazed at the fire.

GUYON HAD BEEN SO ANGRY. She had defied him again, and almost got herself abducted. He had wanted to rage. To break something. His body ached to bed his wife and bury himself in her, to forget that he almost lost her again.

But instead he had seen her fear, her terror at what she had done, so he had bathed her, then put her to bed.

Now, as he glanced over to where she sat, straight-backed and gazing at the fire, he saw she wore an inscrutable expression on her beautiful face that was a barrier, but also revealed her vulnerability. The urge to reach out and take her in his arms and protect her was a living thing in his veins. But her expression was formidable.

You are no breechcloth clodpate. Guyon wondered if in this instance he was exactly that, a callow coward who was fearful of rejection.

Decision made, he placed his goblet of wine on the table and walked towards her, then hunkered down on his heels. "You must still be tired." And terrified. But he didn't say that, instead he just let the unfinished words hang between them.

Slowly she turned her head to meet his eye. Her golden eyes had a haunted look that made his breath catch. Without thinking, he took her into his arms and carried her to the bed, gently laying her on the furs before taking more from the other side and covering her.

"Rest, you are still not recovered from your ordeal." He couldn't give her much, but he could give her time to recover, and that was what he would do regardless of his need to claim her body and convince himself she was safe.

Her hand shot out and grabbed his. "Don't leave me, please."

"Ah, wife, you never have to beg me to stay with you," he replied as he bent and kissed her brow.

He walked around to the other side of the bed, removed his boots then climbed on top of the bed and shifted over to where she lay. Taking her in his arms, his chin resting on the crown of her head, they lay silent for a long time.

Guyon forced himself not to fall asleep by making a mental note of the day's events.

Cicele's soft, even breathing calmed him as he considered Lincoln, and how he could ensure the bastard could never hurt her again. It was pointless to ride to Warkworth and demand Lincoln grant him entrance. The castle was one of the most well defended castles in Northumbria. Guyon would lose men if he tried to take a fight directly to Lincoln. There had to be another way, but what?

There would be a reckoning, but for now he wanted to concentrate on the woman who lay sleeping in his arms.

Warm and soft, Cicele snuggled into his chest, but he drew her closer. His balls ached and his cock was as stiff as the wooden pell in the training yard, but he wasn't about to wake her and plow her when she was so vulnerable. She needed his protection and affection, not his roaring lust.

Still, a little satisfaction wouldn't hurt. He shifted his groin so it rested against her pert bottom, then he pressed himself into her. God's teeth, it was agony.

A moment later she wriggled her bottom into his groin. "I do not appreciate a tease, my lord," she said in a sleepy voice as she rubbed herself against him.

That was all the invitation Guyon required. His body wanted release, but he forced himself to be slow and gentle.

He stood and removed his clothing, not taking his eyes off her.

A slow smile flickered at the corners of her mouth, then she knelt on the bed, sliding her chemise up over her head before lying back, waiting for him.

Hell's teeth, what was a man supposed to do?

Taking a moment to savor her lovely form spread on the bed as a feast just for him, Guyon devoured her with his eyes.

He needed to touch her, to breathe her in.

Leaning over he kissed her lips, then moved to her jaw, her throat. Her skin smelled faintly of lavender, a remnant of the bath. The water cascading over her breasts and the curve of her neck as he washed her had been almost too much for him. He had had to clasp the washcloth in a fist so he wouldn't reach out and caress her body. The heat and steam from the bath had made the hair by her temple curl around her face. The moment was one of the most erotic of his life.

Good God, drying her lovely legs, rubbing the towel down her thighs and along her arms had made him as hard as a rock, but he had refused to succumb to his need, his ferocious hunger to possess every inch of her delectable body.

Her moan brought him back to the present. She wanted him and he would not disappoint her, but instead of the passionate, frenzied coupling they had shared over the past several days, this time he would pleasure her with slow, sensuous strokes of his tongue.

He allowed himself one last scorching kiss of her mouth, then Guyon moved to her feet where he began his slow ascent. He trailed his mouth along the inside of her shin, swirling his tongue around the inner crease of her knee. With slow, deliberate strokes he worked his way up the inside of her thigh, first the right, then the left. Her moan had every fiber of his body tense with arousal. But he would not satisfy himself just yet.

God, she was delicious as he licked a trail up the inside of her thigh before nestling his tongue into the hot wet heat of her.

Her hands grasped his hair. "Guyon, what are you doing?"

Fear, doubt, shame, passion. They were all discernible in her voice and, devil take him, he reveled in it. Instead of lifting his head to look at her he licked the seam of her sex and almost spent his seed there and then, when he heard her groan and felt her body shudder against his mouth.

Hell's fires, she tasted delicious. Wet heat slid over his tongue as the musk of her arousal filled his nostrils. He had to be inside her, to ride with her over the cliff into oblivion.

Dragging himself away, he settled himself between her thighs, his cock nudging at her delicious wet seam. But first, he wanted her to taste. He took her mouth in one rough claiming kiss, forcing his tongue into the heat of her mouth. Instead of shying away from what he demanded, she clung to his mouth, sucking every last bit of restraint from him. As she sucked his tongue into her mouth, he plunged into her, branding her his for eternity. "You are mine," he growled as he drove into her liquid heat, her inner muscles clenching around him.

The harder, the faster he thrust, the more she took of him until they both screamed their release.

Guyon's body shook with the most devastating climax of his life. So much for slow and gentle. He'd been a man possessed. And God's bones, she had taken every last bit of him—his body, his mind, and most definitely his heart.

His head rested on her shoulder while he braced himself over her so as not to crush her. His lips skimmed the line of her jaw. "That, wife, was extraordinary."

She stole a cheeky kiss when he raised his head to search her eyes. Would she feel shame at what he'd done? God, he hoped not, for he wanted to do that again. And again. His thirst for her was unquenchable.

"That, my lord husband, was magnificent." She ran the tip of her tongue over her swollen lips, the little minx. "And deliciously naughty."

"My God, Cicele, you undo me."

"Good." The self-satisfied grin on her face made his heart swell until his chest hurt.

Sliding off her he gathered her against him, kissing the crown of her head as it rested under his chin. "Sleep," he ordered as he closed his eyes and inhaled the heavy scent of their coupling. Every fiber of his body relaxed. But he wouldn't sleep.

～

"WHY DO YOU LEAVE?"

Guyon had been lying in the warmth of their shared passion, savoring the languorous feel of its afterglow. Cicele shared his passion, and he never had to hold himself back. She was his equal in every aspect of his life. But the contentment was not to last. She had asked what he had hoped would never be asked. Stupid bastard, had he truly believed he could hide the ugly truth a bit longer? Thomas was right, he should have told her when they first married.

Now he stood to lose everything. Bollocks, what a mess, and he had no one to blame but himself.

Well, he couldn't tell her the truth, but he could pretend he didn't know what she was talking about.

"I don't know what you mean." The lie spilled off his lips with an ease that caught him by surprise.

She turned to face him then, resting on her elbow as she examined his face. The intensity of her gaze forced him to concentrate on her hair as it fell over her exposed breasts screening them from his vision. His cock gave him a reminder that he was well recovered, and perhaps a change in the conversation would be a good idea. But Guyon was no coward. Yes, he was a liar, and a murderer, and even a demon-possessed beast, but he would face her question and hopefully their marriage would survive.

He watched as a guarded expression, almost a mask of indifference, fell over her face. She was no longer the passionate, playful woman he had bedded a few moments ago. Now a woman he didn't particularly like stared down at him, her face showing no tenderness, while her eyes held an expression that chilled his blood.

Deciding to go on the offense seemed the best option, so Guyon clenched his teeth and offered his own version of a person who had been wronged. "What do you accuse me of?" He kept his tone neutral, but his expression was as steely as her own.

To his surprise her face crumpled as she sat up and went to get out of the bed.

He reached out and grasped her arm.

She winced and cried out.

That had Guyon out of the bed and kneeling behind her. "Cicele, you're hurt."

She swiped at the tears running down her cheeks. "It is nothing, let me go," she sobbed as she tried to wriggle from his hold on her shoulders.

Instead of releasing her he gently turned her round so they faced each other. "Show me."

She held out her arm to him. "There is nothing to see."

Had he been too rough? God knows she drove him to extremes with her unrestrained pleasure. "Did I hurt you?"

She gave him a look that made his breath catch. "Physically? No."

Disgust. Deep, gnawing disgust at himself swamped him. He released her arm and rolled as he flung himself from the bed and began getting dressed.

"Where are you going?"

He had to get away, so grasped the first excuse he could think of. "I'm going to see the spy, see what information he has." Impatience and self-loathing made his tone rougher than he intended.

"Will you come back?"

He turned to look at her then. She was so pale and wan sitting naked in the semidarkness of their chamber. When had he begun to think of it as *their* chamber?

He didn't want to hurt her, but he knew his next words would almost certainly crush her, so he walked over to her and gathered her in his arms.

"Cicele, I have to if I am to have any hope of protecting you." It was the truth, but not one she would understand. He spoke into the hair on the crown of her head. He daren't look at her face, for he was terrified that he would see the beast he had become reflected in the golden hues of her eyes.

"Will you come back?"

His heart wrenched, but he would not tell her his reason, merely try and stall for more time. He wasn't ready to lose her yet. And as sure as day followed night, he would lose her when she found out the truth.

So he kissed her brow. "Lie down, and I will be back when I can."

She didn't look convinced, and for a moment he thought she might argue. She gave him a small nod, then lay back down, gathering the bedding up to her chin, obscuring her luscious body. Her eyes closed and she looked for all the world like a princess, hair spread over the pillows, her pale skin reflecting the soft candlelight. His heart ached to go to her, but instead he drew the curtains closed.

She was as lost to him in that moment as she had been for the past six years. It is better this way. He told himself, but he didn't believe it. Not for a moment.

Chapter Twenty-Three

Cicele lay awake for most of the night, her mind and heart in turmoil. She was sure he had evaded her question, but then he had discovered he had bruised her. That changed everything.

He had been so loving and attentive tonight at the beginning of their loving, but she hadn't wanted gentle and affectionate, she had wanted to release the emotions roiling inside her. She had killed de Sayre, and the fear and revulsion that boiled within her needed to be banished.

Guyon had picked up on her need, and they had loved each other with a ferocity that had left her exhilarated, a little bruised, and completely spent. It had been glorious.

Now she lay awake, fretting about his absence. He didn't seem to want to spend the night with her, but was that such a bad thing? Sleeping and sex were two different activities. But she had hoped they could love and then find their sleep together. She longed to wake in the mornings cradled in his arms.

With a resigned sigh, she sat up and pulled the curtains aside. Vite stirred, but she hushed him and told him to stay. Taking her chemise from the chair where she had thrown it in her haste to have him touch her she put it on. A hot flush singed her cheeks as she remembered the look of desire in his eyes. Shaking herself free of the memory, she took her cloak off the peg by her clothes chest and gathered it around her shoulders before creeping from the chamber.

Maude had said that she had seen Guyon go to his solar during the night, so that was where she would go. Taking a lamp from its peg on the wall outside her chamber Cicele walked down the stairs to Guyon's solar. She had never entered without invitation and she felt a slight twinge of guilt as she lifted the latch, opened the door, and slid inside as quietly as she possibly could.

As soon as she entered the small entrance chamber, she heard the most terrifying noise. An animal cry that made the hairs on her head stand up as a shiver skidded down her spine. What in God's name was that? She was frozen in place—unable to move.

Another strangled cry forced her out of her paralysis and towards the sound. It came from behind the inner chamber's door, not the solar's door further to the left. A great oak door separated his inner chamber from the outer. Yet the muffled cries could be heard where she stood close to the door.

A snarl made her jump back in fright. Whatever was on the other side of the door, it was not human.

Without a thought for her own safety she put her hand on the latch, swung the door wide, and entered the room. Guyon was in there, she was sure of it, and something was attacking him. She had to help. Opening the door, she froze.

Holy Mary, mother of God, I should have stayed abed. That was the last thought she had before she fell to the floor in a dead faint.

Dazed, and her head pounding, Cicele recovered almost immediately upon falling to the floor. She noticed that the lamp she held when entering the room was now on the table. Someone had put it there. It took several moments for her to regain her sense of the situation.

The room was shrouded in darkness except for the light from her lamp and a large night candle burning on the table where she could see a jug, mortar and pestle, and goblets. There was a fire in the hearth, but it gave little light.

A noise from somewhere to her right gave her a fright. A cold sweat beaded her brow, and her pulse hammered in her head. She still sat on the floor where she had crumpled in her faint. Gathering her courage, she turned to face whatever it was that lurked in the darkness beside her. To her surprise, it was Warin, Guyon's squire, who stood in the darkness.

She was about to ask what he was doing when quiet sobbing caught her attention.

It couldn't be? She stood, with Warin's assistance, and moved closer to the bed, but Thomas, who she hadn't seen in the shadows, now moved to bar her way.

"It is not safe, my lady," he warned before turning to stand over her husband who was crouched on his haunches in the corner between the wall and the bed.

Horrified, she watched as both Thomas and Warin coaxed Guyon to the bed. They spoke too quietly for her to make out the words, but the intent was obvious. They were cajoling a grown man like he was a small, frightened child.

When they had him settled in the bed, they both stepped away. Warin went to the table and poured some herbs into the mortar and began crushing it with the pestle. Thomas sat on a chair beside the bed, but Cicele was too far away to have a clear view of her husband. As she moved closer she could see Guyon was visibly trembling, and whimpering. His eyes open, but unseeing. Cicele glanced at Thomas, who seemed unperturbed by what she was witnessing.

She moved forward to get a better indication of what ailed her husband. Her great, strong, arrogant husband was weeping like a child who couldn't be consoled.

What in God's name was wrong with him?

Her head throbbed, and she had to force herself to swallow, but her throat refused to open and she almost choked. A warm hand rested on her elbow. "My lady, please sit and drink this." It was Warin, his eyes telling her what she didn't want to admit. They had a tortured look to them that terrified her.

"What's wrong with him?" Her voice sounded unfamiliar to her own ears.

Warin glanced over at Thomas who still sat vigil by her husband's bed. A silent conversation that lasted less than a heartbeat between the two men who were never far from her husband's side irritated her beyond what she could endure. "Tell me," she demanded.

Warin took a step back. Evidently Thomas would explain. He cleared his throat. "He is like this sometimes after he has fallen asleep." He wouldn't meet Cicele's eye, an indication he was not going to offer anything other than the meagre explanation he had just delivered.

Guyon moaned, his eyes now closed in tormented sleep. It was Warin who moved to the side of the bed and felt his master's brow.

"He will sleep now, my lady, and when he wakes his head will pain him." Warin was a young boy teetering on the edge of manhood, yet Cicele had observed that the boy was both loyal and brave, with a fierce humor that often made Guyon laugh. These men were welcome here, but she intruded.

"He usually acts like a scalded cat when he wakes," Thomas offered with a grim expression. "He won't be pleased to find out you were here, my lady."

She bristled at that but thought better of the bitter retort she was about to give. These men loved her husband, as did she, but she was not welcome. A stab of pain in her chest made her gasp.

Guyon had withheld this from her. He didn't trust her, and never would.

God's bones, she was tired of the lies. He had said he wanted her with him always, yet he withheld aspects of himself that created a vast chasm between them.

It was with a sinking heart that Cicele realized her marriage was a doomed affair. Neither of them seemed able to move past the pain and betrayal of their summer in Rouen. She was always too quick to believe he would abandon her again, and he was unwilling to trust her with his secrets.

With a sorrowful heart, she turned and walked from the chamber. Tomorrow she would ask Guyon for a guard to escort her to the abbey at St. Leonard's where she would have time to think about her future. Cicele had met Hild at Ranulf and Isabeau's wedding. Isabeau had been abandoned at the abbey as an infant, and it was Hild who had raised her, and kept the secret of Isabeau's birth.

Cicele had instantly liked the old nun. Hild would give her guidance, and Cicele would be closer to Isabeau when the time came for her sister's lying-in.

Whatever Guyon was suffering, he had taken great pains to make sure it was not known. She immediately thought back to Ebeta, and the crowd who accused her son of being demon-possessed. She gave an involuntary shudder. She may not believe she had a future with the man that now lay quietly on the bed, but she would never betray him to the church. He would lose everything if Henry found out.

Begrudgingly, she understood why he hadn't confided in her, but it still stung. As she reached the door, she cast her eyes back to where Guyon lay. They would have to talk, but she needed to have a plan ready for when he came to see her. For he would, and her heart would break all over again.

By the time she reached the outer door, she had made her decision, and God help her, she had to believe it was the right one.

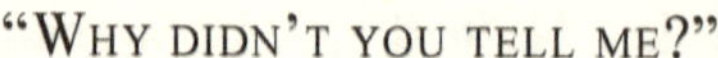

"WHY DIDN'T YOU TELL ME?"

Guyon looked at her but didn't answer. In his own mind he had reasoned that it was best to delay the inevitable confrontation with his wife, but now as he faced her, he didn't know where to start. Not unfamiliar with anger, Guyon had been furious when Thomas had informed him that Cicele had witnessed the full, shameful episode of the previous night. Inwardly Guyon cringed. Guilt at being cursed by God, but remorse for the pain and suffering his affliction had caused.

Growing impatient she raised her voice. "You told me about your father, and the guilt you felt over your marriage to Alice. Surely you could tell me about…this?"

When he didn't answer she began to walk away.

"All right! I'm a coward." He took hold of her arm to turn her to face him. "I was terrified that if you found out about my sickness you would think me possessed of a demon and leave." He was desperate to have her understand. "I couldn't bear the thought of losing you again."

"So you chose to lie to me."

"I didn't lie, Cicele, I just omitted to tell you. There is a difference."

She didn't look convinced, which prompted him to continue.

"What are you upset about? That I didn't tell you, or that you are married to a man who becomes a beast when he sleeps." The weary resignation in his voice must have alerted her to his weakened condition.

"You should sit." She motioned towards a chair.

"I don't need a nursemaid, Cicele, so don't."

"Don't what," she snapped. "I see you…"

She didn't finish. How could she? What words were used to describe what she had seen?

"You saw a grown man cry and piss himself," he raged, not at the woman standing before him, but at himself, and his accursed sickness.

"Is that why you leave?"

"Of course it is. I am terrified that I might fall asleep and the sickness will come. I sometimes lash out, and the thought that I might hurt you petrifies me." He ran his hands through his hair. Nothing would assuage his guilt over what had happened with Alice. That nearly broke him, but if that happened to Cicele he didn't think he would survive.

One of the things he had noticed about Cicele when he had first met her was her perception. He had never met anyone with such astute insight into people. Her ability to parse people was uncanny. It was unnerving to be the recipient of such a gift.

He stood still as she looked at him with those sharp, intelligent eyes. His soul was being inspected and, God help him, he wanted to hide.

"You are not telling me what really worries you," she said as she folded her arms over her chest. "Tell me all, Guyon. If you truly value our marriage you must not hide from me."

He didn't answer immediately, and in that brief hesitation she lost her composure.

"I will not let you destroy my heart again with your sweet words and gentle touches," she yelled. "You spin a web of lies to trap me, but I will not be ensnared again." She spun on her heel and fled the room.

Guyon was momentarily confounded by what she had said, but as the door to her chamber swung open, he regained his senses and ran after her.

Fear. Deep, gnawing anguish tore at his gut. She was fleeing him and running down the stairs. Just. Like. Alice.

He bolted through the door and down the small corridor. Her

skirts were visible as she descended the stone steps that led down to the hall. He had to get to her before she fell.

Heart racing, pulse thundering in his ears he ran, almost tripping on the stairs himself as he took them two at a time. Somewhere in his brain he knew he was taking a risk, but something raw, almost feral, drove him on as he ignored his own safety.

He was behind her now. "Cicele, wait," he pleaded, but to no avail. She didn't even bother to acknowledge him, she just kept running down the stairs.

She had almost reached the bottom when she turned her head to look at him, and that's when Guyon knew what it was to be truly cursed.

Chapter Twenty-Four

In her haste Cicele didn't look where she placed her foot on the narrow stone stairs; she just wanted to escape. His footsteps were so close she could hear the leather soles of his shoes scraping on the stones behind her.

She had to escape. Her heart couldn't stand it, to look into his eyes, and see him lying to her. Again.

Some primal force pushed her forward and away from the man who continued to deceive her. Foolish, foolish woman, when would she learn?

The floor was within sight. Freedom. Glancing over her shoulder to judge the distance between them she missed a step, and her feet went out from under her. Everything slowed, as though she were wading through thick honey. Instinctively, she raised her arms to protect her head as she fell to the flagstones.

Pain. Sickening and sharp, it flared over her body as she hit the floor. Mercifully her arms had done their job, and her head was unharmed. It was her ribs that felt as though they were in the baker's oven. Searing heat radiated out from her chest every time she took a shallow breath, although her hips and arms hadn't fared much better.

Guyon was over her in an instant, crouching down and feeling her body. His hands skimmed over her face, as he felt her head and neck. Then down to her shoulders. He didn't speak, while the scowl that creased his brow seemed slightly comical. She began to giggle. She couldn't control it, the pain in her chest momentarily forgotten as she laughed hysterically. It seemed she was outside of herself looking down at a woman sprawled on the stone floor at the bottom of the steep circular steps. That woman chortled and shrieked like a mad crone caught in the throes of hysteria.

Shock! This was her body's reaction to the shocking pain. The same reaction after her altercation with de Sayre. Was it only yesterday morning that she had killed Lincoln's cur?

She came back to herself as people gathered around her. "Fetch the priest. Go. Hurry." Guyon spoke with a quiet authority that made Cicele take note.

As he picked her up, pain flared through her body, making her head spin. Her face burned, and her skin began to tingle. Without warning she vomited. Mortification was not an emotion Cicele often experienced, but it gripped her with such force it made the pain seem of little consequence.

"I'm sorry," she mumbled as she buried her head against Guyon's chest. Her eyes glued shut. She had no intention of seeing his reaction to her disgraceful behavior.

"It is natural," Guyon soothed. "I once emptied my stomach all over Thomas." There was a forced lightness to his tone, but Cicele appreciated his attempt at levity.

She didn't open her eyes until she felt herself being lowered onto her bed. Pain shot through her chest, making her limbs tingle as she gnashed her teeth to keep from crying out. A strangled gasp escaped her, so she clamped her jaw shut.

Guyon huffed a small laugh. "You are a stubborn harridan." But his tone was gentle. It soothed her. It always had.

An awkward silence followed as Guyon gazed down at her. Neither one spoke but how she longed to say something, anything to break the unease between them.

"God's bones, child, what have you done to yourself?" Maude rushed into the room and over to the bed. A winter's gale would have had less impact as she began ordering servants, and Guyon, to be about her bidding.

To Cicele's surprise, Guyon responded to Maude's orders good naturedly, only muttering under his breath as he was ordered to go outside the chamber to allow Maude to remove Cicele's soiled kirtle. "You might like to have your boy Warin do you the same service," Maude suggested as she brushed past him.

The look of chagrin, then mortification, as he realized he was spattered with vomitus, almost made Cicele forget the pain. Almost.

Changed from her soiled clothing, Cicele lay in only a chemise to cover her when Father William arrived. Immediately he began inspecting her head, then her arms and legs. Murmuring to himself as his hands deftly assessed her injuries. He had been Cicele's chaplain and Lesbury's physician since forever. She trusted the old priest with her life, and her soul. Like Father Orrick, he was a skilled healer who was not opposed to relying on other forms of remedy when prayer was not enough.

Cicele endured his examination quietly until his fingers gently probed her ribs. A scream ripped its way up her throat and out through her clenched teeth before she could control it. She was left panting.

"Take small, shallow breaths, my lady," the priest murmured as he continued to probe along her flank. Finally, his examination complete, he took a small goblet of liquid from his cleric, who stood silently behind his master, and brought it to Cicele's lips. "Drink this," he instructed. "It will help with the pain."

Obediently she sipped at the liquid that smelled strongly of cloves, but as she swallowed it left a minty aftertaste on her tongue.

Cicele began to feel the tea's effects almost immediately. Perhaps having nothing in her stomach helped. It was still early morning, yet it seemed so much had happened. She lay on her back with her eyes closed and let her body relax.

She heard Guyon reenter the chamber and speak to the priest in hushed tones. Annoyed that they would discuss her without including her she braced herself for the pain as she took a breath to speak. "I wish to hear, Father."

Father William stood beside the bed. "It is not a serious injury, God be praised, but you must rest. Your ribs are bruised, but not broken."

"How long?" Guyon's voice was somewhere out of sight.

"I would think by mid-February you would be able to leave your chamber.

Cicele gasped, that was two weeks away. If she waited till then it would be too late to travel to St. Leonard's. It was a disaster.

Only an idiot would risk traveling on horseback in her condition, but perhaps there was another way to travel to the abbey, and away from Guyon and his lies.

"Might I not be able to ride in a wagon, Father? I had hoped to visit St. Leonard's to celebrate the Virgin's Purification Day." Which was in two days. She smiled sweetly at him hoping he wouldn't see through her deception. Guyon would know it for the lie it was, but she didn't care. Only yesterday she had been looking forward to celebrating the feast day, knowing the stonemason would be arriving. How had her life changed in only a day?

The priest gave Guyon a quick glance before he turned his pale gray eyes on her. She immediately knew he saw too much.

"My lady, I would advise against travel until your ribs are healed." He gave her a slight smile. Father William knew her too well. Her trust in him proved valid when he continued, "The damage may be irreparable if you travel, my lady, so I would advise against it."

Cicele understood his meaning. It wasn't her ribs but her marriage that he counseled her about.

Resigned to her fate, she acquiesced. "Very well, Father, I thank you," she replied, but neither graciously or with much conviction.

A heavy sigh caught her attention. She turned to see Guyon visibly relieved. For some reason that angered her, but she was too tired to react.

Maude, as always, anticipated her needs and came to help her to lie a little lower in the bed. "You will feel better after a sleep, child," Maude cooed, as she arranged the mound of pillows for Cicele's head.

Closing her eyes, she heard people leaving the chamber, but she sensed Guyon's presence. "I am tired." She let her pain and anger season her impatient remark.

"I will not leave until you hear me."

"Sweet Christ on his cross, Guyon, leave me in peace."

"I can't. I won't."

A pox on the man.

With a resignation born from years of anger, disappointment, and shame she decided to listen. "Very well, say what you must, then leave, for I wish to sleep." She wouldn't make it easy for him, and she would protect her heart as best she could. And God help her, she must resist.

"I killed Alice."

It was a simple statement, and one that startled Cicele into opening her eyes to look at her husband.

Guyon was many things, but violent or cruel he was not. He didn't mean it the way it had been said. Surely?

She didn't speak, hoping her silence would encourage him to continue.

"Like you, Alice saw me one night and thought me demon-possessed. And like you, when I tried to explain, she ran from me down the stairs and fell." He began pacing, which made Cicele's head hurt.

"Guyon, please, you are making me feel ill with your pacing."

He looked at her as though she had sprouted horns.

"Sit."

Thankfully, he understood this time and came and sat in the chair next to the bed.

"I picked her up and took her back to her chamber. That night she gave birth to a son, but it was too early and the child died soon after." He released a shuddering breath, anguish evident in every word spoken. "The blood wouldn't stop, and Alice was dead by morning."

Cicele stole a glance at him and wished she hadn't. He sat with his head in his hands. She had never seen any man so dispirited, but it was the broken expression on his face that told the truth of his anguish.

He looked up and held her eyes in a tormented gaze. "When you fled the chamber, and ran down the stairs, I thought you would fall and I would be left without you."

"Did you love her?"

His eyes slid to his clasped hands resting on his knees. "No." He lifted his head then, his eyes boring into hers pleading with her to believe him. "I never lay with her," he announced. "But I had vowed before God to protect her, and instead I killed her." It was the desolation in his deep brown eyes that arrested Cicele.

She could see now why he had run after her. And she understood. She could also see why he hadn't confided in her. Shame was a monstrous thing. She had been its prisoner for years. It had coiled around her heart until it was almost too painful to breathe.

"I ran because I couldn't bear the rejection," she confided. "I had begun to love you again, but was too afraid you would abandon me, so when you didn't sleep in the same bed I became convinced that you would leave."

He was about to say something, but she put her hand up to stop him. "I am as broken as you, but in a different way. You believe you are responsible for Alice's death, but it is not true." She had to take a moment because the throbbing ache in her ribs robbed her of concentration.

"Cicele?"

There was some more tea in the jug on the table, so she asked him to pour some. When she had taken a few sips, she continued. "I thought that if I ran from you, I could escape my own fears." Huffing a small laugh, which sent pain radiating through her chest, she clamped her mouth shut and waited for it to subside.

Breathing in shallow breaths, she continued. "We are idiots, you and I, but I must find a way to live without the terror of being left. I do not want to live with this vile thing gnawing away at my heart and mind."

She looked at him with pleading eyes. "Will you grant me time to heal? For if I am to love you, I must find a way to love myself, as I am, not as I wish to be."

That speech exhausted her, so she closed her eyes and relaxed her body.

Guyon hovered over her. His distinctive smell was all male, and unique to him. She could detect horse and leather, and a slight scent of rosemary. She inhaled the familiar aroma. He smelled like home, and God help her, it was where she wanted to be. His lips brushed across her brow. "Sleep."

And she did.

～

THE NEXT TWO weeks dragged by. Cicele was growing impatient with her enforced convalesce, although she wouldn't admit that her ribs still ached. Each day the pain grew less and less.

In those first few days she woke every morning thinking she might be improving, until the pain suggested otherwise. Every part of her body had throbbed. If she tried to move the pain raked up and down her body. Even to slide off the bed to use the chamber pot caused her brow to erupt in sweat and her stomach to heave.

Now, as she lay abed thinking back to those first days after her fall, she remembered how it felt to be thrown from a horse. It had been years since she had fallen from the saddle, but she would never forget the aftereffects of being flung to the hard ground.

Hoisting herself into a sitting position, her ribs instantly protested. "I've been thrown from several horses, then trampled by the cursed beasts," she hissed as she tried to breathe through the pain. "And I won't let a fall down the stairs beat me."

"You look a fright."

Ah, trust Maude to bring her back to reality. "Is that supposed to make me feel better?" She opened her eyes and studied her maid who was standing beside the bed, while servants brought in a tub and water for a bath.

Maude must have interpreted Cicele's anxious expression but wouldn't be swayed. "You will feel better after a bath, and I've steeped some comfrey in the water to help with the bruising."

Unfortunately, Cicele had learned that when Maude used that particular tone, it was best to acquiesce, or suffer the consequences. Clenching her jaw, Cicele submitted to Maude's ministrations, which were neither tender nor quick. But true to her maid's word, she did feel better for having her body bathed. It was the first time in two weeks that she felt clean, and Cicele appreciated it. Until she didn't.

Cicele couldn't endure any more and was about to tell Maude to leave off, when mercifully Maude finished. Cicele was then dressed in a soft chemise and wrapped in her fur lined cloak. Dressing in a kirtle and gown was not an option until Cicele could raise her arms above her head without fainting from the pain in her ribs.

Alas, the ordeal was not over. "Drink this."

A freshly brewed cup of willow bark and clove tea was thrust under Cicele's nose. "I can't," she whimpered. Already her stomach heaved at the bitter smell of cloves. She had endured this brew for weeks and her stomach complained bitterly.

"Come, child, it won't bite."

Cicele wasn't convinced, but obediently, she sipped at the tea. "Wine would be nice," she muttered as she drained the contents. Yes, mulled wine with cloves would be an improvement on willow bark. God in heaven, she hoped she never tasted the brew again.

When she had drained the cup, Maude led Cicele to a chair in front of the fire. When she was comfortable Vite invited himself up onto her lap. "You are a lazy boy, shouldn't you be out catching something instead of loitering about my chamber?" The dog chose to ignore her remark, and instead curled up on her lap and went to sleep.

Although her ribs still ached, she refused to surrender to the lingering discomfort, and let the tea lull her to sleep.

Sometime later she was awoken by a slight sound. Stretching her neck to ease the cramp, she opened her eyes to see Guyon standing near the hearth. He looked exhausted. Dark gray smudges under his eyes told her he had slept ill the past few weeks.

When she moved to put Vite back on the floor he placed his hands in front of him, palms up, indicating he came in peace. "I only came to inquire after you. I won't tire you with my presence." She had hardly seen him, but his absence had given her time to think.

"You may sit," she said hurriedly.

Damn her contrary heart; she craved his presence. It occurred to her that he may not want to. "If you wish," she added.

He sat but didn't say anything for some time. She was happy to stare into the fire and wait for him to speak. Her head still ached, and thinking made it worse, so she was content for him to do the thinking for the both of them.

"Are you well enough to talk about Agatha; she has asked if she might join her husband."

That made Cicele stare open mouthed at him. When Agatha had become her maid several years before, she was told she was a young widow in need of a place.

Was it the fall, or had something happened to her mind? Cicele couldn't seem to unravel what Guyon had just said.

He came to her rescue.

"Lincoln inveigled his way into your life by having Agatha become your maid. He held her husband, who was his liege man, hostage to ensure she would do his bidding." Guyon leaned forward and took her hand. "She has confessed that she was the one who told Lincoln you fished by the weir. When they captured you, she tried to hide, but his men captured her before she could get far."

"Where is she now?"

"She is with Maude, awaiting your decision," he replied. "She expects to be punished for her part in your abduction."

"Will you bring her to me, please?"

He stood up and walked to the door. Agatha must have been waiting just outside in the entrance chamber, because she entered almost immediately.

When she came in, she stood next to Cicele, but didn't meet her eye. Instead, she concentrated on the floor.

Here was another woman who had been used as a pawn in a man's game. "You have been through enough, Agatha, I will not punish you further."

Her maid still wouldn't meet her eye.

"What of your husband?"

Agatha slowly lifted her eyes to look at Cicele. "If it please you, my lady, my lord Cessford has offered him a place."

It took Cicele a moment to catch the conversation. She still thought of her father as Cessford, not Guyon.

Agatha didn't seem to notice Cicele's monetary confusion. "He is, or was, a hedge knight until my lord Lincoln gave him a position," she said proudly.

Cicele tried to hide a smile under the pretext of a slight cough. So, Agatha's husband was a landless knight who had no business being married, yet Agatha's expression reminded her of her own infatuation with Guyon when they had first met. He was so handsome and chivalrous. Her heart fluttered as she recalled the first time she had seen him astride his great courser. She had fallen in love with Guyon then and there.

Forcing herself back to Agatha, there were several questions Cicele wanted answered, but she wanted Guyon present. "Agatha, tell my lord Cessford to come in; I want to ask you some questions."

The girl's face paled. "Don't fret, Agatha, I just want to hear about the Earl of Lincoln, and what you know of him."

Assured, the girl nodded and went to fetch Guyon. The cringing fear on Agatha's face made Cicele's heart snag. She wouldn't add to the girl's pain.

When both Guyon and Agatha were back in her chamber, Cicele asked her questions. "How were you persuaded to spy on me?"

Agatha cast a quick glance at Guyon, then back to Cicele. "My lord Lincoln found out that Hamlin, that's my husband," she gushed, "and I were married without his permission. He ordered me to pretend I was widowed, then he presented me to Sir Nicholas as a widowed maid for you."

"And?" Cicele asked.

"He said if I didn't do what he said, he would make me a widow in truth," she sobbed. "I know it was wrong, my lady, but I love Hamlin and I couldn't bear for him to be killed."

Cicele wasn't cruel or unaffected by her maid's tears, but she was angry at being duped. Cicele also understood what it was to be forced against her will to betray someone. "It is all right, Agatha. I understand the coercion used to make us do another's bidding." She had lived with it all her life. Her father had bullied, threatened, and slapped her to make her bend to his will. It was something of a surprise to realize that of all the men in her life, Guyon was the only one who had not forced her to do things against her will, or her better judgment.

Forcing her mind back to the present, and away from the torment she had endured all her life, she asked, "And where is Hamlin now?"

Agatha looked at Guyon with a vacant expression. So, the young lovers were not together. Yet.

"He is in the guard house. Thomas has men keeping an eye on him. I thought it best to keep them apart until you had a chance to hear Agatha's story."

Guyon had deferred to her judgment? A small thrill fluttered under her bruised rib cage. He would let her make the decision concerning Agatha. That was something Cicele had not expected, and she would tell him later how much she appreciated his gesture.

Turning her thoughts back to Agatha an uneasy question began to form. "Agatha, do you have any family? The truth this time, if you please."

Agatha replied without a moment's hesitation. "No, my lady, Hamlin is all I have."

Cicele looked at her maid in silence for several heart beats. "If I am to let you back into my service, how do I know I can trust you?" Cicele had decided she would allow Agatha back, but she would be wary of the girl until she had proved herself. Cicele was tired of being duped by those she trusted.

Cicele expected all sorts of assurances, but Agatha confounded her with her honesty. "I cannot offer anything that will make you trust me, but if you are willing, I will do all in my power to regain the trust I lost." She was wringing her hands in front of her as she awaited Cicele's decision.

"Very well, I am willing to give you another chance."

The girl's shoulders sagged with relief.

"But, know this Agatha, it will take time, and I will not be so forgiving next time." Cicele gave the girl a cool stare. "You may go."

"Where, my lady?"

Cicele raised a questioning eyebrow at her husband. Where indeed?

"I will keep your husband under guard until Lincoln is dealt with. Lady Cessford will see to your accommodation."

Cicele watched as the girl walked out of the chamber with her head held high.

Now it was time to have a similar conversation with Guyon.

Chapter Twenty-Five

Guyon could tell by the look on Cicele's face that what he was about to hear was not going to be what he wanted. Everything in him urged him to stop her, but he remained where he stood and braced himself for the worst.

"Guyon, come, sit by me."

When he had settled in the chair, she reached out her hand in invitation for him to take it. Which he did without hesitation.

"I have loved you since the first moment I saw you in Rouen." A shy smile creased the corners of her mouth. "But I fear my experience of love has left me battered and bruised, much like my fall down the stairs."

"Cicele…"

"No. Let me finish." She sat back, breaking their connection as she released his hand. That small action left him bereft.

"When you didn't return my heart broke, but a part of me still believed in you. It was a risk giving myself to you, but I believed you hadn't taken my innocence lightly." She huffed a small laugh. "Others were convinced you had stayed away from court because you had seduced another." She gave him a long, penetrating stare.

"Rumors of your exploits were rife about court that summer, but I knew the truth. It was I who lay in your arms, not others. So, I believed you had a good reason to stay away."

"But then a few days before I was to be married to Nicholas, I came across a young woman crying. I had seen her at court, but did not know who she was. So I stopped and asked her if I might aid her. I still remember those pleading eyes staring at me. She told me she was Alice de Percy, and that she was with child, but the cur who took her virtue refused to marry her. Naturally I asked who." Cicele stopped and stared into Guyon's eyes. "She told me it was you, and you had been lovers for months."

"Cic—"

"No. Guyon, let me finish. Please." She wet her lips and looked briefly to her clasped hands resting in her lap. He had never felt so helpless. All he wanted to do was wrap his arms around her and never let her go. Forcing himself to stay still, he waited for her to continue. When she looked up, he saw what this confession was costing her, and it tore his heart apart.

"Naturally I was aghast, for not only had you taken my virginity, but you were sleeping with another. It was Alice's word, and her evident distress, that convinced me you had betrayed me in the cruelest of ways. Then, when I was back in England and heard that you had married her, I realized what a fool I had been. That's when I vowed never to trust you again."

Guyon was incredulous. Hell's teeth, he was furious. Why would Alice do such a thing? It was a heinous lie.

"I think now, after learning about Lincoln's involvement with Agatha, that somehow Lincoln may have either convinced Alice to lie, or perhaps threatened her in some way. But at the time I didn't know Alice and Lincoln were lovers, so I believed her."

Cicele's eyes pleaded with him to renounce the lie that had stood between them for six years.

Guyon was angry. If he didn't control the rage that boiled inside him he would break something. So, he sat, hands curled into fists, and waited for the rage to subside.

"I have told you, Cicele, I never slept with Alice." He looked at her, pleading for her to believe him. "It is the truth."

"I hadn't told you until now, because a part of me believed the lie. I have lived my whole life knowing I was not good enough. My father, my brother, Nicholas, and even you. All of you had either betrayed me, bullied me, or belittled me. And all of you rejected me in some way. I have been wounded in ways that have left deep scars. But I will not let the past, or Lincoln, or indeed my father's pride, destroy my future.

"But you need to understand, Guyon, I will not let anything lie hidden between us."

He was up out of his chair and kneeling before her. "I am so sorry, Cicele. I never meant to hurt you. What I did, I did because I thought it was for the best. I had been injured at the tournament and the fever induced weeks of..." What did he call this demon that reduced him to a beast? "I believed myself cursed, and in my shame, I believed that you would be better off without me." He couldn't look at her, too ashamed to admit his weakness. "I was a coward." He didn't know what else to say. What could he say? He was everything he despised. Weak, cowardly and dishonorable. He didn't deserve her forgiveness, or her love.

"Yes, there is your night terrors, which you use as an excuse to keep me away from you. But I want to be with the person you truly are. Brave, honest, honorable and at times arrogant and overbearing."

Guyon couldn't speak, his tongue was stuck to the roof of his mouth and refused to move. Did she mean that?

They sat in silence for a moment. Guyon desperately tried to think, but his mind was blank. So shocked by what Cicele had told him, he was unable to form a coherent thought.

"Do you remember Ebeta and her son?

Guyon nodded. He wouldn't forget that in a hurry. Or the raging of Master FitzWallah when he confronted Guyon about his daughter.

"I have to confess to something that I have withheld from you."

His mind raced to digest her words, but still couldn't speak. He might actually faint. *God's bones, man, pull yourself together*.

"I came across them as little Moise was convulsing on the ground by the castle walls. I was terrified when I saw him foaming at the mouth, while his eyes stared at nothing. And to my shame I believed, like the crowd gathered about, that a demon had possession of his soul."

Guyon was well aware most people believed the falling sickness to be the result of demons. Shit, he believed it himself, and was convinced that he could lose everything he valued. His lands, his place at Henry's side, such was the fear the falling sickness had over people. But what he feared even more, was the prospect of losing this woman, a woman he loved body and soul.

Terror twisted his guts as he waited. He would rather face a wolf protecting its young, than sit and wait for Cicele to rip out his heart.

He could scarcely breathe when she reached out and took his hand, bringing it to her lips, as she kissed his knuckles.

"Father Orrick saw my horror and set about correcting my ignorance. At first I thought he spouted blasphemy. He spoke of the Iranian scholars who teach that the falling sickness is a disease, and not because of demons. It took some time." A small self-deprecating smile tugged at the corners of her mouth. It made his pulse race, and his stomach tense. Such was her power over him.

"He used their methods, and treated little Moise with herbs, and changed his diet." Pausing she gave him an unsteady smile, "Finally, I became convinced that demons did not possess the child, but that what he suffered was, in fact, a disease."

Their clasped hands were once again on her lap and she was absent-mindedly twisting the ring on his finger. "I neither fear, nor am I offended, by that which reduces you to a beast writhing on the bed." She turned slightly so she could look at his face. "I wish to be your wife, in every aspect. I want to wake in your arms, and have you ravish me at the beginning of the day." Her expression was so fierce he thought for a moment that he had misheard.

"Ravish you?" It was perhaps the most addled-brained thing he could have said, but he was so shocked it was the best he could muster.

Raising her eyebrows in mock horror she teased, "Well, as I am unused to your attention at dawn, perhaps I ask too much."

Guyon didn't hesitate. "I will show you how capable I can be at dawn, or any time of the day for that matter." He stood up and gathered her gently into his arms.

With slow, deliberate care he began kissing the exposed skin on her neck but she placed her hands on his chest.

"Guyon."

He raised his head to look at her.

"Do you promise me?"

What she asked was impossible. "I could hurt you, or worse." He didn't finish that thought, it was too horrific to contemplate. Perhaps when they returned to Alnwick he would seek out the priest and ask his advice. Was it possible to keep the demon—that drove him to madness when he slept—at bay? "Is the child well?"

His wife took a moment to understand his question. He watched in silent fascination as a smile that made her eyes gleam spread across her face. "Yes, he is stronger."

"I don't want to hurt you," he whispered, too terrified to think about what he might do to her.

"You hurt me much more by shutting me out, and I will not live in a marriage where shame and fear exist. Not again." She reached her hand up and tapped her fingers on the side of his head. "And there is always Vite to protect me."

At the mention of his name the dog roused himself from his spot by the fire, stretched, then sat on his little haunches and stared at them.

The absurdity of her statement, and the dog's vigilant pose were a balm to Guyon's tormented soul.

"I promise to try." He leaned in and kissed her. "You are the bravest, most loving woman I have ever known, and I cannot bear to contemplate life without you by my side."

"Then that, husband, is where I shall be."

He chose life. Life with all its complications, frustrations, and fears.

Releasing his wife, he strode to the chamber door, calling for Vite to follow him.

"GUYON?" She heard the note of panic in her voice as she watched him leave.

"I'll be back." He gave her a shameless smile as he opened the chamber door and left, with Vite at his heels.

Pleasure, and more than a little apprehension, filled her as she waited for him to return.

She waited.

And waited.

Finally, he returned, but not alone. Several servants arrived with trays of food and wine. Guyon supervised where the trays were to be placed. Then, like a mother hen, he shooed all the servants, including a very anxious looking Maude, out through the chamber door before bolting it from the inside.

Walking to where the food and wine was laid on the table he poured two cups of wine, brought them to where she sat by the fire and handed one to Cicele. "Let us drink to the dawns we will share together."

The smile that spread over his face took Cicele's breath away.

She had always thought him handsome, with his straight nose, and square chin, but in this moment, it was his eyes that seemed to reach down and search her soul. His searing gaze caught her breath and made her stomach flutter.

"Are you planning on keeping me hostage, my lord?"

Glancing at the food then back at her he gave her what she could only describe as a wolfish grin.

Irrevocably drawn to the handsome, arrogant, and complicated beast who had captured her heart, she was no more able to refuse him than stop breathing.

She took a sip of wine, then handed her cup back to him. Heaven help her, she needed both hands to leverage herself up out of her chair. She moved gingerly to keep the dull ache of her ribs at bay.

Once she was sure of her balance, she drew Guyon to her and kissed his mouth. He held the cups in both his hands so he couldn't touch her and let out a soft growl of frustration.

Cicele laughed against his lips. "I think it is time for me to tame this beast who growls so."

And she would. Be it ever so carefully.

Chapter Twenty-Six

Cicele had not been able to get the image of Guyon's head between her thighs out of her mind. The thrill of it. The knowledge that it was forbidden only made her more acutely aware of her own need. In the two weeks she had been abed while her bruised ribs healed, her mind had replayed their last time together over and over.

He stood before her now, his hands holding the two goblets, so she smiled what she hoped conveyed the seductress she wanted to be and lifted his surcoat aside so she could untie the laces that held his trousers to his undergarments.

She stroked her hands down the front of him and felt the thick, hard evidence of his arousal. She hid a little self-satisfied smile as she continued to tease him with her hands.

Standing up she looked into his eyes. "I want you." It was a declaration of need, of possession.

A lazy smile slid across his beautiful full lips. "Ah, I am your slave, do with me as you will." His eyes burned with desire and his voice was little more than a growl.

She took the cups from his hands. "I have not the strength to undress you, so when I return from placing these on yonder table, I expect you to be lying on the bed. Naked."

She had no sooner retrieved the goblets than he jerked away from her and began tearing at his clothing.

Laughter bubbled up in her throat. "I am so glad you take so readily to my orders."

He didn't respond, too intent on disrobing.

After placing the goblets on the table, she turned in time to see him shuck the final piece of clothing and fling himself on the bed.

Walking with slow deliberate steps, Cicele reached the side of the bed, then carefully climbed up until she straddled him. Her hands rested on his chest for balance.

"I want you to lie still."

"Very well." He sounded smug, but she was adamant.

"No, Guyon, I don't think you understand. You are not to move, you are to remain as you are." She ran her eyes over his body, pausing to admire his chest and taut abdomen. Her gaze shifted to his shaft, a satisfied smile tugging at the corner of her mouth, then she looked back up to his eyes. "Do you agree?"

He let a moan escape between clenched teeth before he answered. "Yes, but God's bones, Cicele, you are driving me mad."

Smiling in satisfaction, she wriggled down his legs and ran her hand over his rigid cock. At her touch it jerked to meet her, while his hips bucked. He growled through clenched teeth, but he didn't move his hands.

She thrilled at taking control of him this way. What a wanton to revel in such power. As she continued her quest to touch him, she had to acknowledge that she hadn't taken control, he had given it to her. She knew that he could easily reverse their position without any effort. She glanced from her hands wrapped around his shaft and looked at his face. His eyes were shut and his jaw clenched as though he was in pain, while his hands were fisted at his sides. An overwhelming sense of power filled her. It was a gift she would cherish. Oh, sweet saints, she was enjoying herself.

Her hand slid up the warm silken skin of his cock while her thumb rubbed at the small drop of moisture that appeared at its tip.

He groaned and bucked as she slid her hand up and down his shaft; as Cicele watched she had an irrepressible urge to taste him.

Lowering her head, she took him into her mouth and laved her tongue over the wet tip. He tasted slightly salty and musky. Her own body reacted to the taste by clenching in anticipation.

"God's teeth, you will have me come in your mouth if you keep doing that," he ground out as his hips jerked, filling her mouth with the length of his arousal.

A deep need to have him inside her radiated from between her thighs.

"Help me," she moaned as she lifted herself over his engorged cock.

Immediately he lifted her buttocks up and placed her over him, then with one quick thrust he was deep inside her. Her whole body trembled as she squirmed down on his thighs. Never had she been so full, so stretched, and her body adored it.

They rode each other in ever increasing haste, each reaching for their own pleasure. She gasped as her body reached that place of exploding pleasure. Guyon gave one final thrust and groaned, his whole body shaking with release beneath her.

Her bones had been replaced with warm wax. Languid and satisfied, she fell over his chest and let her trembling body relax into his. Her ribs protested, but she chose to ignore the pain.

Big, strong hands caressed her hair. Then gently he lifted her head so he could see her. "Are you hurt?" Deep concern and something, possibly love, reflected in his eyes as he searched her face for discomfort.

Still joined, she wanted to keep the connection for as long as she could, so instead of reaching for his lips she kissed his chest. "I want to stay like this for just a little while."

His hands held her as her head rested on his chest listening to his thudding heart.

Guyon was flailing about on the bed, his body rigid as an unholy growl escaped through his clenched teeth.

Cicele jerked awake, her heart pounding as she tried to take in her surroundings.

It had been a dream.

She was lying next to him, her head resting on his shoulder. Relief surged through her body as she raised her head to look at him. His eyes met hers as a small smile creased his lips. "Bad dream?"

She didn't want to worry him with her fears, so instead she asked him a question. "When did the night terrors begin?" She didn't know what he called them, but the "night terrors" seemed apt to her. "Was it when you were hurt at the tournament and couldn't return to me?"

Guyon released a sigh. "No, it was years ago, before I had earned my spurs. I fell in the tilt yard and hit my head. Thomas told me I slept for several days. Not even a day after I woke I had my first 'night terror.' Sometimes they come frequently, like the time I was ill and couldn't return to you, then sometimes not for weeks. But they always come at night when I sleep."

She had been leaning on her elbow as he answered, so she leaned over, her ribs aching as she stretched. She hissed at the discomfort and Guyon immediately rose and lay her on her back. "You little liar, your ribs still pain you."

She couldn't deny it, and a little part of her liked his rough accusation. He cherished her, and it was quite simply wonderful.

GUYON LAY awake with Cicele in his arms. She had been generous with her affection and her passion. Sated in a way he hadn't been since Rouen all those summers ago, he still couldn't bring himself to believe that she would accept him. The torment of his inability to protect her from himself ate at his resolve to remain in bed with her to sleep the night.

A slight noise, a scuffle of feet on the rush matting on the chamber floor alerted him. Guyon tensed, cursing the absence of the knife under his pillow. Never would he bring weapons to a bed he shared with his wife, but now that precaution seemed foolhardy.

"Guyon, do you sleep?"

Thomas. What the hell was his captain doing creeping about his chamber? Guyon remembered that he had unlatched the door so that servants could come in the morning and light the fires.

"You better have a good excuse for disrupting me."

"Lincoln."

That name was enough to have Guyon out of the bed and standing stark naked before Thomas. "Tell me."

"It seems he has amassed a siege force."

"And?"

My informer thinks he will make his move come dawn."

Guyon couldn't see Thomas's face clearly, as the chamber was in near darkness except for the faint light of the night candle and the banked fire in the hearth, but he heard the urgency in his friend's voice. "Does your informer know where he might be leading a siege?"

"Alnmouth, and the port."

Guyon wasn't surprised by Lincoln's audacity; Lincoln was arrogant, and often led with his balls, rather than his head.

I'll meet you in the solar when I'm decent. Tell Warin to have my mail and helm ready."

Without another word, Thomas left.

Dressed and standing before Sir Nigel and Thomas, Guyon strategized. "You know this area better than I do; where would be a good place to intercept Lincoln?" Guyon directed his question to Sir Nigel, who didn't let him down.

"If he takes the road from his seat at Warkworth, then he will have to cross over the causeway on the outskirts of Hipsburn before he can connect with the road that will take him to Alnmouth. Winter rains have made it swollen and difficult to cross. That, my lord, is the ideal place to lay an ambush."

Guyon nodded. "Thomas, take two men and ride back to Alnwick and gather a force of twenty men and meet me at Hipsburn. That's where we will wait for him."

Thomas gave Guyon a feral grin. "Make sure those laces are tight, young Warin, we don't want our lord's family jewels exposed to harm."

Warin, who was tying Guyon's mail chausses over gamboised cuisse didn't bother looking up. "I suggest you look after your own bits, although, truth be told, they are too small to warrant any attention."

Thomas flicked Warin's ear as he strode past, his laughter hanging in the air.

Guyon saw his steward's expression. Warin's impertinent remark was not appreciated by Sir Nigel. Guyon wasn't amused at the old man's silent censure of Warin. "You are much too forward, Warin," Guyon scolded, "but I agree, Thomas's bits are a fraction of my own."

Sir Nigel spluttered. It seemed the old knight didn't have a humorous bone in his old body, more's the pity. Guyon ignored his steward's evident discomfort. A man who couldn't laugh before a battle was not someone Guyon wanted at his back.

"Sir Nigel, I will leave you in charge of reinforcing Lesbury's walls."

The old knight nodded. "The villagers?"

"Bring in their livestock, but they are to leave all their other possessions behind." The castle could accommodate the villagers, and their livestock, but there was no room for cartloads of possessions.

The steward gave Guyon a brief nod before leaving the chamber to prepare the castle's defense.

"Warin, have you finished? I swear by all that's holy you are slower than a monk in a whorehouse."

The squire gave Guyon a lopsided smile. "Wouldn't want to jeopardize your nuts, now that you have a use for them."

Instead of being outraged at his squire's impudence, Guyon guffawed. "God's teeth, boy, Thomas has been a bad influence on you."

Warin rose to his full height, almost to Guyon's chin. The lad was growing like a weed. It would not be long before he would be able to look Guyon in the eye without raising his head. That would be a good day.

"Shall I have Notus readied, lord?" The boy wore a smug expression that implied he was pleased with himself.

Guyon wanted Warin to hold his own and wouldn't censure him for his ribald humor. "Aye, I'll be down soon."

When Warin left, Guyon walked back to Cicele's chamber and waited for her to stir. He didn't want her to wake and find him gone.

Chapter Twenty-Seven

CICELE WOKE WITH A START. HER HEART RACED, THUDDING AGAINST her chest as her mind cleared. A moment later she was fully alert and aware she was alone in the bed, her hand resting on the cool bedding where Guyon should be lying. Suspicion, unreasonable and irrational, tortured her as she lay awake in the dark. He had left their bed. They had shared one night, and now he was gone. *Moron. What did you expect.* The cruel familiar voice scolded. "No!" She wouldn't listen. There must be good reason.

A small noise caught her attention. "Guyon, is that you?"

Immediately the bed-curtains were flung back to reveal a shadowy figure standing beside the bed. The darkness obscured his features, only his outline visible, but he was fully armed.

"I'm sorry, but I have to leave." He leaned over and bussed a kiss on her brow. "There is word of a large force riding towards Alnmouth. They fly Lincoln's banner."

Cicele sat up. "So close?"

Guyon moved aside so she could climb from the bed, but he held her by the shoulders as she stood. "It is safe, Cicele, I will not let Lincoln get his hands on you." He didn't have to finish, he suspected she knew he was about to say *Again.*

"Lesbury can stand against a siege, but we need to get the villagers to safety." She wasn't going to let him deny her the right to protect her own people. "I must get them inside the gates."

The chamber was dark; the fire and night candle the only light in the room, but she could see Guyon's determined expression.

Well, she could be just as determined. "I am going," she huffed. "And if necessary, without you." It was a ludicrous statement, but she meant what she said as she wriggled free of his hold, which was not difficult, and began dressing.

"Cicele, Sir Nigel is seeing to the villagers, and you are not yet fully recovered. I will not allow it."

She turned on him. "You will not allow it," she fumed. "How dare you dictate to me. I am your wife, and Lesbury, and its people, are mine to protect."

She was about to continue, but he put his hands in the air signaling his surrender. He strode to where she stood with her arm halfway through the sleeve of her kirtle. It did nothing for her anger as she struggled with the garment. Her ribs stung as she reached up to pull the garment over her head. An involuntary hiss escaped before she could stop it.

"Here, let me help."

Taking a deep breath, she accepted his assistance. Soon her arms were through the sleeves, and he was tightening the ties at the side of the garment. His attention focused on his task, which gave her a moment to regain her composure.

"I understand it is dangerous." She spoke more calmly, but she was intent on helping Sir Nigel with the villagers seeking protection behind Lesbury's walls.

Buildings could be rebuilt, but lives were irreplaceable, and they wouldn't come without their livestock. Choosing her words carefully she continued, "But surely your men can protect us as we gather the villagers and their stock?" She posed it as a question in the hopes that he would agree.

He didn't answer until he had finished tying her kirtle, which was a serviceable woolen garment with wide skirts that she wore when riding.

"Yes, but that still doesn't guarantee your safety outside of the walls." He was looking at her, but she couldn't face his concerned expression, so she shouldered past him and began pulling on her warmest hose, tying them under her knees so they wouldn't fall down as she rode.

She knew he had agreed when he brought over her high riding boots and placed them beside her. Hiding her face, she bent over to adjust her hose; it wouldn't do for him to see the self-satisfied smile that she was sure was visible.

"You will do exactly as Sir Nigel says," he commanded.

She looked up. "Yes." Then she sat to pull her boots on, but he stopped her. "Cicele, I mean it. You must do *exactly* as he says, or I shall have him escort you back behind the walls."

"I promise. I will be as obedient as Thomas or Warin." She thought that was a sensible response. They were the most loyal of his men, but the look on his face at the mention of their names was not what she expected.

"God help me," he muttered as he handed her her cloak. "We have to go, and now."

She ran to keep up with him as he opened the chamber door and met Warin waiting on the other side. The young squire looked surprised to see Cicele, but wisely kept his comments to himself as he followed Guyon down the steps.

Sir Nigel was barking orders for his men to ready for a siege, while countless numbers of men were mounted and waiting when she and Guyon arrived at the bailey. Notus stood quietly by the mounting block waiting for his master. When he saw Guyon the huge destrier shook his head and pawed the ground. He was a terrifying sight.

Guyon stopped and asked a groom to bring a horse for Cicele.

"I can ride Nyssa."

Guyon took her by the shoulders and moved her away from the gathered men so they could speak more privately. "She is not trained for a fight. If she smells fear, like as not she will take fright. It is safer for you to ride a horse trained for battle."

"But they aren't here."

A resigned sigh, "He is likely to have men hiding in wait knowing you will try to bring the villagers into the castle, but I can't be in two places at once." His eyes gave no quarter. "I must meet him before he lays siege to Alnmouth."

What an ignorant goose. Of course, there was a possibility that Lincoln could use the chaos to try and abduct her. There would be death and blood if he tried. What had she thought?

Guyon regarded her with a scrutiny she didn't appreciate.

"You have turned a little pale, my love." He sounded amused rather than concerned.

Blast the beast. Gathering as much dignity as she could muster, she held her head high and declared that perhaps it was best for her to prepare the castle for the arrival of the villagers.

To his credit Guyon didn't gloat, although she suspected he was sorely tempted. He cleared his throat and arranged his face into a serious expression. "I will be able to focus now that I know you are safe behind Lesbury's walls."

Cicele had never seen Guyon prepared for a fight. The cold, detached glint in his eyes terrified her.

"What will you do when you confront Lincoln?"

"If he fights me, I shall not offer leniency."

"But what if he kills you?" Cicele couldn't keep the anguish from her voice. The thought of losing Guyon now, after they had been through so much, had her fighting back tears. She didn't think her heart would recover if he was killed.

"There are always winners and losers in battle, Cicele," he said as he cupped her chin in his gloved fingers. "But," he flashed her an impish smile, "I have no intention of dying when you are here waiting for me."

His flippant remark didn't allay her fears, but she chose to pretend it had. "Very well, go and deal with the cur," she announced with a bravado she didn't feel. Leaning into him she placed her arms around his neck. Her ribs protested, almost making her cry out, but she forced herself to remain quiet as she pulled his head down to kiss him. "Come back to me," she whispered against his lips.

His hand came around her back and he returned her kiss with a passion that left her panting for breath. "Guyon, the men," she gasped when he released her.

"I don't care who sees me kissing my wife," he growled. "You are mine, and I will kiss you where and when I please." Which he did again, much to her amusement.

When he released her, she became unsteady on her feet and almost stumbled. "I had no idea my kisses were so potent," he drawled. "Mayhap I shall return and finish what I started."

"Go, you arrogant beast."

She could hear his laughter ringing in her ears as he mounted Notus and walked his men out of the bailey, and out of her sight.

A deep emptiness engulfed her as she stood in the now empty bailey.

"Come," a soft feminine voice spoke from behind her. Cicele turned to see Maude standing there. "God willing, he will be back before dinner today with tales of heroics to keep the troubadours singing till St. John's eve," her maid said as she took Cicele by the arm and escorted her back up the steps and into the hall. "But, for now, we must prepare for the villagers."

Cicele followed Maude back into the hall, but as she organized the castle to prepare for a siege, she silently worried that she might never see her husband alive again.

~

Hipsburn was still shrouded in mist as Guyon indicated for his men to spread out and take cover in the nearby woods. The causeway was just visible in the distance, swift flowing water lapping at its banks. It would be a slow, dangerous crossing for heavily armored men and the wagons carrying the siege engine. Sir Nigel was correct, this was the perfect site to launch a surprise attack.

A bleak day dawned to the sounds of men and horses approaching from behind.

Thomas had finally arrived with Alnwick's guard. Guyon broke cover and cantered Notus towards Thomas. "Take your men and seek cover on the opposite bank by those trees," Guyon commanded, indicating the direction with a nod of his head.

Thomas looked over his shoulder, then back at Guyon. "It will be like fishing in a weir." A wolfish grin slashed across his face.

Guyon agreed, but Lincoln was a formidable opponent, and Guyon would take nothing for granted.

"What of Edlington?"

"Rainecourt has seen nothing, but he ordered the villagers outside the walls to be brought into the bailey, just as a precaution."

Guyon nodded. Rainecourt had done precisely what Guyon would have done himself. If Lincoln launched an attack against Edlington Castle, at least Rainecourt would be prepared.

Waiting was the hardest thing to do. Inactivity threatened to rob his men of their concentration, so Guyon quietly walked his mount along the ranks of armed men who were all bristling for a fight. A word of encouragement here, a flippant remark there, and a ribald joke with one of his men who had served him for years. When Guyon made his way back to the front of the column, he waited for the approaching army to appear.

As he waited, Guyon thought back to a time when Lincoln had been his friend. They had served Geoffrey as squires, then knights. But Lincoln—Remeys as he was then—was an earl's son, and impatient to gain glory and wealth. And as was often the way, a woman had destroyed their friendship—Cicele de Saussay.

Did Lincoln mourn the loss of his friend? Guyon thought not. He had proven himself a worthless cur. "A pox on his black soul."

Turning his thoughts back to the present, Guyon surveyed the causeway, and the surrounding land. Lincoln would likely cross with a small contingent of men first, and secure this side of the road, while sending the remainder of his men to protect the siege engines from the other side.

Finally, the waiting was over. In the distance Guyon could see a huge trebuchet. It towered over the mounted men, making Lincoln's men and horses look like ants. One siege engine could wreak havoc on the unprotected village of Alnmouth. Guyon realized that although Lincoln had his eye on securing the port, it was obvious from the weaponry Lesbury would be his next target.

"Pox-ridden fucking cur," Guyon snarled.

"He seeks bigger game than Alnmouth," Warin said as he watched from Guyon's left.

Guyon cast his squire a cursory glance. The lad was turning into an intelligent and astute soldier.

"Aye, but he'll not get the satisfaction."

They continued to watch as Lincoln and twenty of his men made their way across the ford. It was slippery and fast-flowing, making the crossing treacherous for the heavily armed men and their mounts.

It took Lincoln almost half an hour to get his men on the Hipsburn side of the causeway. Only then did the first of the wagons carrying the trebuchet begin to roll towards the ford.

Everything was going as Guyon had planned. That, in itself, was a miracle. War was fickle, and the best laid plan could go awry. No warning. No time to reconsider your options. But this day the Fates were with Guyon.

Lincoln rode with his men to take up a position halfway between the ford and the crossroads that led east to Lesbury, and west to Alnmouth.

"Come closer, you bastard," Guyon snarled as he watched Lincoln gesturing for his men to take up their positions.

"God, be praised," Warin whispered as he watched Lincoln and five men-at-arms ride towards the crossroads.

Guyon raised his hand in preparation for the signal that would lead his men into an attack.

"Come on." Guyon willed his sworn enemy to come closer. He needed Lincoln to be far enough away from his main guard that Guyon could cut him off.

Heaven was listening, Guyon watched with satisfaction as Lincoln and his small guard rode past the woods, where he and his men were hiding, and turned on to the road that led to Alnmouth.

"Now!"

Ordered chaos reigned. Thomas had orders to divide his men, a smaller guard to cut off Lincoln's escape to Alnmouth, while the larger group had orders to surround the men stranded on the Hipsburn side of the ford.

The oxen pulling the wagons through the ford panicked when men began screaming for the guard to form a defensive line. The confused beasts refused to move, although the oxherd viciously whipped them bloody; still the terrified animals refused to budge, thus blocking the causeway and obstructing Lincoln's men from retreating from Thomas's attack.

Guyon watched for a heartbeat to be sure Thomas had this end of the ambush under control. Nudging Notus into a canter, Guyon rode like the Furies to intercept Lincoln before he could make good an escape.

Whoreson that he was, Lincoln broke from his men and rode towards the forest on the northern side of the town. But Notus was stronger and faster. The horse devoured the ground with every deadly stride.

Five of Guyon's guard had followed him while the rest surrounded the small guard Lincoln had abandoned.

Surrounded, and with nowhere to go, Lincoln dismounted and drew his sword, an ugly smile spreading across his face. "Today is a good day, le Loup, I plan to slit your throat and take your whore."

Guyon took his time to dismount, handing the reins to Warin who had just arrived, the lad and his mount puffing from the exertion of keeping up with Notus.

Guyon's men also arrived and made a large circle with their mounts, effectively trapping Guyon and Lincoln in the middle. This would be a place of death. Guyon prayed it would not be his.

Lincoln's comment created a rage that bristled beneath Guyon's skin, but he refused to give Lincoln the satisfaction of seeing his taunts had hit the mark. "The king has issued a writ for your arrest, and I have no intention of denying the royal executioner his due." Guyon gave Lincoln a lazy smile. It was a lie, but Lincoln didn't know that. Guyon would use any tactic he could to unsettle the bastard.

"Or course, you may prefer to fight for your freedom," Guyon goaded.

"You killed one of my men. Justice dictates that I avenge him with his killer's blood," Lincoln snarled, as he readied himself to lunge at Guyon.

Both men were fully armed, but neither wore their helms, only a mail coif to protect their head and necks.

Guyon didn't take his eyes off the man in front of him, but he continued to goad him. They were equally matched, but if he could incite Lincoln's temper, then Guyon could slit the cur's throat and be done with him forever. "Your dog never did learn to keep his hands to himself." Guyon circled as Lincoln tried to gain an advantage. "To be felled by a mere woman, it's lucky he died, or he would have been the subject of scorn for the rest of his pox-ridden life."

Lincoln curled his lip in disgust, and without warning lunged for Guyon, but Guyon had anticipated the move, and evaded it with ease. Lincoln had expected to connect with Guyon, and when his sword struck air he lost his balance. In that instant Guyon saw his chance and took it. He made a savage slash to the Lincoln's exposed flank.

Hissing through his teeth Lincoln recovered and turned to face Guyon, his face a snarling rictus of fury.

"You do tend to overreach, Remeys." Guyon baited as he watched for his opponent's next move. "But while you regain your breath, tell me how you managed to get Alice to lie to Cicele. I must confess, even for you, it is extraordinary that she would willingly deceive another."

Lincoln smiled. "It wasn't Alice. Although the irony appeals. But alas, it was someone who owed me a favor." A sly smile slid across Remeys's face, making Guyon's gut clench.

Guyon didn't recognize the man standing before him. Although it had been six years since they had seen each other, loathing made Lincoln's face almost unrecognizable. Hate radiated off him as though a living thing.

"You took everything from me," Lincoln spat. "A mere grandson of a wolf catcher. You stole my reputation. Cicele, then Alice. I was left with nothing."

Guyon watched Lincoln's eyes bulge as spittle foamed at the corner of his mouth. Never had he seen a man so possessed of hate and loathing.

"I will slice you through and stuff your balls down your throat." Lincoln sneered. "Then I'll march on Lesbury and fuck your whore." Then he lunged.

It came at lightning speed, but Guyon saw the telltale sign of Lincoln's left eye. It always twitched before he lunged, so Guyon deflected the killing blow with a defensive sidestep, then spun to slash across Lincoln's exposed cheek.

Guyon missed. Instead, the sword sliced through the bridge of Lincoln's nose. Blood spurted in an arc as the sword sliced through flesh, muscle, and bone.

Lincoln fell, his ruined face a mask of gore as Guyon watched the life flow from an enemy who had once been his closest friend.

It had happened too swiftly. Almost before it had begun it was over and Guyon was left with a pulsing rage that had no outlet.

A howl, savage and menacing, ripped through his throat and filled the strangely quiet air. Everything in him wanted to slash and kick and pulverize the thing that lay at his feet. Shaking with the need to release all the emotion that pulsed through him, Guyon walked away. It was over. The threat. The fear.

When he had control of his emotions, he walked back into the circle where Remeys de Roumare, the Earl of Lincoln, lay. Guyon's men hadn't moved.

Leaving the corpse on the ground Guyon wiped the blood from his sword on Remeys's surcoat, then sheathed it in the scabbard at his belt. With Warin's help he mounted Notus and rode to where Thomas had surrounded Lincoln's men.

"Take ten men, five to go back to Lesbury, and five to Alnwick, and report what has happened, while I go to Warkworth." Guyon jerked his head in the direction of the clearing where the earl lay. The last thing Guyon wanted was more of Lincoln's mesne lords mounting an attack.

Thomas merely nodded, then began barking orders.

Now that Lincoln was dead, his men would return to Warkworth and wait for a new lord to be appointed. As sheriff, it was Guyon's responsibility to establish an inquiry to determine if any other lords had sided with Lincoln. It would take days, but better to do it now, rather than wait.

Lincoln had no heir to inherit his name or titles. Any memory of Remeys de Roumare and his line would fade. The king would award the Lincoln lands and titles to one of his favorites. Guyon hoped it would be to someone he respected and could trust. It was bloody inconvenient having a neighbor bent on destruction.

Guyon left Thomas at Hipsburn, and with thirty of his men rode over the burn and led Lincoln's siege force back towards Warkworth. As sheriff, it was also his role to return the body, and consult with Lincoln's clerics.

It took hours for the siege engine to be cleared from the ford and then more as the defeated siege force made its way back to Warkworth.

A great sadness engulfed Guyon as he rode. Another death that he, Guyon le Loup, Henry's beast of war, would carry on his conscience till the day he died.

God's bones, he was tired.

Chapter Twenty-Eight

THREE DAYS, AND STILL NO WORD FROM GUYON. LINCOLN WAS dead, but Guyon was still in danger. Thomas hadn't seemed worried, although he had insisted that Sir Nigel increase Lesbury's guard.

It had been a grueling three days. Fear had made the men and women taking refuge in the castle anxious. There were often fights over food and lodgings. The villagers and their livestock were housed in the lower bailey, which was so overcrowded it was impossible to keep people from squabbling.

Sir Nigel was almost at breaking point as he organized the village men into watches, so they could join the castle guards to keep vigil on the ramparts. Meanwhile Maude and Cicele organized the women to keep the bailey clean and prepare the vast quantities of food required for such a large group of people now residing inside the castle walls.

Any spare energy Cicele had was employed in trying to ignore the gnawing fear that threatened to tear her limb from limb. Blood and death, Guyon's death, stalked her dreams.

"He will return, my lady." Thomas tried to reassure her every day, as they sat at the dais eating the midday meal. Cicele had wanted to retire to her solar, but both Thomas and Sir Nigel had persuaded her that the castle folk needed to see their lady. So each day she had obliged, although the food tasted like ash as she struggled to swallow it.

On the morning of the fourth day, Cicele awoke exhausted. Allowing herself to be dressed, then led to her solar by Maude, Cicele sat silently, unable to gather her thoughts. A darkness had descended upon her mind, and she seemed unable to break free of its oppressive presence. She doubted she would be able to concentrate on anything. Her mind kept going back to Guyon's promise to return. *But what if he didn't?*

"Whatever it is you are thinking about, child, I suggest you think on something else," Maude scolded gently as she handed Cicele a goblet of wine. "Drink, child."

Maude was right, but Cicele couldn't dislodge the persistent thought that she would never see Guyon alive again. Her mouth was so dry and devoid of moisture that it was difficult for her to swallow. And to her shame, tears pricked at the back of her eyes. One kind word from anyone, and Cicele would be sobbing.

"I suggest you eat something." Maude spoke quietly, but her tone suggested that she expected Cicele to comply. Moments later Agatha brought Cicele a plate of cheese and bread.

Thanking her, Cicele laid the plate of food on a small table next to where she sat, but forced herself to take a sip of the wine. Her throat too tight to tolerate food, she continued to take small sips, which thankfully slid down her throat, the wine creating a warm pool in her stomach.

Vite had waited until she had sat down before he scampered up to her, begging for attention. Unthinking, Cicele placed her wine on the table beside her and picked him up and put him on her lap, but before she could control the animal he began lavishing her with wet, foul smelling kisses.

Cicele gasped as the dog stuck his tongue out to lick her chin. "What have you been eating?" she asked, almost gagging as she smelled his putrid breath. The dog, who seemed totally unperturbed by his mistress's rejection of his affections, wriggled and whined as he tried to lick her again. Cicele was forced to hold him away from her face. "No kisses, or I shall put you down."

"You are as bad as Isabeau the way you both talk to your hounds as though they understand every word you utter," Maude muttered as she lowered herself onto the bench where she had been spinning wool.

"What, pray tell, is the difference between my sister and me talking to our dogs, and you conversing with a child who is unable to understand any word that comes from your mouth?"

Maude puffed out her substantial bosom. "Master Edward may be young, but he understands every word I say."

Cicele caught Agatha's eye, and judging by her grin, she had been thinking the same thing. Oh Lord, how Cicele missed her sister and cousin.

"I am happy to talk to young master Edward." Maude smiled. "But that," she nodded towards Vite, "is beyond me."

Both women looked at the dog and burst out laughing. Something in that moment snapped in Cicele. The fear she had been holding so tight had been replaced with something so precious she dared not breathe. Hope. It swirled through her chest, making her heart flutter. Yes, she would hope. Here, with a woman who had been the only mother she had known, Cicele decided to cling to hope.

Agatha, who was probably still a little unsure of her place, remained silent, but her mouth betrayed her amusement.

"Have you heard from Hamlin?" Cicele wanted her maid settled, and back with her husband now that Lincoln was no longer a threat.

"He has been sent to Alnwick, where he will serve Sir Robert."

"And where shall you live, child?" Maude asked.

"My Lord Cessford has arranged for us to live in a suite of rooms in one of the towers." She cast a shy glance at Cicele. "I never could have hoped for such favor, and I thank you, my lady."

Cicele acknowledged her maid with a smile. Now if only she could see Ebeta settled. Cicele had noticed the furtive glances Thomas had directed towards the young widow while they were still at Alnwick. Thomas would be a good match for such an intelligent and kind woman and a fair and generous father for young Moise. Cicele decided that when she returned to Alnwick she would suggest Guyon encourage Thomas to pursue Ebeta. *Guyon, please come back to me.*

Turning her thoughts back to the women who shared her solar she watched Maude settle into her spinning, while Agatha chose something to read aloud to them. They had been reading from a collection of Lais from Marie of France, who was favored at Henry's court.

"Shall we have *Bisclavret*?" Agatha asked.

"No." Cicele didn't want to hear the story of a man who turned into a werewolf, and his wife who betrayed him. "Perhaps something a little more..." What was the word she was looking for?

"Absurd?" Maude shot Cicele a conspiratorial look.

"Yes, perfect. Something a little more absurd please, Agatha."

Agatha turned the pages of the illuminated manuscript Cicele and Guyon had been given as a wedding gift from King Henry and his queen. *"Yonec?"*

What a sad and gruesome, and wholly improbable, story that was. It was perfect. "Yes, Agatha, that will do well, I think."

To Cicele's surprise the morning flew by, and only occasionally did she stop listening to Agatha and worry about Guyon. They were about to go to the hall so she could preside over the noon meal when they were interrupted by Vite who jumped off Cicele's knee and ran to the door. Cicele turned to see Guyon walk through and scoop the little dog into his arms.

"God's bones, dog," Guyon said as he recoiled from the dog's face. "Your breath smells worse than Warin's feet after a week on the road."

The young squire, who had accompanied Guyon into the solar turned an alarming shade of scarlet at Guyon's quip.

Cicele wanted to run to her husband and fling her arms about his neck, but she couldn't seem to move. It was as though her body no longer obeyed her mind. "You are back." Well, that was a goose-brained thing to say. Shyness overwhelmed her as she looked upon her husband.

He didn't seem to notice her dull-witted remark for he strode over to where she was sitting, the smile on his face making his features those of a youth. "Aye, wife, I am."

He put the dog down on the floor, then scooped Cicele into his arms and proceeded to kiss her senseless. Mortified that those in the solar witnessed his show of affection, she tried to wriggle out of his embrace, but he held her to his chest and continued to kiss the sensitive skin of her neck, just below her ear. She tingled all over. He was back. And they were safe.

Finally, he released her, although he had to keep hold of her or she would have crumbled to the floor. "Now, that is a homecoming a man could get used to." He smiled down at her, but she could see the hunger burning behind his eyes. She too wanted more. Sadly, now was not the time.

Trying to regain some sense of dignity she straightened her kirtle and whispered with as much dignity as she could muster. "Perhaps we might continue this after the meal, my lord?"

To her relief, and frustration, he barked a laugh. "Yes, wife, to eat and share the exploits of the last few days."

They turned to see that all the occupants of the solar had become very interested in their various tasks. Each one trying desperately to give their lord and lady privacy. She appreciated their tact, although she longed to be alone with Guyon.

"Patience, wife," Guyon murmured in her ear as he led her from the solar.

Heat rushed to her cheeks. Was her desire so transparent? She glanced up at her husband to see him give her a look that made his intentions clear. That smoldering look had her body quivering with anticipation. It was going to be a very long meal indeed. All the thoughts in her head scattered as she gazed upon her husband's face.

A LANGUID AFTERNOON spent in their chamber left Cicele feeling replete and boneless. They had retired almost immediately after dinner, much to the amusement of several of Guyon's men. Their ribald comments were impossible to ignore as she and Guyon made their way past the benches where his men sat consuming ale and telling tales of their encounter with Lincoln.

Now, as the night air turned chilly, it was time to talk. There had been some details shared during the meal, but Cicele needed to know whether they were indeed free of Lincoln and his scheming.

Guyon lay on his back, with Cicele tucked up by his side, her head resting on his shoulder. "What happened," she asked, as she raised herself up on her elbow and looked down at him.

His contented expression changed in an instant and became shuttered. Cicele wondered if he was going to answer, it took him so long to respond.

Finally, his eyes moved and held hers in a gaze that made her breath catch. "What?" Dread gathered in the pit of her stomach. Something terrible had happened, she was sure of it.

"I killed him. But that wasn't enough. When he lay dead on the ground I wanted to tear him apart with my bare hands." He didn't look at her, but Cicele thought she saw loathing in his eyes.

"But you did not violate his body, my love." She peered into his eyes. Something was wrong, and that left her heart thudding in panic.

Gathering some of the bedding around her shoulders, she sat beside her husband and silently urged him to continue.

"We intercepted him at Hipsburn, his force so spread out it was easy to separate him from the larger force protecting the siege engine." Guyon focused on the bedding above him rather than Cicele. "Like the cur he was, he fled, leaving his men to face us."

Guyon had gathered some of Cicele's hair in his hand and was absent-mindedly twirling it around his index finger.

He turned and looked at her. "To kill someone is one thing. To want to eviscerate them makes me worse than an animal." His eyes beseeched her to understand. "When I think about what he did to you, I wanted to hurt him so badly that even now my body trembles with need to destroy something. I am not satisfied with his death, Cicele." His eyes slid away from her then and focused on something Cicele would never be able to see.

"You will have to find a way to let this hate go, Guyon, or it will consume you, and destroy us."

"I need my hate. That is why Henry uses me," he snapped.

Cicele didn't know what to say, but instinctively she knew that pandering to him would do no good. "Stop feeling sorry for yourself," she scolded. "You are not a mindless beast who is only capable of hate and vengeance. If that is all you were, you would not have me here by your side." She knelt beside him and took his face in her hands forcing him to look at her.

"You can choose who you want to be—beast or man." She was shouting but couldn't stop herself. "You are the most honorable man I know and you live by a code that makes men follow you, even into hell itself if you asked." She huffed a deep breath to regain control of her rising temper. "Don't let him steal this from you," she said, but she was desperately trying to think of something that would help assuage his self-loathing.

Cicele leaned over Guyon's chest so that her nose was almost touching his. "Guyon, your actions prove you to be a man of honor. Feelings are not fact. If they were, I would have eviscerated you with anything I could lay my hands on when you revealed yourself to me in the woods after I'd been abducted." She kissed him then. A soft lingering kiss that she hoped communicated all her trust and love.

When she pulled back so she could see his face again, she continued, "I wanted to hurt you because I feared my own feelings." She smiled then. "I feared my heart would break for love of you." She gave him another kiss. "You have to decide what it is that you fear, and what part Lincoln has in it."

His hand came up and caressed her cheek. "I don't deserve you."

"A harpy with a sharp tongue? Nobody deserves that." She laughed as she pressed her cheek into his calloused palm.

"I happen to like that sharp tongue." He smiled as he traced her lips with his thumb. "I would not survive if I were to lose you again. And I hate Lincoln for his part in that."

She leaned over and kissed him. "He is gone, my love, and you will not lose me. Never, I promise."

He didn't respond, but his gaze lingered on her face.

"I will try to be the man you believe me to be."

"I don't believe it, Guyon. I know it. Now kiss me."

Guyon didn't, instead he reached out and cupped her breast, sliding his thumb over her nipple. Cicele moaned as a frisson of desire knifed down her belly and settled in the cradle of her womb. By God's holy cross, the man could reduce her to a trembling mess with just a touch. But she would never complain.

Her stomach growled at that moment, making Guyon stop his exploration of her breast. "Food, I think, wife."

"I have little appetite…for food," she teased as she drew back the covers and straddled him. "Of course, you, my lord husband, might find you need the nourishment to sustain you through the long hours of the night ahead." She gave him a provocative smile as she leaned forward, her breasts tantalizingly close to his mouth.

A deep growl rumbled in his throat as his hands clasped her bottom and ground her against his arousal.

"You tread a dangerous path with a beast such as myself."

Cicele smiled as she pressed herself into him. "But I am drawn to the beast, my lord."

Neither spoke as they sought their own release. Their coupling passionate, and unapologetic, in their need of each other. Cicele cried out as pleasure pulsed through every fiber of her being.

Panting and sweat soaked, she lay on top of him listening to his heart thumping in her ear.

"I love you so much I think that my heart is incapable of containing it." Her throat was so tight she didn't think the words would come, but they did, as did silent tears. They slid down her cheek and blended with the sweat on his chest.

Gently, as though handling something precious, Guyon placed his hands on either side of her face and lifted her head so she could look at him. "And I love you with my body, my mind, and my heart." His voice was strong and unflinching in his declaration. But it was the expression in his eyes that Cicele found overwhelming. There, in the dark depths of his eyes, she saw the truth of his love for her.

Finally, after so many years of heartbreak and uncertainty, she was home. His arms were the safe place her heart craved.

She lay in his arms as he fell asleep.

Cicele lay watching him, and if the night demon came, she would be with him, soothing his fears and protecting him at his most vulnerable.

IT WAS STILL EARLY, but Guyon had been lying awake waiting for the dawn. Today he would see where their son rested in peace.

Cicele had told him during the night that she would take him; now she lay nestled into him, warm and soft against his already aroused cock. It was the first time he had awoken from sleep since the onset of the night terrors with a woman in his arms. Gently, he flattened his hand over her hip and drew her back towards him. She fit him like a familiar glove. This would be his future, and he thanked God, and Henry, for making it so. He smiled as he remembered his wife's words and as he lay with her by his side, he made his decision. He would banish Lincoln from his mind.

Guyon watched in fascination as Cicele awoke and stretched, her arms and legs moving in one fluid movement. She was magnificent.

"Good morning, wife." He moved her hip back towards him, letting her feel his need for her.

She turned then and lay on her back in clear invitation; a smile that spoke of love and contentment greeted him. "Good morning, lord."

They took their time, giving and receiving. Enjoying the contours of each other's bodies and needs.

Content to lie with his wife in his arms Guyon dozed, but awoke with a start when a servant entered the chamber to rekindle the fire.

"What will the servants think?" Cicele sounded horrified, but Guyon laughed.

"They will think that I am the luckiest man alive."

Her soft, tinkling laughter filled the cocoon they had made of the bed, its curtains drawn to keep out the cold and prying eyes.

And dogs.

A pitiful whine, then a small yip. "I think someone wants

entrance to his favored spot." Guyon tried to sound indignant, but he couldn't keep the smile from his voice.

"He has never had to share," Cicele giggled.

Guyon pulled open the curtain to let Vite in. Which was a mistake. Once on the bed the dog wriggled, licked, and generally created chaos.

THE DAY HAD BARELY BEGUN as Guyon and Cicele rode out of the bailey towards the river and the meadow. A mist blanketed the earth, creating an ethereal beauty as they walked their mounts through the dawn landscape. Cicele didn't want to rush; she wanted to walk towards what she expected would be a poignant meeting. A father bidding welcome and farewell all at once. Guyon hadn't said anything as they walked side-by-side. She was content to let him have this time of silence. She had had her time sitting vigil over her son's little grave. Now it was his father's time.

The meadow was bathed in a wintry sun, the mist swirling over the meadow like a reluctant lover not wanting to leave. Even in winter the grassland would soon be alive with wildflowers and small creatures scavenging for food.

Hobbling their horses at the edge of the meadow, they walked in silence as Cicele led Guyon to the small cairn at the boarder of the meadow. The pungent funk of damp earth met them as they neared the place where their son lay.

Guyon fell to his knees and wept. Cicele had never seen him so broken, but she knew from her own grief that he needed the release. A cathartic cleansing of guilt and loss, and she would not begrudge him. They had both suffered, and God willing, they would forge a future together. A rueful longing brought tears to her eyes. Never would Guyon hold their child. But they had each other, and that would be enough. She would make sure of it.

Guyon wiped his eyes with the back of his gloved hand, then

rose and walked towards her. He cupped her cheek in his gloved hand as his eyes traveled over her face. "I love you."

It was all he said, and it was enough. Together they walked back to their horses, hand-in-hand. Love and loss bound them together, and nothing would ever separate them again.

Epilogue

LESBURY CASTLE

Early July, 1156

Cicele could hardly contain her excitement as she watched the grooms lead the horses from the barge—four mares and one stallion. It had taken three weeks for the horses to arrive. And now they were here.

She had traveled from Alnwick to Lesbury the week before to ready the now completed stables for the new arrivals.

"What do you think?" Guyon's breath tickled her neck as he spoke. She would never get enough of his touches, his voice, but she wouldn't be distracted. Well, perhaps just a little; her body quivered as he continued speaking in a low voice that only she could hear. "Are they all you hoped they would be?"

Oh, yes, and so much more. "Guyon, they are beautiful."

He looked pleased with himself, and Cicele couldn't help but smile. She had missed him, more than she could have imagined.

"I don't think I want you to leave me again."

He gave her a look that made her scalp tingle and her stomach hitch. "I don't plan to leave you again, wife, I can promise you that."

He had gone to London to personally oversee the transport of the horses and had returned only moments ago. Instead of waiting to travel from Alnmouth to Lesbury with the barge, he had saddled his horse and galloped the two miles back to Lesbury, and had run into her chamber, giving her a searing kiss that had left her speechless and a little unsteady on her feet.

Now they were both watching the unloading of the horses at Lesbury's jetty.

"You had no trouble?" Guyon had taken almost all of their silver to buy the horses. The Iberian trader only came to England once a year, and had agreed to sell his horses directly to Guyon. Cicele had been terrified that Guyon might be robbed as he made the journey to London. Every night for three weeks she had prayed and worried in equal measure. All she wanted to do was hold him close and reassure herself that he was well.

She may have even been tempted to return to their chamber now and check for herself, but the lure of the horses was too much.

"I see I have competition for my affections."

"You can read my mind, sir?"

He huffed a laugh. "No, but I can read your face."

She loved her husband and was not about to apologize for wanting him all to herself. "I have missed you."

"And I have missed you, but patience, wife. When I get you to our chamber, I do not plan on leaving it until this time tomorrow, so you had best enjoy the moment with the horses now, as you will be flat on your back soon enough."

She liked the sound of that, and was about to say as much when Harry, one of the young boys who had been caught poaching, came to stand beside them. He had a rare gift with horses, and Guyon wanted to train him up with the possibility that the boy would become head groom to the breeding mares.

"We are ready, my lord." He bowed to Cicele. "My lady, they are right beauties, are they not?"

"Yes, they are, Harry." The lad walked back to where the horses were being led to their new stables. It was everything Cicele had imagined it would be when they had first begun to arrange for the horses and the stables back in January.

Guyon walked with his arm around her waist as they made their way to the new stables. They walked through the gate in the large stone wall that enclosed the stables and yard and over to where the horses were being led to their stalls.

Nyssa had delivered her foal, a beautiful filly with her mother's even temperament. Guyon and Cicele spent some time with mother and foal before moving on to the new horses.

"Let me introduce you." Guyon led her to the next stall. "This is Caesar." She knew all the horse's details, she had made sure of that before they had agreed to purchase them, but still, she was unprepared for the magnificent animal that sniffed at her hand as she reached out to stroke his muzzle. "What a beautiful boy," she crooned as she ran her hand down his neck and over his flanks.

Next, she met Gia, a sweet natured bay mare. Iliana was next, a black mare with a mischievous nature. She reminded Cicele of Vite and loved her instantly. Next, was another bay named Theia. A little shy, the mare sniffed at Cicele's outstretched hand, but wouldn't let her touch her head.

"Here, she likes these." Guyon gave Cicele a piece of apple.

"Theia, my beautiful girl, this is your home, and I will cherish you." The horse twitched her ears and snapped her lips together as Cicele held out the apple. Big brown eyes examined Cicele for several heartbeats, then she gently took the proffered treat. But when Cicele went to pat her, she shook her head.

"Perhaps after a sleep you may feel like being friends."

"Sleep does wonders for me," Guyon murmured close to her ear.

Cicele giggled but didn't respond. It was never wise to tease him, especially since they had been apart for weeks.

Finally, they walked to the last stall. "Latona." The mare was black as night, with a long wavy mane that fell over her eyes and down her neck. She nuzzled Cicele as she began to pat her. "She is without comparison," Cicele whispered to Guyon. Truly, the mare took Cicele's breath away. "I hope you live up to your name and produce a foal to rival all others."

Cicele took several moments to acquaint herself with the mare.

"Are you happy?" Guyon nudged her from behind, his hands resting on her waist as he pulled her back into his chest.

Yes, she was happy. Happier than she had ever been in her life. And it was all to do with the man at her back.

"When my father told me I would be marrying you, I never thought I would be happy, but I find myself more in love with you now than when I loved you all those years ago." She rested her head against his shoulder as he kissed her neck. The stall offered some privacy, and she relished being in his arms, his lips skimming along her jaw and over the swell of her breasts.

"I never stopped loving you. You are my life, Cicele, and where you are, that is where I will be."

She turned and pulled his head down so she could kiss him. "Perhaps now would be a good time to show me just how much you missed me." She gave his lip a small nip.

He responded with a growl, and all but carried her through the stables and back up to the castle.

Yes, she was very happy indeed.

Thank You

Thanks so much for reading **Drawn to the Beast**. I hope you enjoyed Cicele and Guyon's story.

Also I would really appreciate an honest review. Reviews, and telling your friends, helps other readers find books, so please consider leaving a review at Amazon.

Acknowledgments

A great many people make a book a reality. Foremost among them is my developmental editor, Angela James, but I also owe many thanks to my copyeditor, Maria Fairchild. I am so fortunate to work with you.

I also want to thank the Otago chapter of RWNZ. Without your support and encouragement this would never have seen the light of day.

And of course my family, who have been tireless in their encouragement. Thank you!

About the Author

Cate Melville is an emerging author of historical romance. This is Cate's second book in the series, The Brides of Northumbria.

Set in 12th century Northumbria, the trilogy is full of richly researched historical settings, where her flawed heroes, and the strong woman who defy convention to win their happy ending, transport readers to a time when honor and chivalry really were something to fight, and die, for.

When Cate is not writing, she is busy reading, or re-reading, her favorite authors, cooking for friends, and enjoying the best of Central Otago's Pinot varieties of wine, and taking long walks with her own Scottish hero, and their dogs, Poppy and Lily. She lives in New Zealand's gorgeous South Island.

You can contact Cate at:
    Web: catemelvilleauthor.com
    Email: contact@catemelvilleauthor.com

Brides of Northumbria Series

Born in Deception

Drawn to the Beast

Tempted by Beauty

(Coming late 2022)